BROKEN GLASS

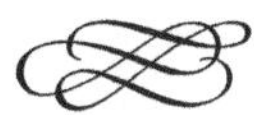

J. D. MASON

SPIRIT IN THE DARK PUBLISHING, LLC

OTHER BOOKS BY J.D. MASON

And On The Eighth Day She Rested

One Day I Saw A Black King

Don't Want No Sugar

You Gotta Sin To Get Saved

Somebody Pick Up My Pieces

Beautiful Dirty Rich

Drop Dead, Gorgeous

Crazy, Sexy, Revenge

The Real Mrs. Price

Seducing Abby Rhodes

The Woman Trapped in the Dark

Without A Song To Sing

ACKNOWLEDGMENTS

Writing Broken Glass is a bittersweet experience for me because I've recently announced my retirement from the literary world, and it's likely the last novel I'll ever write (deep down I know better and will never say never).

I started my first novel, "And on the Eighth Day She Rested" twenty-six years ago. In those twenty-six years, the first thing I've thought about when I opened my eyes in the morning was writing, and it was the last thing I thought about before closing them again to go to sleep. In between, I had a family and worked a "regular" job like most people, but becoming a published author was always my dream. It came true, but now it's time to move on.

Admittedly, I didn't reach the decision to leave the industry, overnight. I thought long and hard before making it official and the more time that passes, the more I'm convinced that I've made the right choice. I have given a thousand percent in each and every story I've written, and I've loved them all. I wrote what was in my heart. I wrote the kinds of stories I wanted to read, and I wrote for all of you, hoping that I offered you something brand new or even, perhaps, a different take on a familiar story. My job, all these years has been to entertain you, and I hope that I have served you well.

I want to thank each and every reader out there who's ever read one of my stories. I especially want to thank those of you who have been with me since the beginning. Know that I could not have lasted as long as I have in this industry without you. Never take for granted how important you are to writers. Your support means absolutely everything, so I encourage you to support your favorite author with Amazon reviews, buying books, or checking them out from the library. DM or email your favorite authors to let them know, personally, how much you enjoyed their story. Your encouragement goes further than you can ever imagine. I know that it kept me going for many years.

I've enjoyed every moment of my literary career and have absolutely no regrets. Along the way, I've met some amazing folks that I hope to stay in touch with for as long as possible.

To Sara Camilli, my agent, you and I will always be friends. Thank you so much for all the support you've given me all these years. Your faith in me has truly, filled my heart.

To Monique Patterson, my editor for the bulk of my career. It has been an honor working with you and knowing you. You've taught me so much and the next time I'm in NYC or you're in NOLA, I hope we get a chance to get together, my friend.

To Carol Hill Mackey, thank you my lovely friend. With Black Expressions, you gave so many of us authors space to soar and because of you, the world "saw" us.

Ebony Danielle Goodrich, thank you so much for editing Broken Glass, and I'm honored to have been your very first customer.

Tina V. Young, you are a beast of a proofreader, and I'm so happy to have been able to work with you.

And a very special thanks to my beta readers, Jemina Harris and LaRael Tunson-Chapman for your time and invaluable input.

In closing, I have to say that, though I have retired from the literary industry, as a storyteller, I can NEVER quit telling stories and I won't. I'll just be telling them in a different way.

Stay tuned.

BROKEN GLASS

"You fake, sneaky, no-class, bad-acting, two-faced bitch!"

There was no moment in her life more sobering than watching, in slow motion, as a $650, red Jimmy Choo stiletto soared across the room, aimed at her face. She slightly leaned to one side, like Neo in the Matrix, watching as it whirred past her, barely avoiding impact.

"I did- didn't," Terri muttered in disbelief as the missile shoe flew passed her.

The scene unfolded like a dream or maybe a sitcom.

The beautiful, cinnamon colored woman with long, expensive, virgin blond tresses cascading to her waist, literally crawled on top of the table, arms outstretched, and inch-long talons clawed space to get to Terri.

"You had no right to tell my business! No goddamn right!"

"I thought she knew," Terri said haplessly, scanning the room for the producer, the one who assured her it was okay to have this conversation with this woman. The one who vigorously insisted on Terri broaching the subject, but the little cow was nowhere to be found.

Camera's rolled. A big brute of a stagehand came out of nowhere, grabbed that wild woman around the waist and lifted her off the table, suffering the torment of her driving her one remaining heel into his shins.

"Th-they told me-" Terri stammered.

A vortex of confusion and disbelief swept Terri up and away to Oz. This couldn't be happening. It wasn't happening... was it?

The sound of laughter behind her caught Terri's attention.

"Told you she was shady," the one Terri thought liked her said to the woman standing beside her, a woman who'd hardly spoken a complete sentence to Terri during this entire season of filming.

"It's the quiet ones, girl," another woman said. "The ones with no fuckin' life."

The word 'fuckin' would be bleeped out for television. Terri had no idea why that mattered in this moment, but it all flowed in slow motion, so details were magnified.

"This is ridiculous," she heard herself say, backing away and shaking her head.

Terri suddenly stumbled, shoved aside by another sister wearing the most impeccable white pant suit she had ever seen.

"She didn't have to tell me shit, 'cause I already knew!" that woman shouted, bounding toward the one shoed woman twisting and fighting to free herself from the grasp of Gargantua. "You still want him! You still throwing your desperate, fat ass at him! Bitch, he don't want you! He never wanted you!"

Another brute grabbed this one and held her back. Arms flailing, legs kicking at air, mouths spitting and cussing. An explosion of ridiculous chaos filmed for the world's entertainment and humiliating embarrassment, as Terri stood like a statue, wide eyed, mouth gaped open, forced to face the mess her career had become.

The magic of make believe.

The magic of Terri.

She used to believe in both but not anymore.

Being an actress was the only thing she ever wanted to be, the only thing Terri Dawson ever thought she could be. Sure, she waited tables, took the occasional temp job to pay the rent, but she'd never committed. Terri knew that Plan A was the only acceptable plan there was, and that Plan B was for losers. Acting was her passion, her dream, but this? *This* wasn't acting.

She got her first big break twenty-three years ago, landing a small, but recurring role on a weekly detective show, *Streets of Vegas*. Terri played a rookie cop with a sharp wit and occasional brilliant deduction who sometimes revealed golden nuggets to the stars of the show. Nuggets that usually led to the capture of the bad guys. She was on that series for six years before they killed off her character. The producers were flooded with angry fan mail for months after that happened, but of course, there was no way for them to bring her back, and they wanted to, but Terri had moved on.

A year later she won her first feature film, not a leading role, but still... a sci-fi flick about a spaceship on a science expedition. The ship falls into a black hole, catapulting the crew into a whole other dimension. Terri played a scientist who ended up getting sucked out into space trying to save the crew, but the film grossed more than fifty-million and she had a whopping, twenty-seven minutes of screen time before she died.

But it was when she landed a part as a regular on a daytime soap opera that Terri really hit her stride. She played Claudia Braxton, a widow and new doctor at the hospital in Ashford, Wisconsin, holding a deadly secret close to her heart. The secret was that she'd murdered her husband using an untraceable drug she'd slipped into his cocktail. But it wasn't Claudia's fault. He was abusive and she thought she was just giving him a sedative to keep him calm. Somehow, the sedative had been switched and what should've been a small dose to put him to sleep, ended up being lethal. Terri played Claudia Braxton for eight years before the character's past finally caught up with her and she was sent to prison.

Commercials, a six-month stint as a daytime talk show host, voice-over work and too many bit parts to count, blurred together in one murky, shit-brown colored career. Terri made enough to keep the lights on, but that big break she'd hoped for, the one with her name at the top of the movie poster, the one that resulted in her walking up to receive that Emmy or Oscar, never came. But reality television did... and she answered.

❧

Boring? Did Terri hear that right?

"That's a bit harsh, David," her agent, Roxy Stewart argued in Terri's defense.

Vivacious Vixens of Atlanta was cable network's highest rated reality show, and Terri had just wrapped up her first season. It was the most brutal thing she'd ever done. Between those vicious women, manipulative producers and ridiculous storylines, every time she was on screen Terri felt like she'd been bathed in cow manure, but she pushed through. Terri showed up on time, repeating the asinine lines they fed her to *keep the drama flowing* without fail or complaint. "You're firing me?" It was Terri's voice, but she couldn't believe those words had the nerve to pass her lips. She'd been in this business for damn near a quarter of a century and never once had anyone complained about her talent, work ethic, or commitment to her craft.

"Viewers can't connect with your storyline, Terri, because there isn't one," David Randall, the show's producer responded, his once inviting green eyes, now cold and merciless.

He'd turned somersaults when she agreed to be on this show. The network had even hosted a cocktail party in Terri's honor, touting her as that breath of fresh air needed to take the show to new heights and add a new level of class. Bloggers, YouTubers, and network entertainment news shows gave Terri more press than she'd ever had in her life, and just like that, she was relevant again. But it wasn't class they wanted. It was trash. They wanted her to make a fool of herself like the other cast members, to roll around in the reality world like a pig in slop, tainting her hard earned and respectable legacy.

The truth was, she never wanted to do the show. Roxy begged her to do it, convinced Terri that reality television was a way to resuscitate her fading career. The women on that show were laughable, overly made-up creatures with small, forest animals for eye lashes, thousand-dollar wigs and stuffed, oversized booties. Terri was the only *real* actress among a cast of women famous for embarrassing displays of over the top, low down, oily drama.

"How can they connect with her, David, when Shannon and Dee Dee get all the screen time?" Roxy continued. "She can't build a storyline if the only time she's on screen is with those two drama queens."

He laughed, "What do you think this show is about, Roxy? Drama. And Shannon and Dee bring it better than anyone, especially better than Ms. Dawson, here."

"She's a respected actress. Surely, you don't expect her to make a fool of herself like the other nobodies on that show."

"That's exactly what I expected," he said, without hesitation. "Transparency is everything on a show like this, ladies. It's called "reality" television for the authenticity cast members bring to the show. That sells it. Viewers want the low-down-dirty-in-your-face-unapologetic ridiculousness of whatever that means. You knew that coming in."

"She's only been on one season," Roxy reminded him. "She deserves a contract renewal, David. Another chance to—"

"Viewers want unscripted reality, Terri. You didn't bring it."

"Unscripted?" Terri huffed at this well-dressed clown. "Do you hear yourself?"

The show was anything but unscripted. Oh, sure, *some* conversations were organic between the cast members, but when producers felt things were becoming a little too tamed and sensible, they'd find a stick to pick the shit with, feeding vomit inducing lines to attention hungry women who'd swallow anything to be relevant.

David slumped back in his chair and sighed, "You know what I mean."

"Oh, you mean when your fuckin' little minions crawl around on their bellies whispering shit, conveniently off camera, telling me what to say? Or, maybe it's all the text messages blowing up my phone from some little assistant snot-nosed producer reminding me of all the things being said about me by all those other bitches behind my back, egging me on about how pissed I should be? You mean that kind of unscripted? This isn't fuckin' high school, David."

His jaws tightened. David glared into her eyes like he hated her. "No, it's reality television, Ms. Dawson. Lucrative, with a formula that works for anyone willing to get off their high goddamned horse and work with it. Obviously, that's not you."

❧

A WEEK LATER, Terri's life was summed up by a half-eaten family sized bag of Lays potato chips, a nearly empty package of Vanilla Oreo Thins, and a two-day old container of fried rice and sesame chicken littering the bed she'd been in since that meeting with David. Remnants of a junk food overdose ushered in a painful revelation; one she could no longer ignore. Her career was over and had been for longer than she wanted to admit.

The day Terri got fired, Roxy left her with an empty parting promise, *"I'm your agent, T, and I'll keep looking for new opportunities until something comes up that's worth the time for someone with your talent. Trust me. The perfect script is out there, and we'll find it."*

Terri forced herself out of that bed and stood looking at her reflection in the bathroom mirror, finally coming to terms with her new truth. She made the gut-wrenching decision to walk away from a career that abandoned her long ago. There was no place left for Terri Dawson in this industry and she was tired. She was mentally and spiritually exhausted.

A normal life. For as long as she could remember, she'd run from the very idea of such a thing and had no clue of what it could look like. Terri thought of her parents, two hardworking people who got up every morning and headed out, rain or shine, to the classroom for her mother, and the insurance office for her father. Normal had been all they knew, and they reveled in it. People did that. As odd as it seemed to Terri, there were folks in the world who were quite comfortable with the nine-to-five existence for forty years of their lives before retiring quietly to fishing trips and rocking chairs.

The idea of routine had always soured in her stomach. She lived for the magic, where she could be anybody and do anything. The world of make believe had always been more interesting to Terri than the real world ever could.

"Not anymore," she murmured, filled with mourning.

Tears flooded her eyes and blurred her reflection, washing away the idea Terri always clung to of who she was... who she *thought* she was.

Maybe now it was time for her to learn who she *really* was. Whatever that meant.

PICK UP THE PIECES

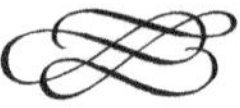

Three months after being fired, Terri left Atlanta in her rearview mirror. She headed to Houston and the sanctuary of her best friend, Nona's, guest house to hide her shriveling soul from the rest of the world until she could figure out what she wanted to be when she grew up.

On the way, she stopped to get gas in a small town. Before she finished topping off the tank, a stomach growl alerted her to the fact that she hadn't eaten since yesterday. Her empty belly led the way to Irma's, a hole in the wall just off the highway at the edge of town.

Devastation, Louisiana.

The irony wasn't missed on her. That a devastated Terri should land here was fate's cruel joke, laughing in her face, adding insult to injury. But the food was delicious. Magical, even. Creamy buttered grits, thick, smoky black peppered bacon, cheese eggs harmonizing in her mouth with buttered pancakes, gave her a kind of joy she hadn't experienced in forever.

"More coffee?"

Terri's appreciative gaze lifted to meet the angel standing over her with a fresh pot of God's nectar, as she held up her cup between both hands.

"Yes, please," she answered. "Are you Irma?"

The loveliest smile spread the woman's lips. "I am."

Terri melted even more in her seat.

"Everything is so delicious," she said, perhaps a bit too passionately.

Full, ebony cheeks blossomed on Irma's pretty round face. "Well, we always like to hear that," she chuckled. "You need more cream, honey?"

"Oh, yes," she said, inhaling the rich aroma wafting from her cup. "And some more orange juice, please."

"Of course." Irma leaned her head to one side, propped her hand on her hip and studied, Terri. "You look familiar. You from here?"

A moment of truth. A year ago, Terri would've erupted inside like a volcano that a random stranger would recognize her. Quite humbly, she'd tout her achievements, probably sign a few autographs, and then walk away shining like a bright star with the affirmation that she still mattered.

"No," she responded, simply. "I'm just passing through."

She'd focused on one thing on the drive from Atlanta. Terri fixed her mind on coming to terms with the fact that who she used to be was not on that highway. She made up her mind that the life and the career she had convinced herself she couldn't live without, no longer existed. Terri drove away from the past and onward to something else.

"Irma," another customer called out, mercifully drawing the woman's attention away from Terri. "You heard what happened to Tanya?"

"I heard she put Ron out the house," Irma said, floating across the small diner to the other table. "Again."

"You want a paper?" an old man asked, pausing at Terri's table.

"Thank you."

In the grand scheme of things, his small gesture meant nothing, but in this crux of Terri's life, it meant everything.

Small.

Small town.

Small town people.

Small Terri.

Inside she was crumbling, but these grits, miraculously, held her together. Irma's smile kept her from falling apart, and that old man's newspaper reminded her of those Sunday mornings when she was a child growing up in Victoria, Texas, sitting across the table, sharing the paper with her dad. Terri read the funnies. Because of those Sunday mornings, those ordinary Sunday mornings, she'd always had a thing for newspapers. Every city she'd ever visited, Terri made a point to grab a copy of the local paper. She'd read it in her hotel room or on set between scenes. It was her way of staying grounded when she was surrounded by the grandeur of Hollywood. She never understood why she needed to feel grounded when all she ever wanted to do was soar… but it mattered.

Terri took her time, soaking in every page of that thin newspaper, catching up on small town news with slices of bacon. This was escape. This was a way to forget all those things she'd failed to achieve and for forgetting all the wishes that never quite came true.

The Mayor of Devastation declared that fishing season would begin a little earlier this year due to overpopulation in the lakes. Mrs. Betty Lenoir was celebrating her one-hundredth birthday at St. Mary's Catholic Church this Sunday at eleven. Marcus Brooks received full athletic scholarship offers from Tulane and LSU. Ordinary people, living ordinary lives still managed to make headline news. Terri marveled at that fact and wondered what the hell was wrong with her that her life never seemed to be enough for her.

For sale: Bungalow, Needs Work, 1124 Dupelo Street. Asking $10,000.00.

The image of that small, wooden fixer-upper stayed with Terri, even as she gazed out the window at the sunlight slicing through moss-covered tree branches. Her mind worked in mysterious ways. It always had. Terri was a creature of risk, emotions, and gut instinct, despite the fact that those things had failed her time and time again. It was in her nature to follow her heart, and ever since she sat down at the table in Irma's restaurant, she felt like she wanted to stay awhile.

❧

"It's two bedrooms," Bobby Johnson, the realtor explained, holding the door open for her at 1124 Dupelo Street an hour later. "One bathroom, sizable. Got a tub."

The soft pink paint peeled on the exterior. The white columns on the front porch had been charming once. Wooden floors creaked underfoot with each step she took.

"How many square feet?"

"Just over a thousand," he said, as if she should be impressed.

The black and white tiled floor in the kitchen had seen better days. Half the tile was missing. Terri ran her fingers along the edge of the pea green Formica countertops, feeling a sense of purpose, something she hadn't felt in ages. This place could use someone like her to make it what it once was. Better. But she was just passing through. Terri was on her way to Nona's in Houston to recover. To heal. To figure out what to do next. To lick her wounds.

"That old tree has got to be well over a hundred years old," Bobby announced, holding open the back door for Terri, who was greeted by that massive, century old soldier standing guard at the far end of the yard.

"A hundred?" she asked, staring at the impressive fixture.

"At least. The house sits on three-quarters of an acre," he said. "Lotta yard for a such a small house."

"How's the plumbing?" she asked, sounding like she was actually interested in buying this house on a whim, in a town she'd never been to before.

"Bad. So's the electrical. That's why it's so cheap."

Terri had just closed on her Atlanta condo. She'd loved her place because it was brand new when she bought it. She loved this place because it wasn't, and because she was as fragile as this house was. She was broken too.

"They're asking $10,000?" she asked, gazing at the tree gazing back at her.

"That's what they're asking."

Terri smiled. "Think they'd take eight?"

❧

"WHAT THE HELL do you mean you just bought a house, Terri?" Nona damn near shouted over the phone. "I thought you were coming here?"

It was right there, skimming the surface of her right mind. Doubt. Was she really doing this?

"I was," she responded sheepishly.

"Terri," Nona sighed and paused. "You can't just be- Why would you do something like that? Especially now, girl."

Nona, the voice of reason. Her best friend. The one she shared all her secrets with, and the one who helped keep Terri motivated, cheering her on and being her biggest fan.

"Terri, this isn't the kind of decision you need to be making right now. I know you're going through some things, sis, and that's why you need to come here. We can talk."

Sure, they could talk. And talk. And talk. And talk some more. But the answers she needed weren't in Houston, or in talking to Nona or anyone else, for that matter, about the newly formed void inside her. Maybe there weren't any answers.

"I need time, Nona," she finally admitted.

"You can have time here. Close to people who care about you, T," she sighed. "You're wounded, sis. I get it."

No, she didn't. Nona pointed to a dream when she was six-years-old on a school yard playground and said, 'There. That's the one I want.' Poof. Just like that, it came true. She was never desperate for it. Never had to be. It was as if, her dream needed her more than she needed it, and would stop at nothing to get to her. Terri's, on the other hand, had ducked and dodged her from the beginning, pausing long enough for her to pull it into focus and want it even more, only to take off again, just when she thought it was within reach. So, no. Nona absolutely did not 'get' it.

"It's cute," she finally said, recalling the devastated and broken little house in Devastation, Louisiana that reminded her so much of herself. "I can't wait for you to see it."

TWO SIDES OF THE SAME COIN

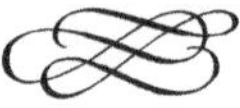

Nick Hunt sat in his car, parked outside of Luther's Bar & Grill for ten minutes before finally deciding to go in to see the owner, his father. The last few times he'd come back to his hometown, Nick stayed with extended family and never once attempted to see the man. He was only here now because he'd made a promise to his uncle.

"You need to go see yo' Daddy," his Uncle Don had told him as soon as Nick walked into their house this morning.

"I'll swing by and see him."

"Don't lie to me," he fussed. *"He ask 'bout you and he paid for that fancy doctor school you went to, so, you need to quit actin' like he ain't shit."*

Luther Hunt might not have been shit, but he wasn't much better than that. Yeah, he'd paid for college and medical school, but those things didn't make him father of the year. Nick grew up without him, taking care of his mother, who battled Lupus for as long as Nick could remember. The illness attacked her kidneys and her heart until both finally gave out. Meanwhile, Luther traveled the world with the likes of Earth, Wind, and Fire and Janet Jackson, living his best life, while Nick fed soup to his mother because she was too weak to lift the spoon. Nick cleaned up after her, stayed up all night lying in bed next to her, scared to close his eyes, afraid that she might not ever again, open hers.

Luther partied.

Nick walked into the dimly lit bar, not yet open for business, and stood just inside the doorway, surveying the place. The rich, dark, ornate wood trim seemed more suited for a posh mansion than a bar in Devastation, Louisiana. Dark, marbled tile floors, mirrored walls, circular tables covered in white tablecloths with lighted candles surrounded a dance floor with a cheesy disco ball hanging overhead. It was all Luther… garish, over the top, dark, and not quite pleasant.

"Well," Luther's baritone voice seeped from a shadowed corner across the room and filled the space like a spirit. "Look at what the wind blew in."

Luther emerged from the shadows like an apparition, wearing a black tee-shirt tucked into jeans that probably cost more than the new living room set Nick had just sprung for.

"You always did know how to make an entrance, Pop," Nick quipped, recalling all those times his father came home, lighting up Nick's mother's eyes like Christmas.

Luther grinned, showing off perfect white teeth behind a perfectly coiffed beard. He was a star, maybe fallen, but there had always been something about his dad that wouldn't let him be ordinary.

"It's good to see you too, son." He said like he meant it.

Luther went behind the bar. Nick joined him and sat on the customer side.

"What can I get you?"

Nick shrugged. "Beer."

Luther expertly filled two glasses from the tap, then came around and sat next to Nick.

"I hear you're a full-fledged doctor now," he said, cocking a thick brow.

Nick was dark like his father and almost as tall, but people always said he looked more like his mother.

"I am as of a week ago."

Luther raised his glass to toast. "Cheers to you and all your hard work, son."

Nick had just turned thirty-five, well past the age when he felt the need to have to forced conversation with his dad because the sound of silence between them was unnerving. He'd learned how to be comfortable in his own skin and to not try and impress a man who didn't deserve the effort.

"How's New Orleans?" Luther eventually asked.

"You know." Nick smirked. "It's New Orleans."

"Yep. Had some memorable times there."

"Well, it's not like it's on the other side of the world, Pop," Nick reminded him. "It's only two hours away. You can always go back and make more memories."

Luther returned a half smile. "How long you here for?"

"Few days," he said. "Wanted to come check on Grandma."

"Give her my best, if you don't mind."

"Why don't you give it to her?" Nick challenged.

"You know better." Luther finished the beer in his glass. "She gives less of a shit about me than you do."

Truth. There it was and leave it to Luther to ruin a semi-pleasant visit by bringing it up. What kind of son would Nick be if he let a comment like that slip by without a response?

"That's nobody's fault but yours."

Luther laughed, "Indeed."

There was no need to go into the details. They both knew them. The older Nick became the less respectful he was about voicing his opinion to his dad, letting them fly like poison darts too many times to count.

"So, now that you're finished with learning to become a doctor," Luther continued, expertly changing the subject. "You seeing anybody?" He cut a side eye at Nick. "Or, you still sowing oats and shit?"

"Is that what you were doing when you were my age? Sowing oats?"

Luther raised both brows. "Me? Nah. I had your mom."

Nick laughed.

Luther didn't. "Believe what you want, son."

"I already do."

His father was a good looking dude. It didn't take a medical degree to figure out that women threw themselves at him, and he'd caught more than his share.

"Don't get me wrong. Pussy was readily available," Luther said with thick introspection. "Too available, which is why it wasn't worth a damn."

"Doesn't matter," Nick interjected. "Those days have come and gone, Pop. Whatever you did or didn't do is none of my business."

Luther stared back at Nick from the mirror on the other side of the bar. "Naw. It isn't."

"Guess what?" Yolanda Johnson asked blowing through the front door. "Nick?"

The two of them had gone to school together since kindergarten.

"Hey, girl," he said, standing to give her a hug.

She looked cute with locs hanging down her back, a nose ring, a cutoff top hugging some surprisingly nice curves, and a full skirt, dragging the floor.

"You moving back?"

"No," he said, admiring the freckles spraying her pretty honey colored complexion. "I'm just visiting."

Yolanda hurried around to the other side of the bar and shoved her backpack underneath. "You will never guess what I heard?" she said, staring at Luther.

"What'd you hear, Yo?" he asked, unimpressed.

"Well, seems you're not the only celebrity in Devastation, Mr. Luther," she said, propping a hand on her hip and looking like whatever news she had was about to bust her wide open. "A real life movie star just bought that old house on Dupelo," she announced. "You know that little one that's been vacant for years."

"A real live movie star," Luther repeated with sarcasm. "Why the hell would a movie star move here and buy that house?"

"Why'd you move here, Mr. I know Janet Jackson and Teddy Riley and Jesus?"

"Not Jesus," Luther corrected her. "And this is my hometown."

"I think you're jealous," she said, leaning across the counter, putting her face close enough to Luther's to kiss.

Nick quickly concluded, that yeah. His old man was doing a chick the same age as his son.

"Why would I be jealous?"

"Because there's someone living here more famous than you now."

"Who?" Nick probed.

Yolanda leaned back and asked, "you ever watch Vivacious Vixens of Atlanta?"

Luther and Nick exchanged glances before turning their attention to Yolanda.

"What about Beyond Time?" She looked back and forth between the two of them. "Shadow Lane?"

Nick shook his head. "Nothing."

"Damn, where y'all been living? Under a rock?"

"She obviously isn't famous," Luther responded with a glint in his eye like he was picking on her.

"The deodorant commercial," she exclaimed. "Pretty black woman, fro, inhales that deodorant and the scene behind her transforms from her bathroom into a meadow filled with pretty flowers?"

Nick looked at his father looking back at him. "Oh, yeah," he said, his tone filled with sarcasm.

Luther cocked a brow. "Her?"

Yolanda returned a broad smile. "I wonder if she'll give me an autograph?"

STILL SHINING

This cute little house gave Terri the tingles. In the three months since she'd moved in, she'd had the plumbing and electrical redone, replaced the roof, and had the outside painted an adorable yellow and white. Terri refinished a lovely, little antique porcelain tub by herself, thanks to YouTube.

She'd hired contractors to do most of the work, but this riding mower was her baby. This little beauty had a ten horsepower, single-cylinder engine, hydrostatic transmission, and an eighteen-inch turning radius. Donning a ball cap, oversized sunglasses, sunscreen, shorts, black Chuck Taylor's, and an Atlanta Falcons' tee-shirt, Terri drove it like she'd been born to ride this thing, the vibration of the engine underneath her ass, fueled her with super human power.

The locals had been parading past her house since she'd moved in. She had even been interviewed and featured in the local paper a month ago, with the headline, "Devastation Has a Brand New Celebrity Calling It Home".

Terri smiled and waved at people gawking at her from the street, and like good, small town people do, they waved back. For the first time in years, she felt relaxed. Authentically relaxed, like, she looked forward to waking up in the morning, relaxed. Terri's mind was focused on her next project instead of wondering whether or not the phone was going to ring that day, offering her a new role, and then going to bed at night, pretending she wasn't broken when it didn't happen.

In Devastation, Terri could breathe. The mental exhaustion weighing her down all these years, had been rising from her like steam since leaving Atlanta. Terri was alive again here. She had no idea what tomorrow held and that was okay.

Terri had no idea how long Lanette Dole had been yelling and waving to get her attention over the roar of that mower, but she pretended not to see the woman for as long as she could. Not that it mattered. Lanette had hiked along the narrow trail through the woods from her property to Terri's the way she'd done every day since Terri had moved into this place, making it her mission in life to indoctrinate Terri into the community of Devastation and to dig in as Terri's new BFF.

"Hey, Lanette," Terri yelled, back, forcing a smile and turning off the engine. "How are you?"

Those three words were all it took for Lanette's enthusiasm to take over, sending her bounding like a child in Terri's direction, with a smile broad enough to split her whole head in two.

"You look so cute on that thing," she said, wrapping arms ladened with beads, bangles and bobbles around Terri, damn near knocking Terri off her seat.

"Thank you, Lanette."

Lanette drew back, eyebrows raised in surprise, an entanglement of lavender braids piled on her head like a nest. Intense, wide, amber eyes bore into Terri's.

"You are amazing. Most people don't work in the yard in the heat of the day. That's insane. They mow the lawn early in the mornings or before sundown. This heat will melt your brain, make you have a sunstroke or something, Terri."

"Well, I— ""

"Stop being stupid and get in the house, girl."

The pained expression in the woman's eyes bordered on a weird mix of an irrational and demanding fear. Madness. Yeah. That was the word.

"I'm fine, Lanette, and far from stupid."

"Oh, of course," she blurted out, lacking the essence of an apology. "Maybe lacking common sense, though. A vegetable garden would be nice, right over there in the corner." She pointed. "Some turnips, carrots, tomatoes, onions, maybe even some potatoes."

"I'll certainly think about it," Terri said, hurriedly.

"You got a hoe?"

"A what?"

Lanette laughed. "Silly. I'll bring mine over next week and we can get started. It's a little late in the season, but something ought to come up."

"No, thanks, Lanette," Terri hurried and said. "I'll wait until next year."

"We gonna have to get started a whole lot earlier in the morning," she continued, as if Terri hadn't said a word. "I'll bring sunscreen because I know you probably don't have any. Dark skin folks don't ever think they can get sunburn, but they can."

"I have plenty of sunscreen."

Lanette's biracial ass had just crossed the line of unacceptable with that dark skin comment.

"And like I said, I'm not planting a garden this year."

"Oh, I don't mind," the woman responded. "I'm thinking six in the morning ought to be a good time to start."

Terri was just about to snap back, but Lanette interrupted, "Have you made up your mind about tonight?"

"Tonight?" Terri feigned ignorance.

"Line dancing class at Luther's? Duh," she said, rolling her eyes. "Boss Man's teaching this week and he's got new choreography."

"Oh, yeah, no. I'm not going to be able to make it. All this work on the house has me exhausted."

"Mowing the grass in the middle of a hell hot day ain't helping. Get inside, shower, and take a nap so you'll be nice and rested for tonight."

"The sooner you leave the sooner I can finish."

Leave it to Lanette to ignore the rude implication behind Terri's statement.

"We need to get there early to get a table. Half the town shows up every time he comes to town to teach. I'll see you tonight. Get some rest."

Terri turned the key in the ignition to drown out the inevitable retort from the woman, mouthed the words, "It was good seeing you," and drove off, leaving that crazy broad to swim alone inside the chaos of her own crazy mind.

❧

A SHOWER and a few hours later, Terri donned a cute, floral, spaghetti strapped sundress, Tori Burch flip flops, slathered her body with lemongrass scented shea butter, and picked her fro to perfection, all for a trip to the grocery store.

"The famous Ms. Dawson."

It's impossible not to get all weak kneed over a baritone that intentional. Terri looked up into the stunning face of a god and suddenly flashed a red carpet worthy smile.

"Hello," she practically sang, extending a limp wristed hand to shake.

He was leading man handsome, tall, six-two or six-three, strong, square jaw, close cut salt and pepper beard, dark, broad shoulders…

"And you are?" Terri asked.

He gently wrapped that big, paw of his around her dainty hand and said, "A fan. I read the article about you in the paper a few weeks back. Needless to say, it was impressive."

Her cheeks flushed warm, but not because of the compliment about her career. A man like him simply raised temperatures.

"Well, thank you very much. My career has been rather interesting, to say the least."

She was a big deal in this town, and Terri relished it.

"From Hollywood to Devastation." He grinned. "Sounds like a movie title."

Was he being sarcastic? Funny? Terri resisted the urge to laugh or to cry. If her career had gone the way she'd hoped, she'd be living large and in charge in a high rise condo in Manhattan or in a fabulous Malibu beach house. Instead, Terri was standing in the grocery store of a town she'd never known existed until the day she grabbed breakfast one morning at a dive off the highway.

"Everybody needs a change from time to time," she explained, making sure to maintain the *smize* in her eyes.

"We all do," he agreed. "Moving to a place like this is a big one, though. You got family here?"

She wasn't looking for a man. In fact, it had been years since Terri had been in a serious or semi-serious relationship. She'd always had an unnatural aversion to the "M" word. Marriage.

"I need to be related to someone in this town to live here?"

"Absolutely not." He shrugged those massive shoulders. "Forgive my short sightedness and welcome to Devastation."

"You're forgiven," she said, with a wry smile. "And you never told me your name."

"Luther Hunt. I own a bar and grill here called Luther's," he continued.

He was *that* Luther? The one Lanette had told her about?

"You should stop by sometime. I'll buy you a drink."

"What makes you think I haven't stopped by?"

"I'd have remembered if you had." He grinned.

Score!

"Maybe I will pay your place a visit."

"Tonight? Unless, you have other plans."

Line dancing night. Lanette night. No. No. No. Luther night? Well…

"I'll think about it," she said with the coyness of a character she might play, before turning back to her cart and pushing it away.

Terri made it to the end of the aisle and glanced back over her shoulder one last time, pleasantly not so surprised to see him standing there, watching her.

LOOKING FOR SOMETHING

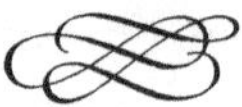

Luther watched appreciatively as the beautiful woman exited the condiments aisle. The flowers on that dress undulated against hypnotic swaying hips. Pretty, chocolate, toned calves, flexed with each step she took in those high heeled sandals.

Without a doubt, Terri Dawson was a welcomed addition to Devastation. Standing in front of shelves lined with bottles of ketchup, Luther dared to contemplate possibilities. When was the last time that happened? His wife passed away five years ago. Since then, Luther skirted encounters with women, meaning sometimes there was conversation, dinner, sex… but never more than that before he'd conveniently become too busy to get together or "forget" to return a call. Not that 'more' was on his mind now, just admiration of a gorgeous little movie star with pretty legs.

❧

LUTHER LIVED in a loft apartment above his bar. He still owned the house he'd shared with Ava but rented it to a family of five. He couldn't bring himself to sell it, though. He'd bought it outright with the first check he'd made from touring with Tina Turner. Back then,

Luther and Ava had been married for a few years. He begged her to move to Los Angeles with him, but six months later she told him she wanted to go home.

"Me and Nick don't belong in L.A., Luther," she argued, incredulous, nursing their three-month-old-son. Her beautiful, shoulder length hair was parted down the middle and braided on both sides. "I don't know anybody. People are rude, and I miss my family." Her beautiful, brown eyes blinked back tears.

"I need my family close to me, Ava," he reasoned. "I'll be spending a lot of time in studios when I'm not on the road, baby. I need to come home in the evening to you and Nick just like any other working man."

Ava challenged him with a look. "And that's the problem. You're always working or on the road, and we're stuck here in this apartment or trying to navigate a city so big it makes me feel like a minnow."

Luther understood. Hell, he was small town too, but the work was here. Luther wasn't good at shit else but music, and he made damn good money playing. The kind he'd never make back home. Ava looked as if she could read his mind.

"We'll be fine, Luther. You come home when you can."

"I can buy you that house you been wanting, baby," he said, kneeling next to her, "I can fly home on weekends when I'm not on the road."

It was a shitty arrangement, but he couldn't think of another one.

"When ain't you on the road, Luther? My momma's there," she said. "My family and your family are all there, and I need all the help I can get with this boy."

Luther ended up being on the road eight, nine months a year, and the truth was, he felt better knowing she was safe at home with family.

YOLANDA HAD SPENT the last three hours creating a chalkboard mural at the entrance of the bar, complete with colors, swoops, swirls, flowers, butterflies, and an image of a fancy glass full of the drink special for the evening; Elderflower and Herb Cooler.

"What the hell is an Elderflower Herb Cooler?" Luther stood back, folded his arms, and asked.

She took a few steps back to admire her own work. "It's delicious. That's what it is," she answered with pride.

"What's in it?"

When it came to alcohol, Luther was basic. Beer, wine, gin, vodka, or whiskey. Yolanda's creative little brain took shit to a whole new level. Most of his customers seemed to appreciate it.

"Thyme and rosemary, which I grew in my garden," she said, counting off on her fingers. "Edible flowers, posies and rose petals, elderflower, cordial, and liqueur."

He looked at her. "We have that?"

"We do now. All mixed together and topped off with sparkling water."

"The cheap kind?"

"Of course not. We're all about class around here, boss. Trust me. People appreciate it."

Line dancing wasn't Luther's thing, but it drew big crowds and was great for business. Luther was old school and preferred one-on-one dancing with a woman. That group shit was too damned impersonal. Doors opened at six. By six-thirty the place was packed and waiting on what's his name to come in and show everybody his latest dance steps, which all looked the same to Luther.

Luther split his time between greeting customers, helping to wait tables and serving up drinks. Stella and Ronnetta, line cook duo of any restaurant owner's dreams, flawlessly managed the kitchen, serving up a native Louisianan's dream of gumbo, red beans and rice, boiled crawfish, fried catfish and snapper, étouffée, alligator tail, and whatever other delicacy they decided to conjure up.

It did his heart good to see his son in the mix. Nick drew women like flies to shit and was loving every minute of it. He might never give a damn, but he did his old man proud. But then, Luther had always been proud of his kid. No matter how many times he said it, Nick never bought it. His son, the doctor, was blessed with his mother's charisma and good looks. Through the years, Luther was out of

Nick's life more than he was in it, doing a better job of bankrolling his family than being an active participant.

Chris Ardoin's lyrics and Zydeco sound filled the room, creating a magnificent wave of dancers moving in a fluid sway. Luther stood behind the bar and took a moment to marvel at the beauty of the scene unfolding here in his place. Every once in a while, his life still held wonder and even a little bit of awe.

Speaking of wonder and awe…

Lanette Dole abruptly dropped out of her place in line on the dance floor, squealing, and making a bee line for the front door.

"Terrrrrrrrriiiiiiiiii!"

Luther's own heart, surprisingly lurched a little at the sight of the woman as Lanette grabbed hold of Terri's hand and dragged her across the room to a small table near the dance floor. All eyes fell on the two women, or rather, the newest resident of town.

"Is that her?" one of his bartenders, Amanda leaned in and asked Yolanda. "She looks famous."

Luther cocked a brow. "What does that even mean?"

"Expensive. She looks… expensive,"—Yolanda looked Luther up and down— "kinda like you."

"Luther," Stella called to him from the kitchen doorway. "That door's stuck again."

He groaned in annoyance and reluctantly headed back to the kitchen. Duty called.

❧

"MAN, told you this is where all the honeys are," Nick's friend, Donny explained. The dude huddled over their small corner table, gawking like a vulture waiting for one of them to pass out so he could swoop in and start pecking at her.

The two of them grew up together. Donny was one hell of an artist, capable of creating museum quality shit. Every now and then somebody would pay a ton of money for one of the pieces posted on his website. Dude had even done a few years at NYU before dropping out and moving back home.

"Man, they play a different kinda game on that East coast. Tried to talk to females and they walked away before I even finished telling 'em my name. I couldn't even buy a phone number."

The truth was, in New York, Donny was an amoeba in a city that stomped his ego like a grape. But in Devastation, he didn't have to lift a finger for women to fall at his feet, despite knowing he was a dog. Donny's ass was lazy, but not so lazy that he hadn't left some babies in his path. At last count he had four.

"I thought we were meeting up with Joe and the boys to play poker," Nick retorted. It wasn't that the ladies in the room didn't look lovely, but Nick had grown up with most of them or had been babysat by a few. So, no. He wasn't interested in any woman on the dance floor.

Donny shook his head. "Joe and his cousin cheat. I don't play with them fools no more."

"I ain't staying long."

"That's cool, Doc." Donny shrugged. "Get yo' high and mighty ass back to N'Awlins, Dr. Nick."

"You don't have to tell me twice."

All of a sudden, Donny's eyes stretched so wide Nick feared for the man's health. "Whoa—" he reached out and slapped Nick's arm—"Check it out."

She was petite, five-four, maybe. She came in rocking a perfect fro and showing off a lovely figure. Without saying a word, she caused a commotion. People bumped into each other staring at her, but dude leading the class just snapped his fingers and barked orders.

"Y'all keep up!"

Crazy Lanette Dole possessively dragged the woman across the room behind her, and Nick's heart immediately went out to her. Everyone in town knew better than to get too close to Lanette. Her crazy could spread like a curse if you weren't careful.

"Yo, that's that movie star who just moved here, man," Donny announced. "Damn, she fine."

Without saying another word, Donny was up and making a beeline for the woman, rubbing his hands together and licking his lips in that creepy way he did when he was about to pounce.

Nick bowed and shook his head, glancing up a few moments later, just in time to see Lanette's scowl, the movie star's confusion, and the lame lip licking, squinting game Donny had been throwing since the seventh grade, collide. All of a sudden, Lanette stood up, grabbed the woman by the hand and dragged her out onto the dance floor, placed her in line, and commenced to following the lead of the big dude leading the class. Donny sat there, watching, waiting, the wheels spinning behind those crazy, obsessed eyes of his, considering his next move.

She was cute and did look vaguely familiar. Maybe it was because she was cute or maybe it was because she was a new fixture in town, but Nick found himself staring too. Irritation started to mask her pretty face. An angry glance at Lanette, a jerk of her arm, and catastrophe!

"Oh shit!" someone yelled, before bodies scattered, some toppling like dominoes.

"Terri? Terri are you alright?"

"No, I'm not all right, Lanette," she snapped, from somewhere on the floor of that crowded dance floor. "Get away from me."

"I'm just trying to help," Lanette snapped back.

"Come on." Donny magically appeared, emerging from the crowd with the woman limping at his side and carrying a blue, high heeled shoe with a lethal looking heel. Donny eased her into her seat and the doctor in Nick bolted to action and hurried to her side.

"What's the problem?"

She grimaced in pain and pensively balanced her foot on the tips of her toes. "I twisted it."

Nick knelt beside her and gently examined her ankle, being careful not to hurt her if he could help it.

"Ah," she exclaimed, when he touched a particularly tender part he knew to be a tendon.

"It's starting to swell," Lanette said, hovering over Nick's back. "Looks broken."

"Can you straighten it and put any weight on it?" he asked.

She attempted to flatten it and managed to press about forty percent of her foot to the floor.

"Why'd you wear those shoes?" Lanette blurted out. "You don't see anybody else in here with no shoes like that."

If looks could kill, Terri Dawson had just slayed the hell out of clueless Lanette.

"How about I take you to the hospital," Nick offered.

"I can take her," Donny chimed in.

Nick looked at him. "You don't have a car."

"Let me borrow yours."

"She's my best friend," Lanette snapped. "I'll take her."

"Let's go," he said, offering to help the woman up.

It was evident, as soon as she stood, that she wasn't walking on that foot. Without thinking, Nick scooped her up and carried her out the door.

IT TOOK ten minutes to fix what he'd been promising to hire someone to fix. Luther came back into the bar, cursing himself under his breath for procrastination that cost him *opportunity, just* in time to see his son, Nick, holding Terri Dawson in his arms and carrying her out the door.

A LITTLE SOMETHING

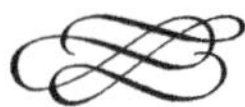

"You sure it's not broken?" Terri asked the nurse wrapping her swollen ankle, bracing herself for one wrong move by that woman's hands that would send a shockwave of pain through her whole leg.

That damn Lanette.

"Not broken," Dr. Nick said, casually leaning against the wall with his arms folded.

Teri's tall, dark, handsome knight had swept her up in his arms like she was as light as a feather in that club. She felt like a regular damsel in distress for the first time in like, ever. But damn, her ankle still hurt like hell.

"Lanette Dole is the enemy," she said out loud, staring at the swelling.

"As are those shoes you decided to dance in," he chimed in with a smirk.

Terri glared at him. "I've danced a thousand miles in those shoes."

"You can walk a thousand miles across a tightrope over the Grand Canyon," he explained. "Doesn't make it safe."

"An extreme analogy."

So, he was a cute asshole. She'd met plenty of those in her time.

"But you see my point."

She wanted to argue. Terri searched her wit for a snappy comeback but came up blank.

"You'll need these," the nurse said, handing her crutches. "But for the record, those shoes are dope."

Terri smiled. "Thank you."

Dr. Nick shook his head and said an exasperated, "Wow."

"So, you're a movie star," he commented on the drive back to her place.

"Yes," she responded, simply.

Terri had acted in some movies. Was she actually considered a "star" among her peers and in the industry? Maybe, not quite, but still...

"What's a famous actress doing in Devastation, Louisiana?"

Something about the way he said it hinted sarcasm, and she found his question a little offensive.

"I'm semi-retired."

"What movies have you been in?"

Was she offended that he didn't know? Yes. Yes, she was.

"Streets of Vegas," she shot off first. *"Beyond Darkness. Lives of Ashford."*

He cocked a thick eyebrow. "That soap opera?"

"You've seen it?"

"No, but I heard about it. My great-aunt watches it every day. She'd love to meet you."

"Your great-aunt?"

"Yeah," he said with a smirk and a side glance. "She's eighty. I'm sure she'd recognize you if she met you."

Terri decided, in that moment, that she didn't like him.

"You've got this old house looking great," he said, pulling up to the curb in front of her house.

"It's getting there."

Dr. Nick helped her out of the car and up the steps to the front door. "Are you going to be okay from here?"

Terri rummaged through her purse for her keys. "I got it, hero."

She hobbled inside, turned to him, and smiled. "Thank you, Dr. Nick."

"Happy to help, Miss Movie Star. Keep it elevated and stay off of it as much as you can. Ice it to help with the swelling."

"Ice on my foot sounds unpleasant." She frowned.

"It is... but it works wonders."

"If you say so."

"Can I see you again?" He asked, surprising her.

Terri's smile disappeared. "What?"

"I'd like to check up on you the next time I'm in town, if that's okay."

"Oh, you don't live here?"

"Not anymore. I mean, I was born and raised here. It's home, but I practice in New Orleans."

"I see."

Did he really just want to come by and check on her or was he sort of, in a roundabout way, asking her out? When was the last time that happened? A long time ago. When was the last time she'd said yes? Even longer.

"Sure," she said, trying not to turn this into something weird.

"I just feel responsible," he added like he was trying not to make this weird too.

"Why? You were not the one grabbing hold of me like I was property and making me fall down in a room full of line dancers."

Evil Lanette.

He smiled. Good Lord! All the man's superpowers were in that smile.

"Following up with my patients is not only my duty as a professional, but also self-serving."

"How so?" she probed, searching for a hint of a come on to emerge from this man.

"I just like helping... if I can," he said, humbly and convincingly sincerely.

"Well, I appreciate it. It's not often that I get to see a doctor without having to pay a copayment."

"Exactly," he shot back. "I'm saving you twenty dollars."

"Awesome."

"All right then," he said, turning to leave. "You take it easy, and I'll see you in a week or two."

"Goodnight," she called after him. "And safe travels."

Just after nine, Terri lay in bed with her foot propped on a stack of pillows, sipping Merlot and watching *The Devil Wears Prada, again*. She must've watched this movie a hundred times, marveling at the artistry of the Magnificent Meryl Streep and how she'd shed her own skin to become Miranda. Performances like that raised her pulse and electrified the desperation in her to raise the bar for herself as an actress and to be better. To always be better. If only she'd landed a role like this. If only, someone would've given her a chance, a role where she could've truly showcased her talents, then Terri would be up there with the A-list actresses of the world.

The phone rang, bursting her bubble of wishful thinking and regret. Thank God. Terri answered too hastily and without checking to see who it was.

"Hello?"

"Oh, Terri, girl, are you okay? I've been so worried."

Lanette. Terri rolled her eyes so hard; it was a wonder that they found their rightful place again in her head.

"I'm fine."

"Is it broken? You looked like you were in so much pain…"

"Not broken."

"It was those shoes, Terri. Everybody knows you don't wear shoes like that to—"

"It's late, Lanette," she said, cutting her off. "I'm tired."

"I'm just saying. This ain't Hollywood and you don't have to be extra like that around here," Lanette said with a bitter version of sympathy. "I'll come by and check on you in the morning."

"Don't, Lanette."

"It's no problem, Terri. I don't mind."

"Lanette— ""

"I'll bring biscuits and bacon. You got eggs?"

Without saying another word, Terri ended the call.

She'd made the mistake of being polite to Lanette when she first moved into the house. It didn't take long for Terri to realize the woman was desperate for interaction because everyone else in town already knew her ass was a lunatic. One simple, "It's nice to meet you, too," from Terri was all it took to get hooked by Lanette and dragged out into the sea of her insane mind. But after tonight, Terri knew it was time to stop being nice and to cut the fishing line on this relationship.

Bright and early the next morning, Terri, balancing on crutches, stared into the face of Lanette Dole. She was standing on Terri's front porch, holding an aluminum covered plate, grinning from ear to ear.

"Hey, sweetie," she practically sang, pulling open the screen door and coming inside without being invited, then had the nerve to stop in front of Terri and deliver air kisses. "How you feeling?"

Lanette looked like a meadow, wearing a floral maxi dress and a wreath of baby's breath circling her colorful braids.

"I hope you're hungry. I've been up since three this morning making these biscuits," she said, continuing into the kitchen.

"Lanette," Terri called out, following her.

"It's my great-grand mommy's recipe," she continued, unabated. "If I told you what the secret ingredients were, I'd have to kill you."

"Lanette," she said, more insistent.

"A nice pot of coffee, some scrambled cheese eggs… Mmmmm." Lanette closed her eyes and sighed.

"Lanette!"

"Your foot hurt?" she asked, staring back at Terri with concern.

"I didn't invite you over."

Lanette smiled. "You know I don't mind. It's my pleasure and I had a feeling you wouldn't be up to cooking. A nice breakfast will make you feel better."

"I don't want a nice breakfast," Terri snapped.

What the hell was wrong with this woman? Terri was sending signals, major signals, in the form of arrows, daggers, and bullets.

Lanette acted like she was Superman and the damn things just bounced off her chest.

"Are these dishes clean?" she asked, pulling a plate from the cupboard and scratching the face of it with her finger.

"I wouldn't put dirty dishes in the cabinet, Lanette," Terri snapped.

Lanette insisted on running it under tap water. "You sure about that? Anyway, you were all anybody was able to talk about last night after you damn near broke your foot."

"You damn near broke my foot," Terri shot back.

"Oh, shoot," Lanette exclaimed. "I forgot the preserves." Lanette immediately opened the refrigerator, found a jar of grape jelly, held the jar out to Terri and grimaced. "This all you got?"

Terri's ankle throbbed as she hobbled lover to the woman and snatched the jar from her hand.

"Did they give you any pain medicine?" Lanette continued, reaching back into Terri's refrigerator, retrieving eggs. "Pain is making you a little cranky."

"No. You're making me a little cranky. In fact, you're pissing me off."

That got her attention. Lanette stared wide eyed at Terri like she was actually seeing and hearing her for the very first time.

"I did not invite you over, Lanette. I don't want your great-grand mommy's biscuits, and I'd appreciate it if you'd stay the hell out of my refrigerator."

Tears? Like real tears? A lip quiver? Seriously?

"I only came by to help," she said, her voice quaking.

Terri had spent months working in reality television with some of the biggest drama queens in the history of drama queens. Lanette was a rookie.

"I didn't ask for your help," Terri continued. "I didn't ask for you to drag me onto that dance floor and damn near break my leg."

"You shouldn't have worn those shoes," Lanette shot back. "Out of all the people at the club last night, you were the only one to come strutting in with red-bottoms on, Terri."

"I can wear what I want, Lanette. You had no right putting your damn hands on me, just like you have no right bullying your way into my kitchen with biscuits I don't want."

Lanette seemed to fold in on herself and for a brief, millisecond, Terri almost wanted to take back everything she'd just said. Thank God, she knew better.

"Fine." Lanette swiped at a tear rolling down her cheek, pushed past Terri and headed for the door. "Keep the biscuits, and you don't have to worry about hearing from me again."

"Good."

"May God's grace continue to shine down upon you, Terri," she said, letting the door slam shut behind her. It was Lanette's one last attempt to go for the jugular with her passive-aggressive ass. "I'ma pray for you, girl."

Terri took ten deep breaths before finally making her way over to the tray of biscuits and inhaling. She'd been doing pretty good with curtailing emotional eating, lately. Terri slathered a little butter and jam onto one of the biscuits and took a bite.

Damn. Great-grand mommy's recipe was to die for.

COME MY WAY

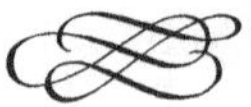

Nick Hunt wanted to impress a woman. He'd been thinking about Terri Dawson since meeting her a few weeks ago and decided to go online to find out everything he could about her. He'd teased her the first time they met, pretending not to recognize her. She absolutely looked familiar, but in all honesty, he couldn't pin down seeing her on television. He pulled up her IMDb page, streamed some movie clips and scenes from that soap opera she was in. Nick even downloaded and watched a sci-fi flick she'd been in. By the time he'd finished, Nick was definitely impressed. She'd recently been fired from some reality show, though. The article mentioned words like "uninteresting", "flat", and "dull". He figured that firing might have something to do with why she ended up "semi-retired".

"It's still tender but at least I don't need those damn crutches to get around the house."

Pretty legs.

Terri walked back and forth demonstrating her recovery to Nick wearing a pair of cut off jean shorts and a fitted New Orleans Saints tee shirt. Her lovely halo of dark curls was pulled back, framing a pretty heart shaped face and wide, brown eyes. He'd made his way back to New Orleans and as soon as he had a few days off, he was back in Devastation.

"Good," he said, trying to sound more impressed by her healing than all of her. "But don't overdo it. If you have to be on your feet for long periods of time, please use your crutches."

"Oh, yeah," she assured him. "Thankfully, I work from home."

Terri sat on the sofa across from him.

"So, what do you do now that you're semi-retired from acting?" he probed.

Terri blinked in confusion. "Do?"

"I mean"— he shrugged — "you work some other type of job?"

Beautiful eyes darted back and forth between Nick and a beautiful philodendron plant on the windowsill across the room.

"I'm considering some things," she offered. "Voice over opportunities... things like that."

"Yeah. That's cool."

"I sold my condo in Atlanta, and I still collect royalties from— ""

"I wasn't prying," he interjected. "I'm just trying to get to know you better."

She raised a brow. "Why? I thought you just came to check on my ankle."

"Well, I did, but... it's not obvious?"

Terri sighed, "I mean, I could speculate that this is a come on, but I'd rather not."

He couldn't help it. Nick laughed.

"What's so funny?"

He stopped laughing, composed himself and sighed, "Will you have dinner with me?"

"I was going to speculate that you wanted to ask me out," she said, smirking.

"Well?"

Terri turned her head slightly, narrowed her gaze as if sizing him up. "How old are you, Dr. Nick?"

He resisted the urge to ask the dumb question, 'how old do I look?' but it was hard not to feel dejected by her response. Still, Terri was a straight shooter, so Nick decided to shoot back in a straight line.

"Thirty-five. How old are you?"

Yeah. No. He hadn't really paid attention to that part during his research, or, maybe he just hadn't cared.

"Forty-three. A little too old for you." She smiled.

Was she being apologetic? Condescending? He couldn't tell.

"I disagree," he said, returning a smile of his own.

Confidence. Nick reached down deep and pulled it from his ass. She was a grown woman. A beautiful woman. A woman who'd probably dated her share of leading men, and Nick had to believe, no, he had to *know* that he was a leading man in his own right. Shit! Since when had he ever felt insecure with a woman?

"I am flattered," she chuckled.

"Is that a yes? You'll have dinner with me?"

"Didn't I just tell you that you're far too young for me?"

"No. You indicated that you thought you were a little too old for me, and I disagree."

"Semantics, Dr. Nick, but the fact remains that there's nearly a decade between us."

"What difference would it make over dinner?" Nick felt damn proud of himself for that response. Witty. Mature. "I've given you free medical care," he continued. "I've even gone so far as to make a house call. Who does that?"

"No one that I'm aware of," she reasoned.

"Exactly. So, in return, I'm just asking you to have dinner with me. That's all."

"Free medical care, a house call, *and* you want to buy me dinner? Or am I supposed to buy you dinner?"

"That's totally up to you," he responded.

"Since you asked me out, you'd be the one paying."

"No problem. Is that a yes?"

"Not yet." She pursed her lips in contemplation. "Just dinner?"

"Food."

Hope rising? Dare he let it?

"Fine," she reluctantly agreed. "I accept your invitation, Dr. Nick."

"Good," he said, playing it incredibly cool. "Tonight? Six?"

"I kind of wanted to wait until my ankle healed so I could wear—"

"Tonight," Nick interrupted. "You can wear sneakers or flip flops."

Terri wrinkled her nose. "Sneakers?"

"You'd look damn cute in sneakers."

She chuckled, "I think I own a pair. I'll have to check, or, flip flops it is."

Nick couldn't help but to grin. "I'll pick you up at six."

❧

CAVIAR AND FILET MIGNON was rare in Devastation. Gumbo, blackened redfish, and crawfish étouffée were plentiful. Chuck's BBQ was a local favorite. Nick had every intention of impressing the hell out of her and spent the rest of the day driving himself crazy trying to figure out how to do it.

"What about laying a blanket down underneath a tree, with wine and food?" he asked Yolanda who was sitting across the table from him.

Nick had stopped at the diner for coffee and ran into Yolanda finishing up her lunch.

She immediately shook her head at his suggestion. "That shit only works in the movies," she said. "Bugs."

Made sense.

"What's good in Baton Rouge?"

"That's a whole hour and a half away, Nick," she reminded him. "Y'all wouldn't be eating until like eight. They've got a fancy seafood place, though. Clara's or Cleo's or something like that. It's pricey. She'd like it."

"Not a lot of options."

"Luther's has a mean a steak and oysters on special."

"Yeah, I don't want to take her there."

"You still mad at your daddy?"

"Not mad. Just not... anything."

"He's good people, Nick, and I think you'd see that if you gave him a chance."

"Noted, but right now I'm trying to impress a woman."

"You're impressive enough already, if you ask me." She smiled.

He chuckled, "That's because you've had a crush on me since kindergarten."

"I have," she laughed. "And I might kind of wish it was me you were trying to impress."

Nick couldn't tell if she was serious or teasing him. "I'm sure you have plenty of dudes around here trying to impress you, Yo."

"Go to Miss Jolene's," she said, changing the subject.

"On Levee Road?"

Her eyes lit up. "Tell her you have a date with a special woman and want her best table."

"Miss Jolene's got great food, but the place is a dump."

Miss Jolene ran a small restaurant, if you could call it that, out of her house, seating people on her screened in back porch.

"Miss Jolene is the most romantic woman in town, Nick. She's in love with the notion of love." Yolanda smiled. "Trust me on this."

"Love?" he drew back.

Nick wanted to treat the woman to dinner, not get married. Love was premature.

"Don't be bullshitting me, Yo," he half-heartedly warned. "Miss Jolene's? This better not be a joke."

He and Yo went back a lifetime, and neither of them were above, or below, the occasional practical joke.

"Not for something like this, Nick."

"Something like this?" he probed.

"Love." She offered a soft smile. "I'm the second most romantic person in town, after Miss Jolene," Yolanda laughed. "Why do you think I'm still single?"

"Nobody here deserves you," he concluded, studying her and wondering where all this love language was coming from.

"Not a soul."

LOOKS GOOD TO ME

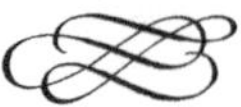

Nick pulled up in front of a small, white bungalow on the edge of town that looked a lot like the one Terri lived in.

"So, we're having dinner with your family?" she questioned, choking back disappointment as Nick helped her out of the car.

This was not her idea of a friendly 'Dr. Nick payback' first date. Terri wasn't expecting this evening to be anything more than it was… dinner with a nice man, but still. Meeting his family was pushing it.

He smiled and brilliant, perfectly straight, white teeth beamed at her like moonlight. "I wouldn't do that to you."

Nick dressed for the occasion, a nice blazer over a fitted black tee, tucked neatly into designer jeans, and leather lace up shoes. Terri, refused to wear sneakers, but managed to find a cute pair of flats to wear with a simple, halter top summer dress. She also refused to drag even one crutch out of the house this evening.

"They don't go with this outfit," she'd told him when he asked about them right before they left her house.

Nick knocked lightly on the front door and a large, older gentleman, the color of charcoal, wearing a crisp, white button down underneath his finest khaki overalls, greeted them with a welcoming smile and slight bow.

"Welcome to Miss Jolene's," he said, ushering them inside.

Once inside, Terri's nostrils were greeted with the most heavenly scents she'd ever encountered, savory, buttery aromas made her mouth water, and even Nick licked his lips after getting a whiff.

"Follow me, please," the kindly man said, leading them through a small living room that looked like something off the set of that old Archie Bunker sitcom.

A brown, plaid sofa, worn leather recliner covered with a crocheted blanket and doilies made Terri feel like she'd walked through a time portal back to the seventies. Terri glanced over her shoulder at Nick, offering an uncertain smile in response, as they trailed behind the giant man to a creaky screen door opening to what looked like the back porch. Yeah. This was going to be a tough night and the last date the two of them would ever have.

"I'm Bruce and I'll be your waiter for the evening," he said with an accent somewhere between American south and the queen's English.

Bruce pulled Terri's chair from the table for her to sit. The look on Nick's face was just shy of full-on terror. He'd fucked up and he knew it.

Bruce stood by and recited the following:

"On tonight's menu is our creamy and delectable crawfish bisque with delicately toasted and buttered sliced baguette, pan seared red snapper with a delicious garlic-herb vinaigrette and a side of dirty rice," he said, grinning and licking his lips as if he'd already sampled the food. His eyes lit up even more, "and for dessert, a slice of Miss Jolene's famous eight-layer yellow Doberge Cake with chocolate butter cream frosting."

"Tell me you like seafood," Nick said, staring at her with a concerned look on his face.

"I love seafood."

"Splendid," Bruce exclaimed, clasping large, calloused hands together, looking as relieved as Nick. "May I start you with some wine? I recommend the white to go with the fish."

Again, Nick glanced at Terri, who smiled her approval. "Perfect."

The whole set up was so fairytale-ish that it was actually charming. Theirs, was the only table on the back porch of Miss Jolene's house. It was screened in, which was nice because it kept the bugs away, and strings of soft lighting hung all around, setting a surprisingly romantic atmosphere.

"I took a chance," Nick blurted out after Bruce disappeared inside. "A big one, on a recommendation from a friend."

"Boy, was it a big one," she agreed.

The two of them stared at each other until Nick laughed first. "I kind of dig it."

Terri smiled and bobbed her head from side to side in consideration. "I kind of do, too."

Nick sighed and slumped slightly in relief, but it was true. Surprisingly, Terri found the whole scene scripted to perfection and like something out of a Reese Witherspoon movie.

"This is a real restaurant?" Terri probed.

Nick shrugged. "Apparently."

She laughed.

"One of Devastation's best kept secrets," he added.

"I'll say. It's nice, though, in an unassuming kind of way. Miss Jolene is the chef?"

"That's my understanding, and the owner."

Miss Jolene must've been listening. Suddenly, the screen door magically appeared to open, and Miss Jolene floated over to their table like a fairy godmother. A bright, welcoming smile exploded from her taupe, full moon, freckled face. She was the roundest thing Terri had ever seen and absolutely adorable. Sandy brown waves of hair pulled away from her face, covered in a hairnet that, upon close scrutiny, appeared to be adorned with glitter.

"Welcome," she beamed at the two of them. "Welcome, and it is so wonderful to meet you." She turned specifically to Terri when she said it.

"I've never had a celebrity come here before. I read all about you in the paper, and I watched you on my favorite soap opera, *Lives of Ashford*," she chuckled and lightly touched Terri's shoulder "Dr. Claudia Braxton."

"Thank you," Terri said, smiling and resisting the urge to glance at Nick after recalling his comment about his great-great whoever being a fan of the show.

"I never believed you deserved to go to prison for killing that brute of a husband," she said with earnest.

"Well, my contract was up so..."

"He deserved everything he got. Had it coming," she said with tears glistening in her eyes. "I kept thinking they were going to find a way to bring you back."

Actually, Terri didn't want to go back.

"It was just time to go."

Miss Jolene blinked and the tears disappeared. "You're here now," she chuckled. "In my house, and that's all that matters."

"It's lovely here, Miss Jolene," Nick finally chimed in.

"Oh, thank you so much," she said, pouring on thick, syrupy appreciation. "My establishment is small, but I prefer it that way, especially for lovers."

"No, we're not— "" Terri tried interjecting.

Nick grinned.

"I can't tell you how many couples have come here who ended up married or with new babies." She winked.

Nick looked at Terri, brows raised, eyes wide. "Is that so?"

"Yes, it is," she assured them both. "If you ain't married to each other when you come here, give it a minute."

Miss Jolene chuckled, turned, and left, disappearing back inside, and leaving that damn threat hanging in the air like a dark storm cloud.

"You look scared," Nick commented, leaning on the table.

"This is just dinner," she reminded him. "I don't plan on letting you get me pregnant."

He leaned back, smirking. "That's too bad."

The food was breathtaking. Bruce deserved the Wait Staff of the Millennia award, and Dr. Nick was most charming. At the end of the meal, the two shared a slice of Miss Jolene's decadent cake.

"I can't remember the last time I've enjoyed myself on a date as much as I have tonight," she admitted, admiring the handsome man across the table from her.

"Quit playing," he joked. "A beautiful woman like you? I'd imagine you have all kinds of leading men chasing you down."

"A few," she admitted, introspective and trying to resurrect the memory of any that actually felt legitimate. "Dating in my line of work isn't for the weak."

"No privacy?"

"No authenticity," she admitted. "Everybody's clawing their way to the top, and if dating a particular person can get them there faster, then..." she shrugged "or, they're looking for that cheerleader, that ride or die, someone to hold it down for them while they chase what's damn near impossible to catch."

This revelation surprised her, but it was the truth. Terri had been one of the players in that game for years, and tonight, this date with Nick was probably the most authentic she'd had since her high school prom.

"This was nice," she said, leaning back and smiling. "Very."

Without realizing it, that fine young man sitting across from her had come dangerously close to making Terri long for something she never realized she'd missed. A relationship. A real one.

"It's still early," he said, glancing at his watch. "Wanna go walk off this cake?"

She curled her lip, "I didn't bring my crutches."

"Then let's go sit somewhere nice."

"That'll work," she laughed.

❧

"I COULD'VE HAD Parker drop this off, Luther," Darnell said as he helped Luther load boxes into the back of his truck. "He could've swung through, day after tomorrow."

"Nah, I need some of this in the morning, D," Luther explained.

A woman's group was having a brunch at his place tomorrow at eleven, and the cook, Brenda, had just informed Luther they were out of cooking oil, flour and cinnamon.

"Next time I'm sending Brenda's ass to come pick it up if she don't give me more notice," he complained.

"I hear you."

Half an hour later, the truck was loaded. Luther sat behind the wheel for a few moments before starting the engine but stopped short when he saw his son.

Nick sat on a wrought iron park bench with his arm draped over the back, behind Devastation's newest citizen and celebrity, pretty Miss Dawson.

"Well, damn," he muttered with a slight smile.

An air of unexpected pride filled his chest at the sight of his son, wooing the woman on the radar of just about every man, single or otherwise, in Devastation. Nicholas Hunt, doctor, grown man, and looking pretty damned pleased with himself. Good. Good for him. Luther had never been the father Nick wanted, but he'd only ever wanted his son to be happy.

Seeing the two of them together gave rise to memories Luther put away a long time ago. He'd spent so much time on the road that sometimes he'd forgotten the moments he shared with Ava when it was just the two of them. Memories of a time when Luther didn't have to hurry up to be somewhere. Before *'I love yous'* were said over the phone, stretching across oceans and continents. She was his love, heart, and soul, but that love came in tiny pieces, having to be assembled like a puzzle to remind him of what they had before she got sick.

Luther started the engine, watched his son laughing and enjoying the company of a beautiful woman, and envied him.

TAKE EVERYTHING IN

"How's that dreadful little town treating you?" her agent, Roxy, asked, her question lacking any real enthusiasm or interest.

"Small. Quiet. Quaint, and no over the top drama," Terri shot back.

"When are you moving back to the A?"

Terri sighed and rolled her eyes, not that Roxy could see them. "Never."

"You stay there, Terri, and you won't have to worry about dying from old age. You'll die from boredom."

"I'm retired, Roxy. For real, but if any decent voice over gigs or even commercials come across your desk, give me a shout."

"You keep saying that," she whined.

"Because it keeps being true."

"You know Tyler Perry is always hiring."

"Yeah, and by the time my chance for an audition comes up, his shows are already casted. You got to know Tyler or one of his people to get one of his roles."

"You know how this business is. The pendulum swings back and forth. You hang in there long enough and it'll swing your way. It's physics."

"Do you have any idea how exhausting and demeaning all that is, Roxy?"

"I know it feels like it."

"Countless auditions, sitting and waiting by the phone for that call telling me I got a part, hoping and praying that some punk ass casting director deems me good enough is belittling, Roxy. I'm tired."

Silence hung between them. Roxy was a great cheerleader, but Terri didn't want to play anymore.

"So, what do you do for fun?"

Terri laughed, "I've got an unhealthy fascination with a fabulous riding mower."

"Cool."

"And… I've been dating."

"What? When's the last time you said that to me?"

"Years."

"Anyone in particular?"

"His name is Nick."

"Nick? I'm listening."

"It was just a friendly dinner, Rox."

"I see."

"No you don't. It's not like that."

"But is it on its way to that?"

"Probably not. He's cute, but young."

"How young?"

"Thirty-five," Terri said, wrinkling her nose.

"That's not young, Terri. That's grown."

"Not grown enough, and it's really not serious. I fell and hurt my ankle dancing. He picked me up, carried me to his car and took me to the hospital. He's a doctor. He just wanted to be sure I was okay."

"A doctor? Is he cute?"

Hell yeah!

"He's alright." Terri grinned.

"Just alright?"

"A little better than alright."

"And just a friend… like platonic?"

"Absolutely."

Terri hadn't lied. She and Nick had gone out once, talked on the phone a couple of times, and even bantered back and forth in a way that could be considered flirting, but she wasn't in a hurry to get serious with him or anyone else.

"Fine," Roxy continued. "I won't push for you to tell me more because I know you won't."

Terri laughed. "If it turns serious, you'll be the first to know."

"Promises. Promises."

Another call came through. It was Nick.

"I gotta take this call," Terri told her friend.

"Tell Nick I said hello," Roxy laughed before hanging up.

"Hey," Terri answered.

"Hey. Is this a bad time?"

She was starting to look forward to hearing the sound of his voice, but it was a platonic appreciation. That's all.

"It's a fine time. How are you?"

"Exhausted. Been working a crazy schedule the last two weeks covering for another doctor in the ER."

"Sorry to hear that."

"Don't be. It's my job, right? I was thinking about you," he admitted.

He was thirty-five, eight years her junior. Terri looked at herself, wondering if what was happening was *really* happening, or even if it should.

"Still worried about my ankle?" she teased.

Eight years was a big difference, but for the first time in longer than she could remember, Nick brought a kind of real to her life that she couldn't remember ever having.

"I'll be back in town this weekend. Think we can get together?"

She smiled. "I'd like that, Nick."

Terri had walked away from her career. Maybe now, it was time to walk away from that other version of herself, the one that could never quite grasp the idea of tangible.

"Cool," he said. "I was thinking—"

"Dr. Hunt. You're needed in emergency," Terri heard someone interrupt.

"I've got to go," he said, abruptly. "But I'll call you later."

"Okay. Talk to you soon."

She'd spent her life chasing a dream only to end up here, in this small bungalow, in Devastation, Louisiana, with just herself. Terri dedicated all of herself to that dream and ultimately, she was all she had left. There was never the time or even the interest to seriously pursue romance. Marriage, a family, not even a dog played into the theater that was her life, but now she had this... this new existence and this new opportunity to explore what it was really like to get to know someone with the intention of forming an actual relationship. Sure, other actors did it all the time, but Terri had married desperation a long time ago, clinging to her career, her hopes for it like a buoy. Terri had lost everything she feared losing, and she was still here, still breathing, and that anxiety she'd clung to all those years was gone.

She smiled, but the tears came. Not sad tears. Not even close. Tears of relief, of release, and tears ushering in this new phase of her life. Terri, surprisingly, was looking forward to seeing Nick too.

❧

LANETTE'S SERVING tray had been sitting, nicely washed, on Terri's kitchen counter for the past two weeks. She'd eaten so many biscuits, if she never saw another one, it'd be too soon, but dang, they were good. Terri hadn't heard a peep out of Lanette since the day the woman abruptly showed up at her house for breakfast, which was fine by her, but she needed to return that dish to the woman so there'd be absolutely no ties between them.

"What's, what's happened?" Terri asked, stunned at the sight of Lanette being carried out of her house on a gurney and loaded into the back of an ambulance. "Is she, she alright?"

"You a relative?" one of the paramedics stopped to ask.

"No. No, I'm her... Is she okay?"

Lanette's eyes were closed. She wasn't moving.

"Do you know her family? Anyone you can get in touch with?"

The paramedic rushed over to the ambulance and climbed in behind the wheel.

"No, I… I don't know."

"We're taking her to St. Agnes," she informed Terri.

"Let's go," another paramedic shouted from the back.

"Can you please contact her family and let them know where she is?"

Terri nodded and backed away as the ambulance peeled off, sirens whirring. She felt like she'd been kicked in the gut.

They'd left the front door wide open. Numbly, Terri went to close it, but before closing it all the way, remembered that she'd come to drop off the dish. It was silly, but…

Family. She needed to find Lanette's family and call them. Terri went inside and stopped just inside the doorway, bewildered by the scene.

Sunflowers on decorative pillows, painted on the walls, flowers in vases, some dead, some alive. The woman was obsessed with sunflowers and not in a good way. Terri winded through the living room crowded with too much furniture, tables, vases, and figurines, all in the shapes of or decorated with sunflowers.

Terri made her way to the kitchen, littered with Styrofoam containers, empty soda cans, and candy bar wrappers. She searched through kitchen drawers looking for a phone number or book with contact information for someone she could call. The search was futile. People didn't write down phone numbers anymore. They kept their contact information on their…

"Cell phone," she muttered, going back into the living room, then the bedroom looking for the woman's phone.

Eventually, she found it underneath one of the pillows on the bed. Terri prayed it wasn't locked, and it wasn't. She clicked on the phone icon, then searched recent calls, but all she could find were calls to the electric and water companies, eight-hundred numbers. It was odd. Not one personal call to or from anyone. Terri decided to check her contacts list, and again, there were no personal contacts, except for one. Terri Dawson.

A sinking feeling weighed in her stomach. Crazy, Lanette had no friends. She had no one, because no one wanted to be bothered with her. There was no one to call. Not a single person who would be worried about her in that hospital... who would know if she lived or died.

Terri moaned, plopping down in a chair across from the woman's bed.

Lanette had no one.

Terri uncovered her eyes and took a deep breath. "Shit, Lanette. Isn't there anyone?"

As much of a pain in the ass as that woman had been since Terri first met her, she shouldn't have cared. But she did.

Terri walked back across the clearing to her place, grabbed her purse and keys and got in the car, headed to St. Agnes.

HARD TO BREATHE

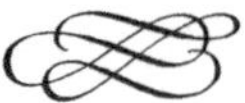

"Holding up good, old man."

Luther sighed with relief after finishing up his exam.

"Old," he repeated, taking a seat across from Ryan, his doctor. "I ain't claiming that."

"Good," Ryan said, finishing up his notes. "Cut back on the salt and get back in the gym to get that blood pressure down."

"Can I pick one or the other?"

"Nope. Both. It's manageable now, but only if you make some lifestyle changes. Otherwise, I'll have to put you on medication."

"I don't like medication."

"Then follow my orders."

"Roger that."

Luther was fifty-four. Seemed like yesterday, he had finally managed to wrap his mouth around the word 'fifty', but sixty was coming at him like a bullet. It wasn't that long ago when time didn't mean shit because he had so much of it. At least, he thought he did. Time turned toxic when Ava got sick, though... as toxic as the Lupus gnawing on her.

"See you in a year," Ryan said, following Luther out of the exam room.

"Same time, same place," Luther agreed.

❧

"LANETTE DOLE? They just bought her in less than an hour ago," Terri explained to the receptionist at the front desk.

Luther was on his way out when he noticed her.

"Are you a relative?" the young woman asked, typing into the computer.

"No. I'm her neighbor. I tried find a relative, but — ""

"What's going on?" Luther asked, appearing next to Terri.

Terri looked at him like she didn't remember him.

"Luther," he reminded her. "We met at the market. What's going on with Lanette?"

"You know her?" Terri asked.

"Yeah. What's up?"

"I don't know," Terri frantically said. "I went to return something to her and an ambulance was at her house. They brought her here. I tried to find family. Do you know any of her relatives?" Terri asked Luther.

"I'm her brother," he lied.

Lanette had no family. At least, none that would come see about her.

"*You're* her brother?" Terri asked.

He turned his attention to the woman behind the counter. "Where is she?"

The receptionist sent them to the third floor where they waited until the attending physician came out and told them what had happened.

"The doctor is with her," the nurse, a young blond woman, told them.

"What happened?" Terri asked, before Luther had a chance to, though he suspected he already knew the answer.

"Overdose," she explained. "The doctor will be out shortly to give you an update."

"Overdosed?" Terri asked, stunned.

"Why would she do something like that?" Terri muttered, looking lost, and then looking up at Luther. "Why would she do that?"

"Is she going to be all right?" he asked.

"It looks like she'll be fine," she assured them before leaving. "Physically."

"Why the fuck would she do that?" Terri blurted out, lowering on shaky legs to the seat behind her. "Are you really her brother?"

"No," he admitted. "But I knew they wouldn't let us see her if I didn't say I was."

"We need to call her family, Luther," she reasoned. "They should be here with her."

"They won't come, Terri."

She looked surprised. "What? Why not?"

Luther sat next to her. Understanding Lanette wasn't easy. Explaining her was hard as hell. She was younger than Luther, but older than Nick, and everything he knew about her was second-hand information.

"From what I hear, Lanette's family doesn't have anything to do with her."

"So, we need to call them anyway and let them know she's in the hospital, Luther."

"It won't matter," he told her.

She looked like she didn't believe him.

"Look, families have their differences, but when something like this happens—"

"It's happened before. I've heard that this is what she does. Lanette takes pills, tries to kill herself and then calls the paramedics to come get her before it's too late."

"That's crazy."

"It is, but it's not the first time I've heard of it."

"Gossip. Stupid gossip. Who'd do that?"

"Look," he said, exasperated. "From my understanding, there is no one in her life. You're the only friend she has."

"I'm not her friend," Terri admitted, lowering her head.

"You're here."

"Because somebody had to be here. I tried to find a number for someone close to her."

"Nothing?"

Terri was silent.

"Because there probably is no one. People steer clear of Lanette. I don't have first-hand experience. I don't know the details." He shrugged. "As far as I know, she's got no one."

Tears glistened in her pretty eyes. "That's so fucked up."

"It is."

Minutes passed before she finally spoke up again. "She tried to be my friend," Terri told him. "I pushed her away because..."

"She's a lot?"

"That's the understatement to end all understatements."

"I've heard that too."

"Pushy. Presumptuous. Irritating. Sarcastic. Bossy. Demanding."

"I get it."

"She doesn't listen. Lanette does what she wants and drags you with her because she doesn't see you, or hear you, or care, but she pretends you're all she cares about until it becomes smothering, suffocating—"

"I get it, Terri." he said, cutting her off. "She's a lot."

"Nobody likes her?"

He shrugged.

"It's understandable," Terri concluded. "But sad. Sad enough for her to do this."

Terri looked into his eyes. Luther's heart kicked.

"Does she have family in town?" Terri asked him.

"I think she's got sisters in town, Liza and Lilly or Lola, something like that. I think her mother died, and I don't know about her father."

Terri stared straight ahead. Luther stared at her, moved by her concern for a woman she didn't even like.

"Hi," the doctor said, approaching the two of them. "Are you here for Lanette?"

Both stood.

"How is she?" Terri asked.

"She's fine. Resting. We had to pump her stomach." Concern creased the woman's brow. "This isn't her first suicide attempt," she explained. "We'd like to put her on a 72-hour psychiatric hold for evaluation."

Terri looked at Luther. "Do you need permission to do that?"

"Not for 72 hours. After that, she can refuse care. I think it'd be in her best interest that we evaluate her."

"Agreed," Luther offered before Terri could even think of arguing. Lanette obviously needed help.

"Can she see anyone?" Terri asked.

The doctor smiled. "Sure, but only for a few minutes. She's exhausted."

Luther followed Terri, taking cautious steps toward Lanette's bed. It didn't take long for him to realize Terri had no idea what to say to the woman. Lanette managed to open her eyes and turned her head towards Terri.

"You okay?" Terri asked.

A tear streamed down the side of Lanette's face. She looked away and closed her eyes again. Terri hovered over her for a few moments before turning to leave.

Luther managed to convince her to go to the coffee shop to compose herself before getting in the car and driving home.

"I UNDERSTAND DEPRESSION," she told him, hovering over a cup of hot tea. "We all go through it from time to time."

"We all do," he agreed. Luther knew it all too well.

"I feel guilty," she admitted.

"Why?"

"Because I told her that I didn't want to be her friend, not knowing that she didn't have any, and then this happens."

"What's that got to do with you?" he asked, a bit taken aback by her believing she had that kind of impact on the woman.

"If I hadn't pushed her away..."

Luther cocked a brow. "She wouldn't be here?"

"Exactly."

"You're not that important, Terri," he blurted out, clearly insulting the woman.

"That's not what I meant."

"Lanette has issues. Issues that she had long before you showed up in town."

"That's not what I mean," she argued. "Why are you trying to make this sound so—"

"Egotistical?"

She pushed her cup away and slipped the strap of her purse over her shoulder. "Thanks for the tea."

"Terri," he said, knowing it was too late.

She left him sitting there, feeling like a complete ass. Luther rushed after her to apologize.

"Terri," he called out, racing to catch up with her. "I'm sorry. I didn't mean—"

She spun to face him, pissed. "I am not so full of myself that I think I'm to blame for what she did."

"I know."

"No, you don't know. You don't know me. I was mean to her. I was impatient. Maybe if I'd been more empathetic, she wouldn't feel so alone. Maybe if we were all more empathetic with her, she wouldn't be here."

"You're right."

"Goddamn right I'm right," she said, storming off again.

"Or,"—he continued following her— "she's got deeper problems than just needing empathy or patience."

"What's your point?" she stopped and spun to face him again.

"My point is don't blame yourself. Lanette needs help. Maybe now, with you pushing her away, she'll finally get it."

That was better. He hoped.

She took a deep breath and seemed to deflate before his eyes. "Broken people," she murmured, lowering her head.

"Don't be hard on yourself," Luther continued, resisting the urge to pull her into his arms. "You're here for her now when no one else would come. She might not have said it, but I have a feeling, it matters."

Terri wrapped her arms around him, rested her head against his chest, and exhaled slowly. Luther hesitated before wrapping his arms around her.

"You're right on both accounts," she murmured. "I can be full of myself and she does need help."

Luther swallowed. "Uh, okay."

She pushed back, looked up at him and smiled. "Thanks, Luther."

"For what?"

She shrugged. "For pretending to be her brother. For staying and for listening."

"No problem."

Something happened. A pause between them. A look. They both noticed and without saying a word, they both acknowledged it.

"I should be going," she said, stepping away.

"Yeah, uh. You going to be alright?"

She nodded and smiled. "I'll be fine. Thanks again."

Terri waived and left him standing there, feeling the kind of school-boyish shit he hadn't felt since high school.

TRAGEDY

Terri was all up in her feelings. What else would compel her to wrap her arms around that tall, dark, pillar of a gorgeous man she barely knew? Luther smelled like ocean air, Redwood trees, a thick, warm blanket, a cool fan, a burning candle, and fresh water. He smelled wonderful and felt as solid as iron, as valuable as gold, as coveted as ivory, and as precious as platinum. Damn!

Terri managed to make it back to her car on legs that were, hopefully, unnoticeably wobbly, tossing one last wave over her shoulder, and topping it off with a friendly smile. Superman had kryptonite. Terri, obviously, had Luther. The thought that a man could have this kind of effect on her was unsettling, and she desperately needed to put some distance between him and her before she did something stupid, like get pregnant.

He stood off in the distance and waited for her to pull out of the parking lot. Terri's heart lurched as she drove past him, waving. What in the world was in the water in Devastation, Louisiana? Tall, handsome men were casting all kinds of spells on Terri, melting her resolve like butter in a hot skillet.

"Geesh," she said in exasperation. "Get it together, T."

To be thinking about a man right now, with Lanette laying up in that hospital all by herself, was ridiculous. The fact that there was no one from her family who cared enough to check on her was insane. Luther said she has sisters. Maybe he was wrong. Maybe, they would be concerned if they knew.

Instead of going home, Terri drove towards Lanette's and continued another quarter mile past her house to the neighbor living on the other side of Lanette. She parked, walked up to the door, and knocked.

A young woman, in her twenties, maybe thirties, balancing a toddler on her hip answered.

"Hi," Terri began. "I'm one of your neighbors. Actually, I live closer to Lanette Dole? You know her?"

The girl brushed long, dark braids off her shoulder. "Ma!" she called out. "A lady here about Lanette."

She turned and waked away, and was eventually replaced by an older, slightly heavier version of herself. The woman glared at Terri without offering a greeting.

"I'm here about Lanette?"

The woman pursed her lips. "Next house over." She motioned right. "That way."

"Yeah, I know."

She propped her hand on her hip. "Then, why you asking?"

"She's in the hospital. I'm trying to locate her family. I heard she has sisters."

The scent of marijuana, cigarette smoke, and maybe greens wafted through the screen door to Terri.

"Liza Cook," the woman said.

"Liza," Terri repeated. "Yes. Do you have a number for her or know where I can find her?"

"Over on Birch Street," she explained. "What's wrong with Lanette?"

"She's in the hospital."

It wasn't Terri's place to give this woman the details.

"Tried to kill herself again?" she asked, looking absolutely unmoved.

Terri cocked a brow, then turned to leave. "Thanks for your help."

"Uh-huh," the woman muttered, walking away, and slamming the door shut.

A quick Internet search on her phone pulled up Liza Cook's address on Birch Street. Terri sat in the car for several minutes, considering that she might be overstepping her bounds. After all, she and Lanette weren't friends, and the last thing she needed was to be pulled into some drama that wasn't any of her business. Terri started the car and pulled away from the curb.

❧

THE HOUSE LOOKED like something out of a storybook... white picket fence, perfectly manicured lawn, colorful rose bushes framing the foundation, and a porch with a charming swing set of a scene that reminded Terri of one of those old seventies shows. In the front yard was a handsome, white man with blond hair and a close cropped beard, tossing a baseball to an adorable curly haired boy.

"There you go, Taylor," he said, grinning with pride at the boy making a diving catch for the ball. "Good job."

He paused and looked at Terri. "Can I help you?"

Terri was starting to wonder if she had the wrong house or if there was more than one Liza Cook in this small town.

"I'm looking for Liza? Liza Cook?"

"She's in the house," he said, leading the way to the front door. "Honey, got a visitor."

As if scripted, a gorgeous golden retriever bolted from inside, stopping for a quick sniff of Terri's skirt before racing over to the boy.

Moments later, a beautiful, blue-eyed, auburn haired woman appeared, drying her hands with a towel. "Hi," she said to Terri. "Can I help you?"

Wrong Liza Cook.

"I'm sorry," Terri immediately said.

The husband brushed passed her and headed back to the yard.

"I was - I think I have the wrong house."

"Oh. Okay."

A teenage girl, looking just the woman, pushed passed the woman. "I'm going to Tasha's, Mom."

"You have your phone?"

"Yes," she said without looking back.

"I'm sorry," she said, turning her attention back to Terri, and then her eyes lit up. "Are you the actress?"

Terri blushed.

"Oh, my goodness. I saw you on the news, and I've seen you on television, too. I've never met a famous person before."

"Yeah, um... look, I'm sorry. I have the wrong house."

"Well, who were you looking for?"

"Liza Cook?"

She smiled. "That's me."

"I'm looking for the sister of a woman named, Lanette."

Just like that, her brilliant smile faded.

"Do you know her?" Terri took a chance and asked.

"How do you know her?" All the blue seeped from that woman's eyes. She looked absolutely miserable.

"We're neighbors. Lanette's in the hospital."

This was her sister? Lanette was light skinned. She could be biracial. This woman didn't look biracial at all, but that didn't mean shit.

"Come in."

Inside was as perfect as outside, gleaming hard wood floors, a show room living room, antiques, and family portraits. Terri sat next to Liza on the sofa.

"How long have you been in town?" Liza asked.

"Several months."

She nodded.

"Lanette's your sister."

"Half."

Like, that sucked. Terri never could get with that half or step bullshit. Either you had a sibling, or you didn't.

"She's my older sister. Our mother married my dad after Lanette's father left. A year later, she had my other sister, Lenore, and then me."

"She was admitted earlier today."

Liza dropped her gaze to her hands, "Another suicide attempt?"

"How does everybody know that?" Terri blurted out without thinking.

"Because it's what she does." She stared hard into Terri's eyes. "Lanette takes a handful of pills, just enough, then calls 911 telling them what she's done and cries about killing herself. They show up, take her to the hospital, pump her stomach, start counseling, and then they send her home." She pursed her lips, briefly, before continuing, "She goes to counseling for a while. She calls me and Lenore and tells us that she's doing better... until she stops therapy. Then she, starts making crazy phone calls to us, stalking and scaring my kids... and when me or my husband tells her to leave us alone, it starts all over."

Terri had nothing to say.

"I get it," Liza went on. "Things were tough for Lanette growing up. Her dad abandoned her. Mom got a new husband and new kids and she probably felt left out, but she's always done things to draw attention back to herself when she felt she was losing it."

"She's done these things with your other sister?"

"No," she shook her head, "Lenore gave up on her a long time ago. She's got a restraining order against her because things got way out of hand once. It got physical between them, so..."

"Is there anyone else?" Terri asked, feeling hope sink for Lanette with every passing moment.

"Lanette has made sure that there is no one else."

❧

THE DRIVE HOME was a lonely one. Lanette was a handful. Terri had experienced that firsthand, and she was no fan of the woman. She wasn't her friend and never wanted to be, but the idea of anyone being so alone was heartbreaking. According to her sister, it was her own fault, but still...

Her phone rang as she pulled into her driveway. It was Nick.

"Hey," he said, his voice magically bringing a smile to her lips. "Is this a bad time?"

"No," she said, filled with introspection.

The last six months, Terri had purposefully pulled away from people who loved her, who cared for her. She'd avoided phone calls from her parents, Nona, even her agent. Shame on her.

"I miss you," she admitted, fighting back tears.

"Why do you think I'm calling? I'll be in town this weekend. Can I see you?"

"You'd better."

LEAN IN

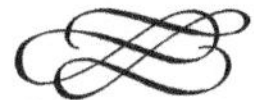

It was her idea to stay in for the evening.

"Dinner was delicious," he commented.

Nick and Terri sat side by side on a loveseat inside an enclosed gazebo underneath that huge, old tree in her backyard.

"Thank you," she said with a proud smile.

Nick nodded slightly. "You made it?"

"No," she admitted. "But I plated it."

He raised his beer bottle to clink with her glass of wine. "Well done."

"I'm not big on cooking."

"Your presentation is unmatched, though." The two of them laughed.

They'd been seeing each just over a month, now. This was the most time he'd spent inside her place. Dates like this were tricky. A brotha could jump to all kinds of assumptions. Terri was comfortable in a flowing maxi dress. She'd slipped out of her shoes and sat next to him with her knees drawn, toying with her hair. Man 101 told him that hair twirling, smiling, and fingers lighting on his arm were signs telling him that she was interested in things getting a little more personal than they had been. The intelligent side of him, the side that excelled in science and was smart enough to get his medical degree, warned him not to jump to conclusions.

Terri was flirty, but subdued. Nick wasn't sure what to make of it. What confused him more was when she leaned over and kissed him. And not one of those friendly pecks on the lips either. She lingered, stared into his eyes the whole time, and leaned back with a coy smile.

Yep. Finally, he was getting some tonight. Nick turned on the smolder and leaned in for a tongue wrestling kiss, when he noticed tears glistening in her eyes, conceding to all kinds of warning signs he hadn't expected.

"What's wrong?"

Terri shook her head slightly and let that doggone tear stream down her face squashing the whole vibe.

"Terri," Nick put down his beer and took hold of her hand, but not in that *'I'm trying to get with you'* way. More like that, *'I'm a doctor so tell me where it hurts'* way.

"I'm just..." she shook her head slightly and shrugged. Terri's gaze drifted to a thread from the throw she picked at on the loveseat. "My life is so different from what it used to be."

And that made her cry? She'd moved from Atlanta to Devastation. Of course, it was different, but different enough to cry about? Women were complicated.

Terri swallowed. "I've chased a dream my whole life, Nick," she explained. "Chased it until I became it."

Nick leaned back and listened because that's what she seemed like she needed.

"Acting has always been more than a way to make a living," she continued. "It's been my obsession. I woke up thinking about it, went through the day thinking about it, and thought about it some more when I closed my eyes to sleep for as long as I can remember."

More tears.

Should he do something? Say something? That small voice in his head, the one he'd mostly come to trust, warned him to be quiet.

"I'm a fuckin' has been," Terri admitted with a bitter chuckle.

"That's not true," he blurted out.

"It is and I know it. I've been knowing it."

"You're a celebrity, Terri."

"I'm a celebrity living in Devastation, Louisiana, and most people I run into here remember me from a toothpaste commercial."

Nick knew where this was going, and he sighed.

"I walk around here like I've won a goddamned Oscar, but I got fired from a reality television show because I wasn't interesting enough." Terri pursed her lips together. "And it was true. I had no real friends, no lovers or even hobbies. Because my whole life was about landing that role, the big one, the one that would finally put me at the top of the food chain and make my name a household word."

Terri finished half a glass of wine in one gulp and then knocked him upside the head with one hell of a statement, random and out of place.

"Lanette tried to kill herself."

Nick arched a brow. "She did?"

"And nobody gave a damn," She went on.

"But she's alright?"

"No," she said, shaking her head. "She's alive, but this is what she does, apparently, and something she'll no doubt do again, according to everybody in town, until she gets it right."

"And that's what's got you upset?"

Terri turned her attention back to that loose string. "Being here is as close to real life as I've gotten since before I moved away from home to L. A., to pursue my career." She looked at him. "I'm surrounded by *real* people living *real* lives right in front of me, and I can't turn away. I can't run back into my condo and disappear behind some script or spend a weekend searching through *Variety* for casting calls."

Terri took a deep breath to try and compose herself.

"For the first time in my life, I have to pay attention and I have to participate." She pursed her lips again. "Because I don't have a career to escape to. I don't have an excuse to bury my head in the sand and ignore the world around me," she sniffed. "Now, I have to pay attention, and not just to a woman so depressed that she regularly attempts suicide just get to get somebody's attention... but to me" she—"lighted her fingers on her chest— "the most self-absorbed person I know. Who am I if not the actress? What am I supposed to do now that I know I'm never going to land the role of a lifetime?"

Terri had gone down a rabbit hole, trying to drag him with her, but Nick couldn't wrap his mind around the gravity of what she was feeling. He wanted to, but she might as well have been speaking a foreign language. Terri Dawson was a celebrity, just not the caliber of celebrity she'd dreamed of becoming? Still, he listened. It was all he had to offer. Hopefully, it'd be enough.

"I sound crazy," she smiled. "Right?"

Truth or dare? *Tread lightly, man. You dig this woman, and you don't want to blow this.*

"You sound... lost."

She nodded. "I have lived my whole life wanting one thing, fighting for that one thing, and now that it's gone..."

"But is it really?" he questioned. "I mean, what's to say the call for the role of a lifetime still can't come, Terri? Of course, it can."

Terri shrank a little and turned to a silent introspection before answering, "I'm tired, Nick. So tired that I don't even know if I'd take it if was handed to me on a silver platter." She offered a vulnerable smile. "The thing about being here and having to face myself is that, for the first time, I feel three dimensional. I feel like I'm just waking up and seeing me in a way I never have before. I am not some character on a television screen that somebody made up. I am Terri Dawson, and now, as hard as it is, as heartbreaking as it feels, I get a chance to play the real role of my lifetime. I get to be me, and I have no idea how to do it."

"You look scared," he said, noting the trepidation in her voice, in her eyes.

"I'm terrified," she sniffed, wiping away tears, and took a deep breath. "But I think I'm finally ready."

"Well, that's a good thing, Ter—"

Before he could stop her, before Nick had a chance to prepare himself, Terri straddled him, tugging and pulling on his belt, his jeans.

Terri stared wide eyed at him, pressed her mouth to his and slipped her tongue past his lips. Her fingers slipped into his underwear and grabbed hold of Nick's dick. It was swelling by the millisecond in her palm.

Fuck! What the hell?

Terri hiked up her dress, slid her panties to one side and…

"Shiiii -"

Warm. Wet. Terri lowered herself onto him, pressed her third eye to his, stared at Nick. and stopped.

"I need you," she whispered. "I need this."

Nick nodded. "Yes," he said, wrapping one hand around her waist, cupping the back of her head with his other hand, and pushing one long, slow thrust into her. "I know."

Terri released a trembling moan and pressed her hips against him. "Slow, Nick," she pleaded, closing her eyes. "Don't rush."

Fuck, he didn't want to rush. Nick absolutely didn't want to rush, but she felt so damn good. Yes, he wanted to rush. He wanted to tear that shit up, but… no. No, Nick. Slow!

Terri kissed him. She wrapped both arms over his shoulders and held on to Nick as if her life depended on him, setting a pace all her own and challenging him to match it.

Slow, goddammit, Nick!

He was not a one-minute wonder, but everything about this woman threatened to pull that orgasm from him too damn soon. Nick grabbed hold of her hips with both hands to stop her momentum and gain control.

"Wait, Terri," he muttered in her ear. "Just… stop."

Terri stopped. Nick shrugged to catch his breath, and then she…

"Aw, shit!" he exclaimed, squeezing her ass and pulling her closer to him.

It was too late. Nick bucked like a rookie getting laid for the first damn time until he exploded inside that woman and everything went black.

GET USED TO YOU

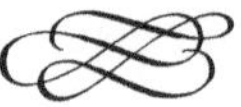

"Huh," Nick drove his hands deep inside his jean pockets and teetered back and forth a bit in front of her house.

"Enjoyed our evening together?" Terri smiled, answering for him.

He chuckled, "Absolutely."

"You heading back to New Orleans tonight?"

He shook his head. "Nah, in the morning."

The pause between them left plenty of room for her to invite him to spend the night, but Terri wasn't ready for a sleepover. Sex was one thing. *Spinin the night* was something else, altogether.

He leaned in for one last kiss and planted pillow soft lips to hers. Nick drew back, and stared into her eyes. "I'll see you again… soon."

She smiled. "Counting on it."

He waited until she was inside the house before easing his car away from the curb. Terri hadn't planned on sexing the man, but vulnerability led her to the comforts of his lap. Terri closed the front door, leaned against it, and released an audible sigh. She'd expected to feel regret. Nick was so much younger than she was, and Terri wasn't interested in a relationship with him, just friendship. The last thing she wanted to do was to lead him on, but is that what she'd done, or did two grown, consenting adults simply have sex because they wanted to?

She made her way to the bathroom, turned on the shower, started to undress and paused.

And what if she did want to have a relationship with him?

"Dag, Terri," she said out loud. "How long has it been?"

Years. She'd dated, had a few trysts, but Terri was married to her career and there was never time to focus on anything or anyone else but that. Until now.

She stepped into the water and pondered the concept. "A true, blue boyfriend."

Normal people dated. Hell, even actors had relationships, complete with full-blown husbands, wives, kids. Terri had never even allowed herself the luxury of a pet, but that was before. Her life was different now and there was space to explore all the things she hadn't had time for when she was scratching and clawing her way through her obsession. The revelation washed over her like this water. Yes. She was officially retired, and it was time to move on to the next half of her life.

"I wonder if I can still get pregnant?"

Kids? Terri got a visual of her pregnant, then her trying to breast-feed, changing a diaper and... crying?

"I'm good," she said, quickly dismissing the thought. "Maybe I'll get a cat."

The phone rang just as she crawled into bed.

"Hey, Rox," she said, slipping underneath the covers.

"Don't tell me you were sleeping," she fussed. "It's not even midnight."

Terri groaned, snuggling deeper into fluffy pillows. "You know I'm on country people time now, girl. Quit playing."

"Well, wake up. I've got something important to tell you."

"I'm listening," she sighed.

Roxy had that tinge of enthusiasm in her tone, that in the past, would've had Terri standing at attention, eager to hear what she had to say. This time, though, Terri had to fight the urge to end the call before the woman could delivery her news.

"Now, it's not official, but I've been told that that something big is headed our way, Terri."

"Don't, Roxy," Terri warned, sitting up in bed. "Please."

She knew where this was headed, and Terri didn't want to go there.

"Just listen, T. This is major, honey, and I think it's the role you've been waiting for... dreaming of, Terri."

"How many times have we had this conversation?" Terri interjected, not bothering to hide her frustration.

"I know. I know, Terri, but this could be the one. Word has it that an announcement is going to be made soon in *Variety* and that you're being considered for the lead role in a feature film."

Word has it.... being considered...

Ambiguous words that meant nothing. Terri couldn't touch rumors and speculation. She had banked her heart and soul on them so many times, only to have to pick herself up off the ground, dust herself off, nurse bruises and wounds and march on to the next disappointment like a good little soldier.

"Terri," Roxy continued. "I know how hard the last several years have been."

"No, more like the last decade, Roxy," she corrected her.

"I've been here with you, every one of those years, sis. So, I *do* know. Believe that. I wouldn't even mention this if I thought it was a bust. I wouldn't set you up like that, especially not now."

Tears clouded her vision. Getting news like this from her agent, should've put Terri on top of the world, but instead she felt detached from the one thing she'd wanted most in the world. Maybe Roxy was right and it was a sure thing. Terri had been riding the rollercoaster of her career for so long, that she never believed she knew how to get off. But she *had* gotten off. Terri had walked away from her dream but nobody believed that she really had. Especially not Roxy. Not even Terri had believed it, until this moment.

Terri lay back down and pulled the covers to her chin. "I had a date tonight," she said changing the subject.

It took Roxy a moment to respond, "A date? That's nice. How was it?"

She smiled at the memories of the evening spent with Nick. An evening spent enjoying his company, dinner... intimacy.

"I enjoyed it."

"So... you'd rather talk about your date instead of the movie role of a lifetime?"

"For the first time in a very long time, I'm living my life, Rox," she explained, full of introspection. "A normal, boring life in this tiny ass town, surrounded by the kind of people I'd have never even noticed before getting fired from that damn reality show."

"Terri..."

Terri needed to drive the point home to her agent that she really was finished with the business of acting and that there was life outside the film industry—good and bad and Terri was neck deep in it, finding her place in it.

"He came over to my place for dinner."

"You cooked?"

"You know better than that," she laughed. "We ate, talked about real shit, Rox, and then I sexed the man so good he came in minutes."

"Damn."

"Right? I'm not even mad because he wasn't ready."

"Why are you telling me this, Terri?"

She sighed, "Because I'm not sitting around waiting and biting on my nails for you to call me about a role. I'm not sick to my stomach when the news comes that I was passed over. I'm not jumping out of bed at the crack of dawn checking the internet for parts or counting my pennies to be sure that I'll have enough money next month to pay my mortgage."

"I get it," Roxy softly responded.

"Do you? I've lived for my dream and it's kicked my ass almost the whole time. And now, I'm living in this tiny house, in a tiny town with people who treat me like I'm Regina King, and I'm happy, Roxy. I've been featured on the local news, in the paper. I've signed more autographs here than I have in my entire career. I've got a handsome man that I'm seeing and another one that I have a mean crush on, and I'm enjoying how I'm living."

Roxy laughed, "Two dudes, Terri?"

"I'm not seeing both of them. But my point is, being a retired actor has freed up all my time to do the kinds of things other people take for granted, to discover, not only the woman I truly am, but other people. It sounds crazy, I know, but I don't want to go back, Roxy. I don't want to go back to being that crazed, obsessed woman who believes she's nothing because she didn't get the part."

Roxy laughed, "Your life sounds way more interesting now than it did when you were filming *Vivacious Vixens*, girl."

"It is more interesting. The whole time I was on that show, I was on the phone with you talking about a part in a movie or commercial. And when I wasn't talking to you, I was talking to one of them crazy bitches, trying to pretend I didn't see the eye rolls."

"Yeah, you really were boring." Roxy laughed.

Now you tell me."

"You were too good for those people, T. I hope you know that."

"Thank you for standing by me all these years as my agent and thank you for being my friend."

"How come I feel like there's a "but" coming?"

"But now, you're fired, Roxy," Terri said with finality. "I don't need an agent anymore, but I will always need my friend."

And there it was. Cut. That's a wrap. Terri was done.

WHY?

Lanette was drama. She was the town crazy. She was annoying, condescending, and presumptuous. Most of all, she was sad. Not that it was any of Terri's business, and not that she should've even given a damn considering the woman had damn near broken Terri's leg, but for whatever reason, Terri felt compelled to call and check on the woman. The day Lanette was released, Terri found herself standing in the lobby, waiting to take her home.

Dark, sunken half-moons cradled Lanette's hollow gaze when they wheeled her to the exit. Her colorful braids had grown out, exposing sandy brown natural roots.

"What are you doing here?" she asked, glassy-eyed at Terri.

"Came to take you home."

Lanette looked like she didn't believe her. "I was going to take an Uber."

"Let's go," Terri said, turning to leave.

Five minutes into the drive, Lanette made a statement, "I need a drink."

Terri glanced at her. "Aren't you medicated?"

Lanette shrugged. "Not enough."

Lanette is not your friend. Lanette is not your responsibility, Terri.

For some asinine reason, Terri drove to Luther's. Ten minutes later, the two sat in a booth across from each other sharing a pitcher of mango mimosas in complete and utter silence. That was the best way to share space with Lanette as far as Terri was concerned. Of course, Lanette had to ruin it and start an actual conversation.

"Why'd you come get me?"

The thought briefly crossed Terri's mind to be kind with the woman, to be empathetic and tender toward this wounded soul, but it kept on crossing until it was gone.

"Hell, if I know."

Lanette took another sip of her drink as if she was cool with that answer.

"Why'd you try to kill yourself?" Terri blurted out, then immediately regretted it because she didn't care. She really didn't. She was curious. Nosey. There. That was it. Terri was being nosey.

Lanette stared at her. That was her answer.

"Ladies." Tall, dark, and good-looking Luther said, sauntering, not walking, over to their table. "You good with the drinks or would you like me to send Yolanda over with some menus?"

That any human being could be so utterly captivating seemed impossible. Sure, he was handsome, but he was also something else. His persona radiated magnetism to the point where it should've glowed nuclear red and flashed a warning to stay out of close proximity to the man.

Terri managed to peel her eyes off him and momentarily divert her attention to Lanette. "I'm good. You?"

A weird little smile curled one corner of that woman's lips. "I'd love a menu, Luther."

"You got it," he said, walking away.

A few moments later, Yolanda flitted over like a beautiful butterfly. "Hey, ladies. So, the lunch special is the Angus burger with steak fries."

Without even opening the menu, Lanette ordered, "I'll take it, medium well, please."

"Yes ma'am," Yolanda said. "And for you, Miss Terri?"

"I'm good, Yolanda," Terri responded, glaring at Lanette.

Terri sure hoped this bitch had money.

"You on a diet or something?" Lanette asked, giving Terri a disapproving side-eye.

"No."

A long, weighted pause hung between them before Lanette, the real one, showed up at that table. "I hear being on television makes a person look ten pounds heavier. Does that bother you?"

Terri rolled her eyes. "Why would it bother me?"

"Cause you ain't skinny."

Terri was just about to say a cuss word when Yolanda showed up at the table. "Figured you two might want some waters."

As soon as Yolanda left, Lanette leaned across the table and said, "What's up with you and Luther?"

For the first time since Terri had picked her ass up from the hospital, life flooded that woman's eyes like she'd suddenly grown a soul.

"What?"

A broad and unexpected smile spread across her face. "And don't you dare try to tell me ain't nothing going on because you'd be lying."

Terri leaned back, crossed her arms, and stared at that woman in dismay. "There you are. The intolerable, insufferable Lanette."

That smile disappeared. "Insufferable? Is that what you think of me?"

"That's what everyone thinks of you."

Terri wanted to snatch back the truth as soon as it flew passed her lips, but it was too late. The woman had just tried to commit suicide because no one cared, and Terri's mean ass was sitting here, driving the point home.

"Because I say what I think?"

"Because you say things *without* thinking. You blurt out whatever pops into your little mind without consideration for anyone else, and it makes being around you… challenging, at best."

A look akin to something manic, filled Lanette's eyes. "You dig him."

Terri huffed and rolled her eyes. "Oh, God, Lanette."

"Don't be ashamed, girl. Who ain't into Luther?"

"I'm not." Terri's eyes darted around the room looking for the man. Thankfully, he was nowhere in sight.

"Ain't a woman in town who wouldn't drop their draws for that man, if he asked," she said, with a nonchalant shrug. "You gonna sit there and tell me you wouldn't?"

"I wouldn't."

"Y'all do have a lot in common," Lanette continued, the wheels of her little mind spinning out of control.

Terri pulled the pitcher away from the woman. "You finish what's left in your glass. No more alcohol because you obviously can't handle it."

Lanette surprised Terri and laughed. "I'm not drunk, and it's okay, girl. It's obvious he's feeling you, too. So, why you tripping?"

Terri studied Lanette, slightly amused by her, mostly annoyed, and not just with Lanette, but with herself for subjecting herself to this woman's company. And why? Because she felt sorry for her. Lanette Dole was a sad and pitiful human being. She tried to take her own life and all anybody in town could say about it was, 'again?' Lanette had family twenty minutes away who didn't even think enough of her to pick her up from the hospital. Terri had been compelled to be there when she was released for reasons she couldn't understand.

"What happened to you, Lanette?" she asked, wondering why it mattered.

In the grand scheme of Terri's life, Lanette Dole was no one, and yet, she held Terri's attention captive. Her suicide attempt left Terri feeling involved and responsible. It was all so odd, like the unexpected twist in a movie no one saw coming. The woman was riveting.

Lanette gazed deeply into Terri's eyes. "We all deal with our demons in our own way, Terri."

In that moment, Lanette radiated an air of sanity and clarity that Terri hadn't known the woman was even capable of. Lanette was absolutely calm, cool and collected and that was scary.

Neither of them said a word for fifteen minutes, until Yolanda appeared with the biggest burger Terri had ever seen.

Lanette's eyes lit up. She licked her lips and rubbed her hands together. "Ketchup?"

"Right here," Yolanda said, pulling a bottle from her apron pocket.

Lanette assembled her burger with the precision of a sculptor, placing the lettuce just so, then topped it with the tomato, sprinkled salt and pepper on top, then finally added the pickles before topping the masterpiece with the thick bun, and cutting it into four pieces and taking a bite, making it look absolutely delicious. Terri suddenly regretted not ordering one for herself, but she wasn't about to order one now and endure this woman's company longer than necessary.

Lanette's eyes rolled back as she moaned the whole time she chewed.

Eventually, she swallowed, opened her eyes and stared at Terri. "You want a fry?"

"Yes," Terri reached across the table, took one and dipped it in ketchup.

"He's been watching you since we came in," Lanette smiled.

Terri cut her eyes toward the bar. Sure enough, Luther was watching, and he smiled. Terri's heart lurched.

"I can pay you back," Lanette abruptly offered.

"What?" Terri forced herself to swallow that fry.

"For the food and drinks. I've got money at the house. I'll pay half."

"Half? You ordered a whole meal." Terri reminded the woman.

"Why don't you ask him out?"

"Who?" Terri asked, taking a drink.

"It's 2021, Terri. Women ask men out all the time. Want me to call him over?"

"No," Terri blurted out. "I don't want to ask him out, Lanette. Stay in your lane."

"You really don't like me. Do you?"

"Does anyone?"

Unexpected tears glistened in Lanette's eyes. "Not like I care," she said, chowing down on a fry.

"You must care, Lanette. Why else would you have done what you did?"

It was a heartless thing to say and Terri felt like shit for saying it, but Lanette had a way of bringing out the worst in her.

"There she is," a woman said in a hushed tone, coming through the front door.

"Maybe we should wait. She's eating," another woman said.

The two women, one black, the other white, huddled together, arm-in-arm, and shuffled over toward their table.

"Miss Dawson?" The white woman nervously asked, gushing at the sight of Terri.

"Hey, Mavis. Lucy," Lanette said to the ladies.

"Lanette," The white woman answered. The other rolled her eyes.

"We hate to bother you," the one who ignored Lanette said, focusing on Terri. "But... well, it's just such an honor to meet you in person."

Terri smiled. "Well, thank you very much."

They were older women, maybe in their fifties or sixties. The black woman is the one who ignored Lanette like she wasn't even on the planet. The white woman at least acknowledged her, but barely. Both women were dressed almost like gypsies, or throwback hippies from the sixties, wearing bold, flowing colorful, maxi-dresses, beaded bracelets and necklaces. The white woman had a mountain of silver dreadlocks piled on top of her head that reminded Terri of a giant beehive. The black woman's head was totally clean shaven.

The black woman placed a card on the table in front of Terri. "Now's not the best time, but it would be lovely to chat with you, Miss Dawson."

"Yes. We're head of the DAC and would love a chance to work with you on some upcoming projects."

"DAC?" Terri probed.

"The Devastation Arts Council," the black woman responded with a whole heap of pride.

Terri picked up the card. "Oh, how nice."

"Yes," the white woman chimed in. "This theater season is approaching, and it would be such an honor to have someone with your credentials be a part of this highly coveted annual event."

Terri plastered on as genuine a smile as she could muster.

"Mavis didn't want to ask," the black woman said, looking at a blushing Mavis. "But I figured why not," she giggled. "What's the worst that could happen?"

"She can say no," Lanette interjected.

Terri cut her eyes at the woman, but of course, Lanette had proven to be oblivious to eye cutting.

"We certainly hope you'll consider our little event," Lucy continued. "It's not Hollywood or Broadway, but even if you'd consider giving a speech or..."

"Some advice to our burgeoning actors would be appreciated," Mavis added. "Anything, really."

"I will certainly consider it," Terri assured them.

The two women fumbled all over her and each other as they said their goodbyes.

On their way out, Lucy blew Luther a kiss. "I'm still single, Luther."

He looked up from his paperwork. "I still know it, Lucy." He grinned.

"You gonna call them?" Lanette asked after the women left.

Terri smiled and tucked the card into her purse.

"You're not," Lanette laughed.

"You finished?" she said, ready to drop this woman off.

Terri had done what her conscious had compelled her to do and was now ready to get on with her life, devoid of Lanette Dole.

"Yolanda," Terri called out to the young woman sitting across from Luther. "Can we get a to- go box?"

"Coming right up, Miss Terri."

"His son is fine, too," Lanette said under her breath to Terri.

"Whose son?" Terri held up her credit card for Yolanda.

"Luther's," she motioned her head in his direction. "Name's Nick. He's a doctor. You met him. That night you wore those dangerously high heels to line dancing and fell and damn near broke your foot. Don't act like you don't remember."

OUTSIDE WORDS

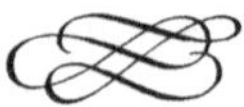

"Can you swing me by Walmart?" Lanette asked Terri on their way out.

"Do I look like a chauffeur?" Terri snapped marching ahead of Lanette like she was leading a regiment.

"I'm just saying, since we're already out… I can pay you back."

Luther couldn't help but laugh. Terri had a friend, or rather, a Lanette, whether she wanted one or not. Luther raised a brow at the unlikely duo and shook his head. Terri glanced at him one last time before leaving. He wished she'd stay.

"I'm heading upstairs," Luther said to Yolanda, gathering his laptop and ledger.

"Don't forget. Cee Cee's coming in early to finish my shift," Yolanda reminded him.

"How many times you gonna tell me that?"

"A lot, because you forget stuff and I don't want you blowing up my phone talking 'bout, 'Where you at, Yo?' like last time."

Luther sighed and headed up the winding staircase in the corner of the restaurant, leading up to his place.

"Leave a note on the counter," he told Yolanda.

He had a serious crush on Terri Dawson, but she was seeing his son, for God's sake. Luther had no business thinking of her any kind of way, except maybe that of future daughter-in-law. She was new to town. A fresh face. Ultimately, Luther had to chalk his interest in her to that and trust it to evaporate like steam and leave him to his old, ornery self.

His home was a hodgepodge of art and furnishings he'd collected from around the world, places like Europe, Asia, and Africa. None of it fit in Devastation any more than he did, but he'd made it work. His place had been little more than an old attic when he'd bought the property. Luther had it gutted from top to bottom, turning the lower level into his business.

❧

AN HOUR after balancing his books and grumbling under his breath the whole time, he concluded, once again, that he really needed to hire somebody else to do this. Every week he complained and every week he spent hours hovering over this damn laptop, looking at numbers until his eyes crossed. Eventually, he got up, went to the kitchen, and poured himself a glass of sweet tea.

He stood at the cathedral window staring down at the cobblestone streets below. Luther's Bar & Grill sat just on the edge of downtown Devastation. He'd opened it because he needed something to do. Pure and simple. He had enough money to last him the rest of his life, as long as he didn't splurge on Lamborghinis and private jets. This life was a far cry from the one he'd lived. Back when he signed on to play guitar for Whitney Houston's first tour, not long after graduating high school.

She was touring the south promoting her latest album and her guitar player got sick in Birmingham. One of the managers at the venue knew Luther because he'd sat in with a few other artists who'd come through, and hours later, Luther's whole life changed.

The call came two weeks later from Whitney's production manager, *"You're a great fit, Luther. Whitney starts recording a new album in a few months and we'd love to have you."*

"You think I should go?" he asked Ava.

The two of them sat shoulder to shoulder on the back porch of her parents' house because they couldn't afford their own porch. She smiled so pretty, and soft curls rested on the tops of her shoulders.

"You're too damn good at what you do not to go, Luther," she said.

"I'll be gone for some months," he explained, excited about the opportunity, but dreading leaving his new wife behind.

"And I'll be right here when you get back."

He'd loved her since the third grade and indicated that fact by pulling her hair on the school bus one day on the way home. She slapped at him, waited for him to get off the bus and slammed her book bag upside his head. He knew then that he'd marry her.

Luther made enough money from that touring gig to buy her a house outright and fill it with everything she could possibly want.

If anyone had told him he'd be standing here, in this old, renovated attic atop the old Crenshaw mansion, turned bar and grill, in his hometown, without her, he'd have called them a liar. Ava passed away nearly five ago, and Luther had tried to move on. He'd tried burying his memories of her. He'd dated, worked double time to let go and move on, but here he was, stuck between a hard place and heartbreak he couldn't shake, and likely never would.

He had a crush on his son's girlfriend and that was all kinds of fucked up. In his fifty-four years of living, Luther had come to realize that fate had a sick sense of humor. It wasn't like he didn't have options. He just wished Terri Dawson was one of them. A few minutes later, his phone rang.

"Hey, you," he said, smiling when he answered.

"Guess who's coming to town and would love to see you?" Cleo Miller, literally sang the question to Luther, sounding like the Grammy Award nominated artist she was.

"Hmmmm," he responded. "Uh... you in Devastation?"

She laughed, "Why the hell would I go to that pimple on a gnat's ass of a town? I'm in New Orleans, which is as close as I'll ever get to your hometown, Luther Hunt."

Luther sank into his cognac colored, buttery-soft leather sofa. "I think I should be offended."

"For skipping over New Orleans to live in no-man's land," she shot back. "Yeah. That is offensive."

Cleo had sung background for some of the industry's superstars; Michael Jackson, Prince, and Luther Vandross. Fifteen years ago, she released her first and only solo album to critical acclaim, was nominated for a Grammy for Best Female R&B artist and went back to background singing.

"Being in the forefront is cool and all," she admitted to him once. "But too much pressure. Everybody watching, listening and judging your every move." Cleo shook her head.

"It's crazy," he chimed in.

"It'll make you crazy. That's for damn sure and we both know I don't need no help in that area."

"How long you in town for?" he asked, glossing over the memory.

"Two nights, performing at a dive on Bourbon Street. You should swing through."

They'd started out as friends. Stayed friends until after Ava passed, though Cleo had been tempting even before that. She offered a good ear for listening after his wife passed, and a warm, soft, accommodating body for other things.

"I will absolutely swing through, darlin'," he assured her.

"I'll text you my hotel info," she added before hanging up.

Luther let himself get swept away by introspection and memories of him and Cleo, huddled up in the backs of tour busses talking dirty to each other, warding off the temptation to cross lines neither of them had any business crossing. Shit happened on the road that stayed on the road, but he'd sworn an oath to Ava that he'd never cheat and he never did. Came close, but Luther held fast in his commitment to his wife. His right hand had its share of a workout though, from playing guitar and jerking off like a maniac.

Cleo's phone call had been sobering and set him back to right... and away from getting worked up over Terri.

Terri was a fresh face in Devastation. That was all. And she had nothing to do with him, except that she was seeing his son. It didn't matter if their relationship was serious or if they were just kicking it. It really was none of his business. *She* was none of his business.

After ending the call with Cleo, his phone rang again. This time it was Nick.

"Hey, pop," he said when Luther answered.

Luther sat up, curious as to why his son would be calling. It wasn't like they regularly shot the shit or anything.

"Is everything alright?" Luther asked, concerned.

"Everything's good. I just um… thought I'd check on you. That's all."

Luther waited for the punchline.

"You there?"

"Yeah," Luther said, surprised. "Just —"

"Shocked?"

"Pretty much."

"Don't be. It's not that serious. Just doing my part to work on things between us."

"Okay," Luther sighed. "Then I'll let you. And I'm fine. How are you, son?"

"Good. Really good."

The familiar weight of silence wafted between them.

"How's business?"

"It's alright. Keeping me busy. How's doctoring?"

As he spoke, Luther quietly concluded that Nick had something else on his mind. And sure enough, it eventually came out.

"Yeah… I think I might be catching feelings for someone, though."

Nausea and elation ballooned in Luther's stomach. "Oh yeah? Anyone I know?"

He knew.

Nick laughed, "The movie star, Terri Dawson."

Luther sighed, "You've been seeing her, huh?"

"Yeah, for a little over a month."

"And you're falling for her already? That's quick, don't you think?"

"I'm thirty-five, Luther. Not fifteen," he said defensively.

“Okay,” Luther quickly added. “I get it. Grown men know.”

“Grown men know.”

After chatting a few more minutes and getting off the phone with Nick, Luther immediately packed an overnight bag and headed downstairs.

“I’m heading out of town for a few days,” he said to Yolanda. “Tell Irene to hold down the fort while I’m gone.”

HAVE IT ALL

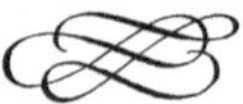

Lanette was an emotional vampire, even after spending four days in the hospital. The woman had picked up where she'd left off, grazing across Terri's nerves like the jagged edge of broken glass. Terri eventually dropped her demanding ass off at her house and drove off before Lanette had even closed the car door.

"Luther is Nick's dad," she muttered, shaking her head, as she paused behind the stop sign at the end of Lanette's street.

Ever since she'd found out, the words played on repeat in her mind, driving her nuts while she followed Lanette up and down every, single aisle in Walmart. A strange, weighted anxiety ballooned in her stomach, one she'd been tortured by for the last hour and a half.

Terri eventually made it home in time to meet the tile guy before he drove off.

"Sorry! I'm so sorry," she said, opening the front door. "I lost track of time and—"

"No problem," he said, pausing while she made her way up the steps to the front door. "My guys are going to unload and we'll get started straight away."

"Thanks, so much," she said in exasperation.

The old black and white tile in her kitchen had, mercifully, been scraped up and in its place, a blue and white swirly patterned tile was being laid. A new subway tiled backsplash was also being installed.

"It's going to be a little noisy," Ned, the leader of the tile-guy pack explained.

"That's fine," she said. "I'll be out back if you need me."

Lanette left her emotionally drained and all she wanted to do was to go outside, sit under her tree, and detox from the residue of the woman's poisonous energy. Terri grabbed a bottle of sparkling, white wine from the fridge, a bag of Baked Lays, and a book before walking through the house and out the back door.

Terri put her feet up, searched Peloton on her phone and ordered one. Her jeans were getting a little too tight and Terri was getting careless with her eating. Just because she wasn't on television anymore was no excuse to go crazy and blow up like Violet after chewing the gum, Willie Wonka had warned her about.

After taking some much needed deep breaths and eating a few chips, Terri relaxed into the loveseat, which she hadn't sat on since sexing Nick nearly a week ago. What the hell had gotten into her? It wasn't that she regretted it, but the whole thing had been driven by a tidal wave of emotions that needed sorting out. Rather than do that, Terri caved to the weight of those emotions and decided to sex the man.

Luther was his father and before Lanette dropped that bomb on her, she hadn't been above wishful thinking about him, too. Terri was a single woman, driving hard and fast into an impressive mid-life crisis, open to exploring her once dormant sexuality, so, yeah. Admittedly, Luther had been on that very short list, until Nick. Until she'd given in to the idea of being the other half of a couple with Nick. Until she found out that Luther was the man's dad.

Not that it mattered. It didn't matter. Of course, it didn't matter because Luther was a nice man who owned a bar. That's all. He'd been patient and kind to Terri when Lanette was in the hospital… which, was nice, but Luther was Luther and no one in particular to her… He was Nick's father, and so what? What? Why was her brain trying to make it a thing when it wasn't a thing? None of this was a thing.

What was it about Devastation, Louisiana that made men so devastatingly handsome? She hadn't noticed a resemblance between Nick and Luther until after Lanette said they were related. It wasn't a strong resemblance. They were both tall, though Luther was taller. Both broad-shouldered and maybe they even kind of walked the same. And, thinking about it, they had similar smiles. Luther was more brooding, and Nick was Mr. Sunshine and Personality.

"Hell, it doesn't matter," she blurted out, spewing chip crumbs onto her lap.

It didn't. She wasn't feeling Luther like that and Nick, was… Nick was sitting here on this loveseat, not all that long ago, all up inside Terri, grabbing hold of her ass like it was the buoy that could keep him from drowning, while she had a mini breakdown. He came. She didn't, but that wasn't the point. Terri had put that thang on him too damn good, so she didn't blame him. She blamed herself.

This was about life. Her life. Her identity. Her. Her. Her, damn it. Because didn't the world revolve around her? She was so sick of herself. Terri shook her head in frustration. She was tired of looking inside and coming up with the same old thing. Terri was a piece of cardboard, a plain sheet of paper that someone—anyone could draw a circle, two dots for eyes and a half moon for a mouth and make her whoever the script said she should be.

Who was she, really? She'd never asked herself that question before and damn sure didn't have an answer for it. Terri was spontaneously combusting on the inside with no idea of how to stop it. It was like, she was unbecoming, being unmade from what or who she'd always believed herself to be. But more and more, she was starting to understand that everything she'd always believed herself to be, was fake.

Ten minutes after she'd sat down, Terri's phone rang. It was Nick. She thought about not answering but did.

"Hi, there," she said, regretting picking up that damn phone.

"Hey," he said, sounding a bit tired, "how you doing?"

Still unraveling.

"I'm fine. How are you?"

"Missing you," he chuckled. "There. I said it."

Terri couldn't help but smile. Dating, for Terri, had never been a priority and it had been years since she spent more than a few hours, maybe a night, with any one, particular man. Nick was dangerously close to becoming a habit.

"Are you in town?"

"Not yet," he said. "But I will be tomorrow. I was hoping to convince you to pack an overnight bag and let me whisk you away for a night, maybe two."

"To where?"

"Here."

New Orleans was a two-and-a-half-hour drive from Devastation. Maybe getting away was a good thing. Escapism, a way to peel her away from the microscope she'd been examining herself under lately might be just what she needed to gain a clearer perspective of... what exactly? She wasn't sure.

"I think I'd like that, Nick."

He was a good man. Nick was fine and young, yes. Too young? Perhaps. But, so far, age hadn't been an issue. He wanted time with her, and Terri had no more excuses for why she couldn't focus on a relationship.

"I'll pick you up at five," he said.

"I'll be ready."

She could tell that he wanted to talk longer, but Terri didn't and ended the call feigning the demand of a contractor needing her attention.

Terri sat there realizing she couldn't spend the rest of her life sitting under this tree, eating chips, drinking, and brooding over what wasn't. She was getting ready to turn forty-four, and she needed a job, a purpose. Terri needed something to do every day. But what?

She damn sure wasn't waiting tables or being anybody's receptionist. Terri had been a presenter at the Daytime Emmy Awards, for crying out loud. So, what could a woman with her experience do in a town like this? Teach? The very notion of being surrounded by children of any age made her shudder.

Write? She perked up a little at the thought. She was a creative person and writing was creative. So, write... what? Screenplays? She'd read a million of them so writing one was a no-brainer. Maybe that was it. Maybe, it was time for Terri to shift her focus from being in front of the camera to being behind it. She sat up and placed both feet on the ground. Her heart fluttered with a hint of excitement.

"I mean... why not?" she said with warm enthusiasm.

She was an industry veteran and Terri knew the ins and outs of the movie industry, so why not?

"Whoa," she said, raising her hands in front of her as if to stop the momentum.

Wasn't she supposed to be walking away from the industry? Terri was supposed to be reinventing herself, starting over brand new, doing something with her life that didn't leave her feeling like she wasn't good enough, young enough, talented, or beautiful enough. She was tired of beating herself up whenever she was passed over for a role or fired from reality shows.

"No," she muttered, shaking her head.

It didn't matter what side of the camera she was on. That old, familiar feeling of anxiousness and desperation came with it, and that's what she was leaving behind. No more rejection. No more waiting, hanging on the edge of a cliff by her fingernails for some producer or studio to validate her, as an actress or as a screenplay writer.

Terri sighed and closed her eyes. That small voice inside, begged the question, "But...why not?"

MENDING, BLENDING

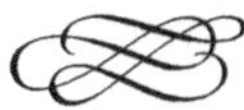

Geraldine's on the Q was legendary for their oysters on the half shell and seafood gumbo. Terri turned her nose up at the oysters, but appreciatively devoured a pan seared sea bass, steamed asparagus, and buttered mashed potatoes. Nick started with oysters, then finished up with rosemary baked chicken, macaroni and cheese, and a small bowl of gumbo.

"Oh, I was ambitious as hell as an undergrad," Nick boasted over dinner, beaming at the memory of his young, college self. "I was Neurosurgeon bound, for real."

"Brain surgeon. Wow. Impressive."

"It was," he said, swiping his napkin across his lips and tossing it on top of his mostly empty plate. "Until reality kicked in, and after that second year of med school, I was like, nope. Not going to happen."

Terri wrinkled her pretty nose. "Too hard?"

"My ass was tired," he admitted, laughing. "Maybe I could've done it, and maybe I still will, but I honestly fell in love with Emergency medicine and all the unknowns that it brings. Something about it feels more organic and feels like what practicing medicine should be. You never know who's going to walk through those doors or what they're coming in for." He shrugged. "I don't know. It's real. Real and unscripted. No pun intended."

Nick had always believed he'd specialize in internal medicine or, at one point, neurology, but emergency medicine chose him during his first rotation in an emergency room as an intern.

"Sounds like you have to be a jack of all trades, though," she reasoned.

"You get to be," he agreed. "That's why I dig it."

She smiled, and he melted a little on the inside. The last time they'd been together, she'd been emotional, even a little down. Tonight, Terri was a beautiful woman enjoying good food, his company, and a night out on the town.

"Well, you don't look like any doctor I've ever had," she admitted, sipping wine. "I prefer my doctors old, mottled, and out of shape."

"Thank you," he said, grinning.

She shook her head and smiled. "You know you're hot. Don't sit there acting like you don't."

He returned an introspective nod. "Yeah."

Terri tossed her napkin at him.

Damn. Nick couldn't take his eyes off her. Terri had pulled her hair back tonight. Bright eyes bore into his, soft lips… taunted him, daring him not to lean in for a kiss. Of course, he did.

"I taste like garlic?" she asked, frowning.

"I dig garlic."

After dinner, they walked three blocks over to Bourbon street and slipped into a club called The Truth. The place was packed, but Nick called in a favor with the owner. He'd treated the man's son a few months ago, and he'd made Nick a promise.

"We almost always have a packed house, Doc, but if you ever decide to come through, give me a call," he handed Nick a card, "I'll save you one of our VIP spots."

Nick gave his name to the hostess and she immediately led the two of them to a table near the stage in the center of the room.

"What can I get you two to drink?" the hostess asked. "On the house."

Nick draped his arm over the back of her chair, and Terri leaned into him. The vibe, all evening, had been perfect. He couldn't remember the last time he felt this kind of a connection to a woman. Nick wasn't a schoolboy. He never rushed into things, especially when it came to relationships. He'd always been levelheaded, patient and objective. Getting his education was his priority when he was younger. Next, he focused on getting his medical degree and finishing his Internship. He'd dated. He'd even had a girlfriend here and there, but he wasn't interested in anything serious back then. Now, his life had settled into somewhat of a routine. Nick was getting older, and he wanted a family. It was time. Not that there were any guarantees with Miss Terri, here. She had an issue with this age difference thing, but she was definitely giving him a taste of the kind of life he wanted, the kind of woman he wanted, and a clear view of what *could* be.

The DJ played for about twenty minutes before the owner, a heavy set, white man, bald, with a funky soul patch, took to the stage with a microphone.

"All right, y'all," he said to the audience. "I'm not going to stand up here and talk too long. This lady is amazing and we're so happy she agreed to bring her show here. Ladies and gentlemen, I give you," —he raised his arm to usher her in— "the incomparable, Ms. Cleo Taylor."

She was old school. Nick dug old school and from the look on Terri's face, she was impressed too.

The tall, light skinned woman, wearing her hair cut nearly as low as Nick's, was stunning, probably in her fifties. She had one helluva voice, covering Chaka, Anita, Whitney and even threw in a little Jill Scott for good measure.

"Thank y'all so much," she said, after finishing Jill's *A Long Walk*. "I have a special treat for you tonight." She smiled at the audience. "A friend of mine… a Louisiana native as matter of fact, has—after much begging and pleading, and flashing a little thigh," she teased, jutting out a shapely leg, "agreed to share the stage with me tonight."

Nick's eyes lit up at the sight of Luther coming out on the stage and kissing Cleo on the cheek. Some people in the audience hooped and whistled at the sight of him.

"Luther Hunt, ladies and gentlemen." She smiled and hugged him.

His father bowed slightly before someone handed him a guitar. Nick's chest filled with unexpected pride. He hadn't seen his dad handle a guitar since he was a kid sitting on the floor at Luther's feet, staring up at a man, larger than life. And he'd never actually seen him perform live. Growing up, the closest Nick ever got to seeing Luther play was catching a glimpse of him in videos or on television. Every now and then, Nick would pull up an old YouTube video and see Luther grooving in the background.

Luther stepped back and played the riff leading into Jimi Hendrix's "Purple Haze." Cleo took to the mic with the lyrics, and the world vanished all around Nick except for him and his dad. Luther was a giant on that stage, and not just physically. His father had an air about him that resonated under a light that shined differently from everyone else's, even Cleo's. She might've been the star, but Luther had a presence that would easily overshadow hers if he wasn't careful. He played like he knew how powerful his presence was on that stage, standing away from her so as not to dull her shine with his own.

Luther didn't notice Nick until he saw him standing and applauding with everyone else after they'd finished the set, nodding an acknowledgment and grinning. Luther, eventually weeded his way through the congratulatory crowd and made his way to Nick, embracing him in a way he hadn't done since Nick was a kid.

"Good to see you, son," he said.

Nick couldn't stop smiling. "You're fuckin' amazing."

Luther reared his head back and laughed, "Coming from you, that's everything."

"Hi," Terri said.

Shit. Nick had almost forgotten she was there.

"Dad, this - this is Terri."

His father nodded, cordially. "I know. Good to see you, too, and welcome to New Orleans."

"Great, great show," she beamed. "I didn't know you were a musician."

"Retired," he clarified.

"Why?" she asked.

"Y'all met?" Nick asked.

"At the bar," Luther said.

She glanced at Nick. "I've been there a couple of times."

"I'm glad you're here," Luther said to Nick. "I mean that."

It was never perfect between the two of them, but every now and then, Nick and Luther had their moments.

"Me too."

Cleo Taylor seemed to appear out of thin air and stood next to Luther, wrapping her arms around him. "I see you have a fan," she said, winking at Nick. "Or two." She smiled at Terri.

"My son, Nick, and his date," Luther said, "Terri."

"Your father and I go way back," she told Nick.

Nick resisted the urge to read more into her sentiment than what she'd said.

"We backed up everybody from Luther Vandross to, shit," —she looked at Luther— "Tina Turner?"

Luther draped his arm over her shoulder. "Yeah. Just about every damn body."

"He used to keep pictures of you and your mother on the walls of the tour bus to mark his seat," she laughed. "Everybody knew that was his spot."

"Oh yeah," Nick said, feeling that pride rising again.

"Talked about you all the time. You're a doctor. Right?"

"Yes, ma'am."

"Bragged about you, long before you became one." She looked at Luther.

Luther sighed, "He doesn't need to know all that."

Nick didn't say it out loud, but yes. He did need to know all that.

Cleo laughed, then looked at Luther. "Can I count on you for the second set?"

He shrugged. "My stamina ain't what it used to be," he joked.

"Oh, your stamina's fine, Daddy-O," Cleo damn near purred.

"Whoa." Luther shot her a warning look. "Not in front of the kid."

She glanced at Nick. "He's hardly a kid. Besides, he's doctor. He knows all about anatomy."

It didn't take a genius to know these two were more than just old friends. Regardless of what Nick suspected might or might not have happened between two of them in the past, when his mother was alive, tonight Luther was back in the one place that probably felt more like home than anywhere else. He was on stage, and for the first time, in a long time, the man actually looked happy.

FROM INSIDE

Luther *was* music, plucking the strings of that guitar like angels had created it *just* for him. The man was mesmerizing, a god, beautiful and commanding, illuminated by a heavenly light. Was Terri the only one who saw it? Watching him perform, bobbing his handsome head to the rhythm ignited a place inside her that had gone dark... that had once believed in miracles. Luther's guitar playing revived her faith in all the things she'd once found magical but had forgotten existed.

"Enjoying yourself?" Nick asked, breaking through the spell she'd fallen into.

Terri managed to tear her gaze from the stage, look into Nick's eyes and force a smile. "Yeah. He's amazing."

He's amazing. A slight Freudian slip, but thankfully, one Nick didn't seem to catch.

He leaned in and kissed her and then turned his attention the stage again. Terri sat like a statue, trying not to swoon or melt. Nick was her date. Luther was her secret wish. Nick was a dream walking. Luther was otherworldly. *Shit!* Terri felt like a rotten person. A bad date. A desperate fan. Jealous of the way that Cleo woman kept smiling at Luther... knowing that she was probably taking him home.

Terri always avoided making a fool of herself over a man, any man, especially the father of the one she was dating. Nick Hunt was his own prize, first prize. He wasn't a runner up to anyone and she knew this. Cleo Taylor flirted. Luther flirted back. Terri was jealous, but perspective crept in with every chord, every note, and by the end of the second set, she realized she was simply being a silly woman with a crush.

At the end of the performance, Nick, Luther, and Terri stood outside the club, saying their goodbyes.

"I had no idea you were that damn talented," Nick said, his tone filled with admiration.

"Yeah, well." Luther shrugged. "I was in my element."

"Why'd you stop playing?" Terri eventually asked.

The two men exchanged quick glances. "My wife passed away," he explained, scratching his head. "Nick's mother. I was on the road and came home when we knew she wasn't going to pull through this time."

"Oh, I'm sorry," she said, looking at Nick.

He'd briefly mentioned his parents in the month that he and Terri had known each other, but he'd never told her that his mother was dead.

"Complications from Lupus," Nick offered.

Terri nodded.

"Anyway," Luther continued. "I didn't have it in me to get back out there, so I decided to stay home and open up the bar."

Body language between the two men, checked glances, told her that there was more to the story than either of them wanted to share and Terri wouldn't pry.

"You and Miss Cleo a thing?" Nick asked with a sly grin.

Luther raked his hand across his head and sighed, "Cleo and I go way back."

"I'm sure you do."

There was no amusement in his tone and Terri caught a look between the two men, signaling tension.

Luther sighed. "'Night, son," he said, heading back inside.

Nick called after him. "Be responsible," he called out after his father. "You know what I'm talking about," he said, sounding light. "I'm too old for siblings."

Luther chuckled and disappeared inside.

Nick's condo was within walking distance to the World War II Museum in a restored cotton mill building, complete with signature New Orleans charms, tall ceilings and windows with exposed brick and wood beams. Not your typical black leather with red and gold accents she'd come to expect from a bachelor, but still, it screamed, 'man'. His condo boasted clean and simple lines and neutral grays accented with splashes of color. It was classic, timeless, and pretty.

He sat her bag down on the sofa, shoved his hands into his pants pockets and stood in front of her. "Can I get you anything?"

She'd had sex with him already. It only made sense that both of them would expect to fuck again. Right?

"How many bedrooms?" she asked.

He raised both brows in surprise. "Uh, one."

Handsome Nick. There was nothing, absolutely nothing, about him that she didn't like.

"Is that okay?" he asked, his tone pensive.

"Why wouldn't it be," she said, smiling.

He lowered his head and turned it slightly to one side. "Are you sure?"

Terri took two steps, stopped in front of him, then took hold of both his hands before looking up at him. "Positive."

This time, sex wasn't some frantic attempt to distract from entangled and overwrought emotions. Nick wasn't caught off guard and nobody was going to be dismissed and sent home when it was over.

He took the lead.

She let him.

Nick took his time peeling her out of her clothes and then stripping down to his skin. Kissing was his thing, lips, face, neck, breasts, stomach, even feet. He worked hard to impress her, probably because he'd come in five minutes the last time they were together, but that wasn't his fault. Terri had come at him like a freight train and taken what she needed from him. That's all. This time, he came at her with an agenda, one proving he was no one-minute wonder. It was hard not to be both amused and impressed.

It took twenty minutes of foreplay and her begging and pleading for him to finally put it in. Nick took his sweet time, working her into a frothy, clawing, clinging mess.

"Oh, Nick," she heard herself say, wrapping arms and legs around him in what amounted to a bear hug.

When it was over, Terri was the one laying limp like a rag doll, too weak to move. Nick stretched out next to her, his broad chest heaving, perfect white teeth exposed in a proud smile.

He held her all night. Terri briefly drifted off to sleep but woke up before dawn, staring out of the window. The sex was amazing. The connection... was not. She wanted it to be. Terri wished it were, but as wonderful as Nick was, she was emotionally absent and had no idea why. He'd come into her life unexpectedly. She wasn't looking for a relationship when she met Nick, but maybe she needed one.

Terri had spent so much time focusing on so many other things that she wondered if it was even possible for her to romantically connect to another human being. Nick was damn near perfect. A bit too young, but still... he was wonderful. She wanted to be wonderful with him, to be excited to be with him. Terri was empty inside, an emotional void, a black hole of cold space.

He moaned, pulled her tighter against him and settled down, back to sleep. She smiled because the gesture was endearing and special. Nick was special, and Terri was going to have to rise to the occasion if she wanted to be special with him. She briefly thought of Luther. Sure, she had a crush on the man. She'd have to be dead not to. But no. This wasn't about Luther. Terri was on a search for her elusive soul, the one that didn't obsess over something she couldn't have.

She could have Nick, and... maybe love Nick. She could have romance with Nick. Marriage with Nick? Wow! Marriage? Where'd that come from?

Wake up, Terri. Wake up and live, really live. Try it. Try being brand new with brand new thoughts, ideas, and courage. Try being open to the possibilities of Nick Hunt and see what happens.

BETTER LEFT UNSAID

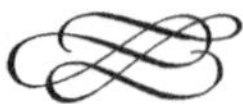

Thick and shapely Cleo slithered into the room, freshly showered and sitting on the side of the bed next to Luther.

"You know I'm jealous." She leaned down and kissed him. "Right?"

Luther sank dramatically into the thick pillows and sighed, recalling his days on the road and hitting the road at the crack of dawn's ass.

She laughed and playfully slapped his chest. "I can't stand you."

"This is what retirement looks like."

She stared down at him. "Looks damn good. That's for sure." She kissed him again, then crawled on top of him, the thin sheet separating the two of them. "You know how long I've been wanting you?"

Cleo had never made a secret of that fact when they toured together. Luther fought long and hard, keeping her at bay despite appearances and gossip.

"Worth the wait," she murmured, grazing a manicured nail down his cheek. "I truly am sorry for your loss. I know how much you loved Ava, but I gotta say," she chuckled. "I have enjoyed my stop here, immensely."

No one believed that Luther had been faithful to his wife all those years on the road. Admittedly, there were some moments when he came a hair-width away from crossing that line, but he never did.

He sighed. "You ain't the only one, sugah," he said, staring deep into her eyes. "You still with Russ?"

Cleo rolled her eyes, pushed off Luther and sat back on the side of the bed. "You know I ain't never leaving that fool."

Cleo had been with Russ for as long as Luther had known her, which had to have been more than thirty years. Nobody believed there really was a Russ at first because they never saw him, only heard about Cleo complaining about *'That fool, Russ'* for hours at a time on the tour bus.

"That damn fool, Russ," she exclaimed, all kinds of pissed, coming out of a restaurant on Boise once, after using the pay phone to call him. "Done burned down my damn house."

"That fool, Russ, smashed my damn car."

"That fool, Russ, said a curse word to my momma then got mad when she hit him upside the head with a baseball bat."

Years passed before Luther finally laid eyes on *That Fool Russ* backstage during intermission at a Boys to Men concert. Russ had Cleo pressed up against the wall with his tongue so far down her throat it was a wonder she didn't choke to death. Cleo clawed him like a predator, keeping him in place until the stage manager told her it was time for her to get her ass back out on stage. She hurried back to one of the dressing rooms, reapplied her lipstick and rushed past Luther with a sly glance and grin.

"That Russ?" he asked.

"That's my baby," she said with the kind of affection he didn't know she was capable of.

But what happened on the road, stayed on the road. Luther suspected that whatever happened on Russ' end when Cleo was touring, happened on Russ' end. Their relationship had withstood the test of more than thirty years. So, who was Luther to judge?

"Who you seeing now?" she asked, putting on her earrings.

"No one."

Cleo rolled over next to him. "You serious? Ain't nobody got you?"

Luther shook his head. "Ain't nobody got me, baby."

"Ava passed, what? Four, five years ago?"

"Something like that."

"You been single all that time?"

Luther didn't answer.

"Honey," she said, raising up on her elbow. "Why, Luther? She's been gone long enough."

"Says who?" he asked, facing her.

What was long enough? Luther had missed most of his marriage to the woman he loved more than anything. Almost. It was that part, the *almost*, that tortured him.

"Your boy is handsome," she said, changing the subject.

Luther nodded slightly. "He looks like his mother."

"And you. Maybe more her, but I saw you in him, too." She pressed a hand to his cheek. "Saw how proud he looked watching you play, too."

Luther noticed.

"Pretty date he had with him."

Yeah. She was pretty. Luther thought about how good the two of them looked together. Nick was happy.

"You ain't a granddaddy yet," she asked. "Are you?"

He laughed, "Lord, no."

"Well, it's coming." Cleo got up and started getting dressed. "So, you need to get ready."

The very thought made him feel old.

"What time y'all heading out?" he asked.

"Less than an hour." Cleo slipped on a loose-fitting maxi dress and flip flops, pulled a ball cap onto her damp hair, and then started shoving her things into a small duffle bag. On stage, the woman was pure diva, but in the trenches, Cleo was a road warrior, capable of being locked, loaded, and packed in a matter of minutes.

"You forgot to put on panties?" he asked, smirking.

"I didn't forget nothing," she said, slipping a purse over her shoulder and kissing him one last time on her way out. "Get yourself something to eat before you leave. The club is paying for it."

"Be good, Cleo," he called after her.

"Define good." She winked, closing the door behind her.

LUTHER EVENTUALLY ORDERED room service and paid for it out of his own pocket. He sat on the balcony, enjoying his meal and his coffee, looking down at the streets of the Quarter slowly starting to come to life again. New Orleans was a little more than two hours away from Devastation and he couldn't remember the last time he'd come here.

Playing last night resuscitated Luther, ignited his whole soul. Damn, it felt good being up on that stage, fusing with his guitar, drawing in chords and melodies. God! He missed playing. For years, he felt more at home on stage than he did in his own house. Last night had been his return to the mecca and it felt damn good.

Luther let himself die with Ava. Guilt buried him a long time ago. Until last night, he was fine with that. Until last night, he'd forgotten that he was still here and that there was some part of him left that relished life.

He hadn't been there for Ava when she needed him. Luther had been punishing himself for what happened to her long before she died, though.

"Lupus ain't cheap," she'd told him time and time again, making light of her illness.

Ava was light in the darkness, even when it was her own. She went out of her way to downplay her symptoms for as long as she could. Luther let her because it gave him the excuse he needed to play.

"That's what insurance is for, Ava. I can come home."

"And be miserable with me?"

"But I'd be with you and you need me."

"How many times have we fought about this, Luther?" she asked. "How many times has it left us nearly bankrupt?"

"It's just fuckin' money," he argued.

"And Nick wants to go to college."

"He can go, Ava. Other kids do it."

"And end up paying back money until they're old and gray. I don't want that for him."

She was strange in her priorities. She convinced Luther to buy into the nonsense that he needed to keep working, keep playing for them to keep living the way they did.

Was she all that convincing? Or did he really *not* need a reasonable argument to be convinced to keep playing, keep traveling, leaving his sick wife and kid alone in a fancy house, while he lived his dream?

A memory crept up on him. One of those he never cared to recall, but some of them left him no choice. It was 2001 and Luther was in Toronto, getting ready to go on with Blackstreet.

"Luther!" One of the managers shouted, shoving a phone at him. "They say it's an emergency."

Dread filled his gut like a balloon. "Yeah?" he shouted over the noise.

Luther could barely hear the person on the other end of the phone, so he ducked into a small equipment closet. "This is Luther."

"It's—Nick," the boy hiccupped through tears. "Mom is..."

In the hospital? Or worse? Luther fought like hell to keep his thoughts from going to that dark place.

"What, Nick?"

"Luther! Anybody seen Hunt? He needs to be on that stage."

"Nick?" Luther yelled.

"She's back in the hospital, Luther," Ava's mother said, replacing Nick on the phone. "You'll need to get home as soon as you can."

"Luther Hunt! Where the fuck is his ass?"

He had no idea how long he stood in that closet with the phone to his ear, listening to nothing. The woman had hung up without saying goodbye.

Some things were automatic, robotic. Luther played that night. Played like a man possessed, focusing so hard on the damn music, to keep his thoughts off of her and the fact that she—and Nick, needed him home. Days later, Luther called to say he was on his way to Devastation.

"It's all right, Dad," Nick told him. The boy had to have been thirteen, maybe fourteen at the time. "She's home."

Memories like that kept Luther grounded, reminding him of why his son resented him and why the two of them would never have that bond most fathers have with their sons. They both had made peace with it.

❧

An hour after finishing the last of his coffee, Luther dressed to leave and head home, realizing he'd repented long enough. Ava was gone, and what he did or didn't do right was gone with her. He still loved music; still loved playing. Luther loved the feel of a woman's body and the comfort that came with it.

He and Nick had reached an unspoken agreement. His son would always have his own ideas about the kind of man Luther was, had been, is... but Nick had come to terms with those ideas and maybe it was time for Luther to stop letting another man make him feel like shit.

Nick was living his life.

Luther needed to live his.

CIRCLE IN THE SAND

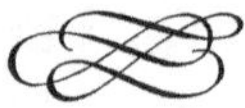

"The theater community here in Devastation has always been vibrant," Mavis Renfrow explained, using delicate hands with long, thin fingers and perfectly manicured nails painted yellow.

"And very respected," Lucy Madison chimed in with a proud smile and bright eyes.

"Oh, yes," Mavis continued. "Why, some of our productions here have won high praise and have even been reviewed in Baton Rouge and New Orleans newspapers."

"Oh, wow," Terri managed to say, eyebrows raised and trying to look as impressed as the two ladies sitting across from her obviously were.

The old, musty smelling theater flourished with character but could do with a facelift. Heavy, wine colored velvet drapes, pinned back on opposites sides of the small stage, matched faded, velvet covered seating, probably dating back to the forties or fifties. Peeling gold paint on oversized columns and railings needed to be touched up, and new carpet wouldn't hurt. From the outside, this place, located in the heart of downtown Devastation, didn't look like much. Inside, it definitely was over the top.

"Mavis and I are the fifth owners of this establishment," Lucy told Terri. "We've owned it longer than anyone, except the first owners."

"Who are long dead, of course," Mavis laughed.

"Of course," Terri smiled.

"Died in forty-one, during the fire," Lucy added.

"Fire?" Terri asked, feigning interest.

"Oh yes," Mavis added. "A terrible fire broke out in the cellar, and Tom and Wilma Benoit both died of smoke inhalation."

"Here? In the theater."

"Only their spirits remain," both women said in creepy unison, and with straight faces.

Terri waited for the punchline or for them to laugh or something. They didn't.

Goodness gracious. Terri still couldn't believe that she'd agreed to be a part of this. But she'd run into Mavis and Lucy twice since the first time she'd met them a few months ago, and each time they asked if she'd be able to spare some time to be a part of their "little" production.

Deep down, she wasn't interested in theater. Terri was through with acting, but she was a resident in this town. A resident hiding out in her little cottage, minding her own business. Terri was part of a community now, and the idea of becoming that crazy, old, washed up actress closed up in the house on Dupelo, who nobody ever saw, wasn't appealing.

"How many people can this place hold?" she asked.

"Seventy-five," Lucy said, glancing at Mavis.

"We usually fill it to capacity," Mavis added. "Especially on opening and closing nights of the season."

"Season?" Terri probed, surprised that this little town had a *whole* theater season.

"Yes," both women said in unison.

Mavis elaborated, "One month a year we open for submissions, that come from as far away as Houston. They send us scripts and entry fees, and we decide who makes the cut."

"We're very selective," Lucy added, raising a sophisticated brow.

"Do you think you'd be interested and have time to contribute to our little endeavor?"

"To read through stage plays?" Terri asked, trying not to sound as pensive as that knot in her stomach felt.

The two women glanced at each other. "It's just that, there are so many, and well..."

"Someone with your expertise could weed through the shitty stories without hardly batting an eye," Mavis elaborated.

"How many are we talking about?"

Lucy shrugged. "This year, I think we got about a hundred."

"A hundred?"

"At least," Mavis answered. "Of those, a dozen were accepted and performed here during the three-month season."

Two pair of eyes locked on Terri, waiting for her response.

"Sure, I could read a few," she shrugged, emphasizing the word *few*.

"Is that all?" Lucy asked, expressionless. "A few?"

She wasn't interested in reading through scripts. Especially bad ones, which she suspected most of the submissions would be.

"How many did you want me to read?" she asked with caution.

Mavis grinned, "More than a few. If you can spare the time."

"She's retired, Mavis," Lucy muttered to her friend, cutting her eyes at Terri. "Of course, she has time."

Terri was just about to mildly protest the woman's bold presumption, when they were suddenly interrupted.

"Ladies."

Luther Hunt appeared out of thin air like a beautiful apparition, towering over the three women and pulling up a chair to join their group.

Terri hadn't seen him since the show in New Orleans a few weeks ago.

Mavis clasped her hands together, "Luther, we're so glad you could make it."

"Yes," Lucy agreed, her eyes sparkling.

"Apologies for being late." He bent and kissed each woman on the check, then glanced at Terri. "What'd I miss?"

Butterflies filled her stomach, but then Terri composed herself and reminded herself that she was, happily, dating the man's son.

"Terri has agreed to read through the play submissions," Lucy chimed in.

"Cool," he said, nodding.

"*Some* of the submissions," Terri quickly added, shooting her gaze back at Lucy. "A few. Time permitting."

"When can you start scoring *The Devil's Run*?" Mavis asked Luther.

"I'm working on it."

Mavis giggled and lightly touched his hand. "I know it'll be marvelous."

"*The Devil's Run*?" Terri asked.

The two women glanced at each other, then looked back at her.

"It's *our* contribution," Lucy explained. "We wrote it."

"And it's the finale," Mavis added, proudly.

"Folks will be talking about it for years to come," he assured them with a wink.

Terri sensed that his declaration was not necessarily a compliment.

"What's it about?" Terri dared to ask.

Lucy took a deep breath and suddenly turned contemplative. "You know, the church used to sponsor the theater festival," she began.

Mavis nodded, "Many, many years ago, before we bought the theater."

"Our vision has always been to make the festival as inclusive as possible," Lucy continued. "Showcasing not only black and white productions, but—"

"Homosexuals," Mavis interrupted. "LGBTQ, transgender, transsexual, everything."

"Non-binary," Lucy added.

"Well...wow," Terri responded.

"*The Devil's Run* is a burlesque number," Mavis offered.

"Think Josephine Baker meets James Brown," Lucy said, her eyes wide with excitement.

Terri tried to picture it, but couldn't. She looked at Luther, sitting there looking absolutely amused. "You're writing the music for *The Devil's Run*?"

"Oh, absolutely. It's my honor."

If the ladies noted the hint of sarcasm in his response, they pretended not to.

"I'll be playing the role of Tonya Boy," Mavis blurted out, gleefully. "A woman pretending to be a man, pretending to be a woman."

Sounded an awful lot like Victor, Victoria.

"She'll be hosting the burlesque show, which will feature several different performers and their tortured behind the scenes stories."

"Two women, one black, one white, daring to love each other despite the fact that one is married to a man," Mavis explained.

"A transgender woman, who identifies as a man, falling in love with another man, who is in love with the woman that she was." Lucy gleefully clasped her hands together. "There'll be dancing and singing, and even a comedian performing on Tanya Boy's stage."

"That's a lot," Terri offered.

Luther chuckled, but the women didn't seem to notice.

"Thank you," Mavis shot back, elated. "We're thrill with the premise. Been working on it for more than a year."

Did she say it sounded good? Terri said that it was a lot. Not that it was good.

"Would you..." Lucy exchanged a look with Mavis. "Do you think you could take a look at it and tell us what you think?"

"What?" Terri asked, trepidation creeping up her spine like a vine.

"We'd be honored," Mavis added. "Maybe tell us how we need to do to make it better?"

"Well, I—"

"I've got a copy in my car," Luther said, staring at Terri. "I'd be happy to let you borrow it."

Terri wanted to punch him in the jaw because, obviously, at least to her, he thought this shit was funny.

"That'd be wonderful," Mavis said, clasping her hands together, tears glistening in her eyes. "Oh, you have no idea how much it'd mean to us for someone like you, a professional and experienced actress, to give us feedback."

Terri smiled.

Half an hour later, Terri walked out carrying four scripts and followed Luther to his car where he handed her the fifth. She held it and stared at it like it was that possessed book in that old horror movie *Evil Dead*.

"Have you read it?" she asked, raising her eyes to meet his.

He took a deep breath, drove his hands into his pockets, and sort of shrugged. Moments later, he laughed.

"Seriously?" she asked, not needing to hear what he had to say because it came through loud and clear from what he didn't say.

"No," he said, trying to compose himself. "It's—interesting. But their plays are always interesting, which is why people pack this theater every year."

She gave him the side eye. "What are you saying? Is it good or not?"

"Read it."

"Can't you just tell me?"

Luther hesitated, sighed again, and shook his head. "It's something I cannot put into words. Just, read it."

She rolled her eyes and groaned, "I'm retired. The last thing I want to do is read another bad script."

"Nah, you're not retired," he, for some reason, felt the need to say it. "People like us can't retire."

"People like us?"

He shrugged. "Artists."

"*You're* retired and you own a bar."

He nodded introspectively. "And I jump at the opportunity to play music every chance I get."

Luther walked Terri around to the driver's side of her car, parked next to his, opened the door for her and closed it after she got inside. The man was dangerously magnetic. Terri concluded, in the short time she'd spent sitting next to him in that theater, that her attraction to Luther had more to do with physics than how fine he was. Nick was fine. She'd been around *fine* plenty of times. This thing with Luther had more to do with neutrons, protons, atoms, and electricity. He couldn't help it and he wasn't doing it on purpose. Knowing that it was science drawing her to him, helped settle her down as she waved goodbye.

Terri's phone suddenly rang. "Hey Roxy," she answered, absently.

"It's been a while, sis. How are you?"

"Oh, I'm coming down from a high from being in the presence of the most mesmerizing man I've ever known."

Goodness, gracious! Why'd she say that?

"You mean the doctor?" Roxy probed, laughing.

"No," Terri murmured and reluctantly admitted. "His father."

"Wait. What?"

"How are you?"

"Don't you dare," Roxy fussed. "Don't you drop a bomb like that and then change the subject. You're seeing your man's father?"

"Nick is not my man, Rox," Terri explained. "We're just dating. And no. Yes. I mean, no."

"Terri…

Terri glanced at the pile of scripts on the passenger seat. "Know how I always told you I'd never do theater?"

"Yeah."

"Well…"

"Wait. You're acting in a play?"

"No," she said with emphasis. "I'm reading play submissions for the local theater company. Which is hilarious."

"Why are you reading plays?"

"Because these really nice, weird ladies asked me to, and I need to keep busy."

"Way to get immersed in the local culture, T."

"It's either this or volunteer with the local 4H Club," she quipped.

"Okay. Local theater is a better fit. Look at you, having a life," she teased.

"I know, right?"

"Back to your boyfriend's dad…"

"Nope. Not back to that, and I'm sorry I even mentioned it. Pretend I didn't."

"Too late. Sounds juicy."

"It's not. It's a harmless crush. Everybody crushes on Luther."

"Well, you know you're at that age."

"What age?"

"Haven't you ever seen that meme? I'm at the age where I can date you or your daddy?"

Terri laughed. "Girl, hang up. I gotta drive."

TALKING OLD SOLDIERS

"It's actually not bad," Terri said, taking a sip of wine.

Luther sat across the table from her, laughing. "No, it's not," he agreed. "It is a little bizarre, though."

"I mean, there's a lot going on but," she said, glancing down at the script sitting on the table between them. "It's not terrible. The other four I've read, however..." Terri furrowed her brows.

"Only what?" he asked. "Seventy more to read?"

In the last several weeks since meeting with Mavis and Lucy, Terri had gone from reading a handful of scripts, to MCing the event, to being dubbed an honorary member of the Devastation Community Theater Board of Directors. Luther Hunt was the other honorary member along with the Director of Music. Terri had come to Luther's restaurant to grab something to eat and finish reading *The Devil's Run* when he joined her.

"I am not reading anymore," she said, emphatically. "My brain is swollen from all that bad writing."

He didn't look convinced.

"I'm serious. I can't." Terri raised her hands in surrender.

Yolanda sat a beer on the table in front of him, then sat down across from Terri. "I'm auditioning for the Broken Hearted Cabaret Dancer."

Terri shook her head.

"And you'll be great at it," Luther said, sounding like he meant it.

"How's the score coming along?" Terri asked.

"Great. Doing a fusion of old rag time and jazz, maybe throw in a little Andre 3000 type hip-hop." He shrugged.

Terri grimaced. "I don't understand."

"You will," he said with a smirk. "Trust me. It'll work."

Yolanda stared at him, impressed. "You think you'll out-do last year?"

"By far," he boasted.

"Last year the sisters wrote a space opera called, "*We Outta Here*". It was awesome. I played a Martian spirit who took possession of Marie Antoinette," Yolanda said with a smirk.

Terri wasn't sure she heard her right. "A Martian —"

"Spirit." Yolanda beamed. "With abandonment issues. It was so deep."

"The music was along the lines of a *Madame Butterfly* / *Aida* kinda thing," Luther explained if he were absolutely serious. "*With a Phantom of the Opera* vibe mixed in. I put some old school hip-hop in that one. Worked great."

"I remember." Yolanda said, with a forlorn look in her eyes. "It was dope."

Yolanda's phone rang. "Hey. You here already?" she asked, getting up to leave. "I'll be out in a minute. See you in a few days, boss. Bye, Terri."

"Bye, Yolanda," Terri said.

While getting to know Luther this past month, Terri had worked through her crush issues and could now sit comfortably next to the man without melting into a gooey puddle. He wasn't as immediately personable as his son. Luther was more aloof, and it only appeared that he was hard to get to know. His sense of humor, though dry and harder to gauge, was rich, but low key.

"I can't tell if you're really serious about all this theater stuff or if you think it's absolutely ridiculous," she mentioned, studying him.

"Why can't it be both?" he offered. "I've traveled the world, Terri. Met people from all over, but none, not one, as fascinating as the people from Devastation, Louisiana."

This time, she laughed. "Yeah, I get that. The people here are unlike any I've ever come across."

"And it's genuine. Theater season is a big deal here, as big as any production on Broadway. Mavis and Lucy may seem crazy, but they're crazy like foxes. They know how to put on a good show, even to the naysayers."

"I'm not a naysayer," she argued.

"No, but you don't expect much," he clarified. "I'm just saying, don't judge too harshly or too soon. You might just be more impressed than you've been about anything in a long time."

Terri gave some thought to what he said. "Noted."

"They appreciate you coming onboard," he told her. "And they really do want your honest feedback."

"They told you this?"

"They didn't have to. It comes through loud and clear whenever you show up at a meeting."

Surprisingly, Terri was actually enjoying being a part of something outside of her own, selfish, self.

"Come on," he said, pushing away from the table. "I want show you something."

Terri packed up her things and followed Luther up the winding, wrought iron staircase in the back of the room. It opened to the most beautifully decorated and elegant apartment she'd ever seen.

"Wow," she said, her eyes widening to take in all the exceptional artwork and dramatic, international décor. "You live here?"

Sunlight flooded the whole place through dramatic cathedral windows.

"This is home," he said, picking up the remote and turning on a television bigger than her whole living room.

Luther punched a few buttons and sat down on the sofa, motioning for Terri to sit next to him.

"You're going to get a kick out of this."

Two hours later, it was over. The two sat silently next to each other for several beats before she finally spoke up.

"A Martian space opera?"

He nodded, introspectively. "That's how it's done."

They looked at each other and without warning, burst out laughing.

"It was actually pretty—unusually—phenomenal," she blurted out.

"I told you," he leaned back and sighed.

"You scored that?"

"The whole damn thing," he admitted. "I've never been so challenged in my whole career. I wanted to put that shit on iTunes or Spotify or something and sell it."

"You could," she exclaimed. "It's that Rocky Horror Picture Show kind of iconic."

His gorgeous eyes lit up. "Exactly."

Terri sipped more wine while Luther talked through his ideas for scoring the new play and even sampled some chords for her on the guitar and the piano, which he played flawlessly.

"The thing is not to take the damn play too seriously, but to respect it," he explained.

She leaned against the piano. "How can you take it seriously? It's not going to win any Tony awards but for what it is, or can be, it's got elements of brilliance in it."

Luther stared at her long enough to make her feel exposed and transparent.

"What are you really doing here, Ms. Dawson?" he asked, his fingers gliding across piano keys, building on a hypnotic melody. "How come you're not over in Hollywood rubbing shoulders with Viola Davis and Brad Pitt? Big star like you?"

Terri shrank a little inside herself. "Is that what you think I am? A big star?"

"That's what everybody in town thinks you are, Terri."

"That's hilarious," she said, not finding it funny at all.

"Why? You're a big deal." Luther knitted thick brows.

"I haven't had a real role in years, Luther," she eventually admitted, fighting back tears. "Lately, it's all I can do to land a halfway decent commercial or voiceover if I'm lucky."

Luther focused his gaze on the keys and his playing. "So, you came here?"

Terri paused before responding. "I got tired of wanting what I couldn't have," she admitted. "I've been chasing that dream for half my life, and yeah. Landing here is what came of it."

Luther continued playing. "You were on your way to someplace else, though." He looked up at her. "Am I right? Nobody like you, finds a place like this on purpose."

"I was on my way to Houston to hide out at my best friend's house. Stopped to get gas and decided to stay."

"Running from something. Running to something." He smiled. "Or, just running."

"Why are you here?" she asked, refusing to let him off the hook. Luther was a big man, with a big presence and talent as wide as the ocean. "And don't tell me it's because it's your hometown. There's more to it than that."

"I was married," he began. "I got married when I was nineteen. She was seventeen. We had Nick, and not long after, I got my first big gig. I took it to make us some money."

He glanced up at her with dark regret filling his eyes.

"You stayed gone?" she asked.

"Until it was obvious that Lupus wasn't letting up," he admitted.

Luther shrugged. "I came home, but by then it was too late. Five months later, her heart gave out. I stayed."

"You miss it, though," Terri noted, recalling watching him play in New Orleans. "Performing."

Luther looked up at her and smiled. "Don't you miss it? Performing?"

Terri shrugged. "When it was good, yeah. But the longer I'm away from it, the harder it's becoming to even think of going back to that life."

"I get it."

She shook her head. "No, you don't," she said, calling him out. "I saw you on that stage, Luther."

He stopped playing.

"You were a bright and shining star, and you were loving it."

He started back playing but stopped again. "You're right. It felt like I'd never left."

"So, why don't you go back?"

"Why don't you?"

"I didn't give up my dream," she responded. "It gave up on me. Yours would welcome you back with open arms. I know it."

"I don't deserve it," he admitted. "When Ava and Nick needed me the most, I was on the road, living my dream. I've had my time."

"I get it," she said. "I'm a failure and you're riddled with guilt."

He looked at her and smiled. "Ain't we a pair?"

SUGAR HONEY

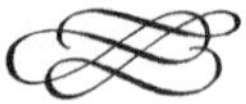

Terri couldn't blame it on the alcohol. She wasn't drunk. She wasn't grappling with confusion or despair. The conversation between them flowed easily. Their vibrations synced. Luther's deep laugh resonated to her soul, striking a chord to something she'd never experienced, but had always wanted to... connection. Not in a friendly, 'we cool' kind of way. Not in a 'we have a lot in common and can make this work' kind of way.

The warmth of his hand touching hers awakened her from a slumber at the soul level. He wrapped his arms around her, pulled her to his chest, lowered his mouth to hers, and the flavor of Luther Hunt, the heat from him, pulled Terri out of the recesses of that emotionless abyss she'd fallen into long ago.

His.

His pussy. His woman. His... Terri.

Surrender.

It was never her thing. Not when it came to men. A man could share her time, her space, maybe even her life, but he could never possess her, not until this moment.

Sex. Fucking. Making love.

This wasn't any of those things, but something else that defied reason, right or wrong, common sense.

No space between them.

No space to let in air or light.

Terri spread her thighs wide, straddling him. Her chin kneaded into his broad shoulder, her arms wrapped tight enough around him to choke the life out of him, but he didn't protest. Muscled arms circled her waist, calloused hands caressed her skin.

He was deep, his stroke steady and filling. The scent and sounds of their lovemaking permeated the room. Time. How long had they…

It didn't matter. Time didn't matter. Nothing did. Except him. Except this.

A gentle tug from him coaxed her back far enough to lock onto the penetrating gaze of his dark eyes. The conviction in them drilled to her core. His lips, slightly parted, inviting her mouth to his. Terri moaned, groaned, and stilled her hips, forcing his movements to stop.

His thick dick filled all of her, and if she wasn't patient or careful, she'd come too soon, she'd make him come too soon and she wasn't ready for this to end.

"You feel so damn good," his deep, soul-stirring voice, melted away what was left of any inhibitions.

This beautiful man kissed her neck, lowered his hands, palmed her ass, pushed into her again, commanding the moment.

Terri cried out, submitting to his rhythm.

"Hold on," he demanded. "Don't let me go, sugah."

She did as she was told, willing time and the rest of the world to stop. Terri trusted Luther with her… trusted him to know what she needed and wanted without instruction or guidance. And he did. His patience transcended to her. His strength, confidence, and steadiness grounded Terri until she felt absolutely, unshakeable.

This was what she wanted, what she'd always wanted. A link to another human being, at the core. To belong and to be the other whole of a half. In this moment, in Luther's arms, that's exactly how she felt.

"Don't let me go," she whispered, pressing against him. "Don't ever let me go."

Luther was perfect and he was right and necessary.

❧

TERRI SLEPT.

Luther couldn't.

You dumb motha fucka! You selfish, dumb motha fucka! He cursed himself over and over. Luther sat up on the side of the bed, coming apart over what they'd done. Another mistake, one in a long list of too damn many. Luther ran his hands down his face, the intoxicating scent of her all over him. God! She was perfect. Luther hadn't believed something so completely about any woman since, since he'd first laid eyes on Ava.

After losing her, there had been no one else, not even a thought that anyone else could fill that empty space in his heart. This one time with Terri had proven him to be a liar, and Luther felt like shit.

He heard her stirring, felt her moving behind him, but Luther didn't dare to turn to look at her.

"What time is it?" she asked, her fingers grazing his lower back.

He glanced at the clock on the nightstand, "Just after nine."

The silence between them was deafening, filling the once sweet space with a toxic regret.

"I'm sorry," he said first.

"Luther, don't." Terri sat up, placed a soft hand on his shoulder. Luther gently shrugged it off.

"Nick and I have never been close," he explained.

"This isn't about Nick."

"Bullshit," he snapped, glancing over his shoulder. "We were trying, Terri. We can't mend what was broken, but he and I have been trying to build on something new."

Luther shouldn't have had to explain this. Terri knew what they'd done was wrong. Fuck, if she didn't know.

"Okay, but you can't tell me this didn't mean anything to you,"

Terri's voice cracked, like she was on the verge of crying. "It wasn't just sex, Luther. Don't tell me you think that's all it was."

"Then I won't. What we did was wrong, and you know it." This time he did turn to her and stared into her eyes, challenging her to deny that he wasn't right.

Tears glistened in her beautiful eyes. "I care for him, too."

Luther swallowed. "He's my son, Terri. What I did—"

"*We*, Luther," she interrupted, swiping at tears. "What *we* did."

What the hell kind of father was he? What kind of man? There was no excuse for what he'd done with this woman, and he hated himself. Nick meant everything to him. He was the only thing Luther had left in his life that he'd be willing to die for, and he'd put it all on the line, for what? Her? Pussy?

"He can't know." He stood, crossed the room to put space between them.

"Of course not," she blurted out. "I would never tell him."

How'd he let this happen? What was the moment that made him forget about Nick long enough for Luther to feel it was okay to fuck the man's woman?

"We take this fuckin' secret to our graves, Terri," he demanded, feeling more convicted and more determined to salvage his relationship with Nick.

Terri drew her knees to her chest, looking as devastated as Luther felt, but there was only one thing left for her to do. If she hadn't reached that conclusion on her own, he needed to be sure she understood it now.

"You can't keep seeing him."

She looked stunned that he'd said it, but she needed to hear it. This wasn't solely about keeping a secret. It was about saving Nick at all cost. That boy could not be played. Not by her. Not by anyone.

"I-I mean, no. Of course, I won't keep seeing Nick. How can I? After this... you ... How could I possibly continue seeing him?"

He'd fucked up. Nick had been happy, and Luther had fucked that up. Terri had been getting her life on track, and he'd fucked it up.

"I'm sorry," he said out loud, more to himself than to her. Luther's voice trailed off.

"I am too, Luther. Believe me, I am so very sorry."

"He won't understand you ending it all of a sudden. You need to let him down—"

"I'm not an idiot, Luther," she said, shucking off the sheet and climbing out of bed.

Terri dressed in a hurry and gathered her things to leave.

"It's over," her voice cracked. "I'll take care of it."

Luther felt as if someone had spooned out his heart.

"Not that way," he told her, just as she was walking down the stairs leading to the bar.

Luther led her to the back of his loft and held open the back door for her. Terri paused, and almost looked up at him before taking the stairs leading from the back of the building into the parking lot.

He waited at the door, long enough to see her get inside her car and pull out of the parking lot before closing the door behind him and walking back to the bed on shaky legs. A lump the size of his foot swelled in his throat. The overwhelming need to be with that woman clouded his judgment to the point of putting everything that mattered to him at risk. He and Nick were on the mend for the first time since that boy had been born. But Nick had been an afterthought. His whole life, his son had been an afterthought. Luther had been lying to himself, convinced that he had become a better man. He believed that shit, until now.

LET IT RAIN

Half an hour after leaving Luther's, Terri, freshly showered, changed into a tee shirt and panties, crawled into bed, and lay in the dark, staring up at the ceiling.

"What the fuck did you just do, Terri?" she whispered, numb and in total disbelief of what happened between her and Luther.

This was the kind of shit that would happen on that reality show, the kind of shit she'd judged her co-stars for, turning up her nose and rolling her eyes in disgust.

Terri covered her face with her hands and cursed, "Damn! Damn! Fuck, Terri!"

"How'd you let that happen?" she asked, rolling over on her side, blinking back tears. "Why?"

It started out as nothing. One minute she and Luther were talking, watching videos, listening to music. Talking. They were friends. Right? Friends talking about their lives. There was an understanding between them centering on similar backgrounds and the worlds they'd come from. They'd related to each other on that level. That's all it was, until...

She searched her thoughts for a moment, the one where it all changed. It was there, but shrouded in a cloud of gray, cloaked in casual glances, coy smiles and touches. More than a gesture or anything either of them said, there was a feeling. Terri felt it and he must've felt it too because nothing specific was ever said, but the energy between them led to one thing. A kiss.

An image flashed in her mind of Terri leaning on the piano, Luther playing, and of a very natural, magnetism drawing her face closer to his, his to hers, and at first, lips. It was a sweet peck that they had no business sharing but did. They drew back and stared into each other's eyes for a moment, and then another one, as light as the first. Luther reached one of those bear paws of his to the back of her neck, pulled her lips to his again and...

The taste, the flavor of him, mixing with her, created a fog thick enough to cloud judgment and impair reason.

Terri shook off the image, covered her face with a pillow and screamed into it.

For years, she'd felt like driftwood, carried by waves at their mercy, desperately seeking to land somewhere, but she never could. Sure, she'd bought places to live, but in her heart, home was temporary until something better came along. In the few hours she was with him, Luther felt like home, like a place she could stay and never leave, because the urge to pack up and move on was gone. So, it wasn't just sex.

She drew her knees to her chest and wrapped her arms around them. Nick was a nice man. He was funny, handsome, smart, and attentive. He was everything she *should've* wanted, but not quite. And it wasn't him. It was her. He was centered and solid in who he was. Any woman in her right mind would turn backflips for his attention. Tonight, however, with Luther, Terri realized she'd only been with Nick because she felt like it was the right thing to do. With him, life was giving her a chance to move back a couple of spaces and take a different path than the one she'd chosen. He was a chance at normalcy for someone like her, who'd avoided the concept like the plague.

Terri cared for him. In the few months they'd been dating, she enjoyed Nick's company and she thought she'd wanted more with him. A life, a future. He was everything.

But he wasn't Luther.

❧

"DID you hear what I just said?" Roxy emphatically asked.

It was just after seven in the morning and she'd ambushed Terri with a surprise video chat. Terri was one of the few people in the world to ever see the woman with her head wrapped, wearing glasses, and without a full face. She actually looked ten years younger in her natural state.

Terri groaned and rubbed sleep from her eyes as she sat up, "I heard you."

"Six-hundred-and-fifty thousand signatures, T. All for you."

"Great," Terri responded, with way too much sarcasm.

Somebodies, apparently 650,000 of them, had decided to get together and petition Terri's return to the *Vivacious Vixen's* reality show.

Roxy sighed, "Terri, it's not ideal, but a show like that could change the whole trajectory of your career, sis."

"What career, Roxy?" Terri snapped. "It's over. How many different times do I have to tell you that? I'm through. I'm done. And I'm certainly not interested in going back into that three-ring circus when I'm living in my own, right here in this tiny ass town."

Terri had never raised her voice to Roxy before, but dammit, the woman wasn't listening. Terri needed Roxy to finally hear her and stop pitching acting opportunities at her.

"It's too early for this, Roxy," she said, her voice cracking. "I can't—"

"Terri? What's wrong? What happened?"

Terri closed her eyes and shook her head. She didn't want to talk about it, but she desperately needed to talk about it.

"I slept with Luther," she blurted out.

Roxy's eyes darted back and forth. "Luther? Luther who?"

"Nick's father," Terri snapped. "The man I'm seeing... I slept with his goddamned father, Roxy."

Tears escaped down her cheeks and the reality of what happened between the two of them came rushing back to her.

"Fuck!" Terri exclaimed. "Who does that? I mean, I'm all for a woman's right to explore her sexuality. I should be able to have sex with whoever I choose to have sex with because I'm not married. I'm not even Nick's girlfriend, but his father?" She grimaced. "Seriously? Who the fuck does that?"

"Whoa," was the best Roxy could do, her eyes glazed over and fixed on Terri, coming apart.

"This is reality TV drama. It's a soap opera. It's humiliating and a small ass town and it wouldn't surprise me one bit if half the people here didn't already know about it."

Roxy finally spoke up after a long pause, "What are you going to do?"

Terri sniffed and wiped away tears. "Duh—I have to stop seeing Nick. Stay as far away from Luther as I can and go back to minding my own, damned business."

"What kind of man is this Luther to do something like that to his son?"

"He didn't do it by himself, Rox," Terri admonished. "I kissed him first."

"You kissed him? Terri—why?" Roxy probed.

"You think I haven't been banging my head against the wall asking myself the same thing?" Terri asked, frustrated. "I'd heard about women slipping and accidentally falling on dicks, but I never expected to be one of them."

"It wasn't an accident," Roxy stated, simply. "Things like that don't just happen, Terri. You didn't *accidentally* sleep with the man's father."

Terri rolled her eyes.

"It's me, T, and you don't need to lie to me or to tell me what you think I need to hear. Truth. Why'd you do it?"

"I don't know," she murmured.

Dead silence from Roxy, which often happened while she gave Terri time to rethink her answer.

"What kind of woman *settles* for a handsome doctor?" Terri finally asked. "One who has made it clear that he's interested in a future with that woman?"

"I'm listening," Roxy responded. "What kind?"

"I'm almost forty-four, Rox, and I have no idea who I am."

"You know who you are."

"I really don't. Practically my whole life, I've been Terri the actress, and that's it. That's all. Being here is forcing me to look inside and to see myself in a whole other light."

"And that's why you fucked your man's dad?"

"Why do you have to say it like that?"

"Because I'm sick of hearing it, T," Roxy complained.

"Of what?"

"Your act."

Terri grimaced. "What are you talking about?"

"You're still on, girl. Still on a movie set or reality show. Still performing. Still drama."

"I am not drama," she shot back.

"Are you really being real with me right now? Because it doesn't feel like it."

"I *am* being real with you," she said, irritated by Roxy's judgment. "I'm confiding in *you*, my friend."

"Then confide, girl, and stop with this bullshit about finding yourself. Why'd you do it? Why'd you sleep with Nick's father? Were you drunk?"

"No," she snapped.

"Did he slip something into your sweet tea?"

"No."

"Did he force himself on you?"

"No, Roxy!"

"Then you fucked him because you wanted to?"

"Yes," she admitted.

Roxy paused. "Was that so hard?"

"I shouldn't have wanted to," Terri stated, bitterness burning the back of her throat.

"But you did and that's your truth."

Terri groaned, disappointment shadowed her face. "It just happened, Rox."

SERVES HIM RIGHT

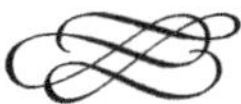

Tyler threw the best parties. A few of Roxy's clients were regulars on a few of his weekly television shows and she'd been invited to this shindig by proxy.

"Roxy," David Randall, Executive Producer of the *Vivacious Vixens of Atlanta,* smiled, impeccably dressed in an impeccable suit. "How've you been?"

"David." She smiled. Roxy sipped her wine. She'd caught wind of the petition weeks ago. "Great seeing you. It's been a while."

"You look beautiful, as always."

"Thank you, and congratulations on the launch of the new show."

That broad chest of his puffed, shoulders drew back, a satisfied and proud smirk tweaked the corner of his mouth. "Thank you. It's exciting and we've already started casting."

"What's the name of the show again?" she asked.

"*The Lavish Life,* set in Los Angeles."

Roxy raised her glass in a toast. "Here's to living the lavish life."

David clinked his glass to hers. "By the way, how's Terri? Have you spoken to her?"

Six months ago, he'd fired Terri, citing the doldrums of her storyline. When viewers found out she wasn't coming back next season, they cried foul and reigned down bullshit all over his perfectly coifed head.

"Yes, as a matter of fact, we spoke a few days ago."

"I'm sure you've heard about the petition," he offered.

"No," she lied. "What petition?"

So, where was this headed? Roxy maintained her cool, hoping to get a glimpse of him squirming.

He paused, looking surprised that she appeared clueless. "It seems fans didn't take the news too well about Terri's unexpected departure."

"You mean, her firing?"

He leaned back on his heels and returned a wry smile. "Prematurely."

Roxy's smug expression caused his face to flush red.

"She's doing well, I hope."

All the conversations she'd been having with Terri, including the one from this morning flashed in her memory and the opportunity to strike back at the man who'd dared call her client boring was too great to just let slip by.

"She single-handedly saved the life of one of her neighbors who broke Terri's ankle some months back. She's smack dab in the middle of the kind of love triangle playing out in one of Mr. Perry's hit shows. Oh, and she's going into theater."

Roxy had embellished, but the way his eyes lit up, she knew her point had struck gold.

"Our Terri?" he asked, impressed. "That all sounds—amazing."

"Never a dull moment," Roxy lifted her glass and took another sip.

"I thought she looked down her nose at drama?"

"The woman's living her best life," she assured him. "It's definitely a side of her you never gave her an opportunity to show."

Not that she'd ever want to put her friend's business in the street like that, or air Terri's dirty laundry on national television. She just wanted this fool to see the woman's potential and how he'd failed to capitalize on a good thing.

"Roxyyyyy," one of her clients, Desiree, squealed floating across the room looking like a dream, wrapped her arms around Roxy. "I'm so glad you could make it." Desiree placed delicate fingers on David's arm. "Mind if I steal her away for a moment? I have someone I've been dying to introduce her to."

Roxy delivered a beaming smile at the man before disappearing through the crowd with Desiree, knowing good and damn well the seed had been planted and was already taking root.

Roxy loved Terri like a sister, and she'd only ever wanted the best for her. She'd lost count of how many times the two of them had been in this space before. Terri was down on Terri. She was tired and she'd made up her mind that she was finished with acting. Only, she was never quite finished.

Terri needed to rest and to heal. She needed to salve her fragile ego, massage her broken heart. And like so many times before, Roxy would sweep in wearing her superhero's cape, in time to rescue her friend with a role, one she deserved, and too incredible to resist.

BOUT YOU

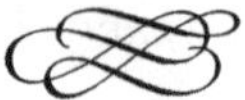

"Hey, baby," Nick said, coming into her place, wrapping his arm around her waist, and planting a thick kiss on her lips.

Nick hadn't been able to get away for nearly a month to see her. He'd called, but Terri had been too busy to talk for more than ten minutes. She'd signed on to work on theater stuff, and Miss Mavis and Miss Lucy had her swamped.

"I missed the hell outta you, girl," he laughed, pressing his forehead to hers.

"I've missed you too," she said, stepping back, and taking hold of his hands.

Terri looked soft wearing a loose-fitting dress, the hem falling at the middle of her thighs, showing off those pretty legs of hers. Nick licked his lips.

"Can I get you something to drink?" she asked, heading into the kitchen before he answered.

"Um, whatcha got?"

"Wine, sweet tea, water..."

"Tea is fine."

Nick sat on the sofa, crossed one leg over the other and kept his eyes fixed on her. Terri's soft fro was tamed in a thick braid down the back of her head. Absence had made his heart grow all kinds of crazy for this woman. Seeing her now, only drove that point home. He was falling for her in a big way, and Nick decided it was time she knew it.

"So, you're in the theater business now," he laughed. "Those old ladies taking advantage of your talents?"

Terri sat his drink down on the table in front of him. Nick pulled her down next to him.

"The Devastation Community Theater Company is more than I bargained for," she explained. "And those two old ladies have the energy of someone half their age."

He laughed, "Miss Mavis and Miss Lucy. Legends."

Terri laughed, "For sure."

"They're characters," he stated with a shrug. "But, progressive visionaries, that's for sure."

"And passionate."

"My pop is writing the music for this year's production," he said, remembering Luther mentioning it. "He worked with them last year, too. Did a damn good job from what I heard."

"I heard that, too," she smiled.

"You and him ought to be seeing a lot of each other. He takes this thing as seriously as they do."

"We've seen quite a bit of each other."

Terri working alongside his old man. Something about the idea set well with Nick. He'd never been this serious about a woman before and he and his dad were starting to mend fences, it felt right that Luther and Terri had a chance to get to know each other.

"So, what do you think of Luther?"

She raised a beautiful brow. "How do you mean?"

Nick turned contemplative. "He and I are trying," he admitted. "We're getting closer and it's important to me to know that the woman I'm seeing, and my dad get along."

"Oh, yeah. I mean, we don't spend a whole lot of time together, but when we do, it's fine."

"Fine?" he shrugged. "Okay. That's cool? I guess?"

"He's a nice man, Nick," Terri elaborated. "And talented. I got a chance to hear the music he'd written for last year's show and it was brilliant."

"Yeah. He's well... You know. You heard him play," he said with pride. "Luther's got mad skills."

"He does."

"And you two have that whole celebrity thing in common," he reminded her. "Might even know some of the same people."

She smiled. "It's possible, I guess."

Terri was reserved, a bit more aloof than usual. Maybe he'd been gone too long, but Nick planned to make up for it.

"So, a friend of mine is having a thing at the lake."

"A thing at the lake?"

"Yeah, it's cool. It's his girl's birthday and he's grilling, got a DJ, drinks. I told him we'd swing by."

"Tonight?" she asked, looking concerned.

"Yeah. Unless you don't want to go."

"Um." She scratched the edge of her brow. "I just promised Mavis and Lucy to have some plays I've been editing back to them by morning. I'd planned on reading tonight."

"Baby," he groaned and took hold of one of her hands. "I haven't seen you in weeks, Terri. Miss Mavis and Miss Lucy will understand. I'm sure of it."

She started to protest but Nick wasn't going to give her a chance.

"Want me to call them? I don't mind." Nick pulled his cell phone out of his pocket.

"No, you will not call them," she protested.

"I really want to spend time with you, sweetheart," he said, lowering his tone a few octaves, leaning in close and grazing his lips against her cheek. Nick leaned back and gazed into her eyes. "We can go to this thing, then come back here and..."

"I've got my period," she unmercifully blurted out.

"I don't care?" he shrugged. "I'm a doctor."

"I care, Dr. Nick." She pulled away from him.

"Nooooo," he groaned, leaning his head back.

"I'm sorry, but it happens."

Nick looked at her, then down at the boner in his lap, then back at her. "We can get creative."

"Nick."

"Too desperate?" he joked.

Nick expected a snappy comeback, pity, something. Terri smiled. Nick was no mind reader, but something seemed to be going on with her. She felt closed off for some reason.

"What's going on, baby?" He took hold of her hand.

"Nothing. I'm just working through some things, Nick," she said, softly.

All kinds of imaginary red flags waved in his mind. "What kinds of things?"

He wasn't a kid. He'd been on the other side of words like that his share of times to know where this conversation was headed. What he couldn't understand, was why.

"You are so special," she said, pressing her hand to his cheek.

Shit! Nick knew where this was going. He could read people. There was a melancholy to her. Sadness in her eyes and a tone of finality in her words.

"What's up, Terri? What's going on?"

Chill, bruh, he told himself. All she'd said was that she was working things out. That didn't mean she was ending this.

"I'm saying that I need space, Nick."

Or did it?

"Okay," he said, pensively. "Um… mind telling me what that means for us?"

Terri momentarily pursed her lips. "I've been thinking… and I really don't think I've been fair to you."

"Don't," he said, getting swept up by pride. "Don't patronize me, Terri. I'm a grown man. Say what you've got to say."

"I just did." She stared back at him. "I need to step back and deal with some issues I've been running from for too long," she sighed. "I'm not in the right head space for a relationship, Nick."

"This is a recent revelation?" he asked, sarcasm slipping through wounded pride.

"It's not recent," she responded defensively. "We were just kicking it in the beginning."

Nick's brows shot up. "Kicking it? Is that what we were doing?"

"See, this is what I mean," she sighed. "Yes. To me, that's what we were doing. To you... obviously not."

It wasn't like he was planning on proposing marriage after the first date, but Nick was well past the age of 'kicking it' with a woman. Terri was eight years older than him. She, should've been past it, too.

"I'm not looking for a serious relationship, Nick. I thought we could just keep it simple, keep it light, but I sense that you want more, and maybe I've let this go on too long, but—"

"No," he said, frustrated. "I get it."

"It's not out of the blue, Nick. I've been halfway straight arming you from the beginning, making it clear that I've got issues."

"Is that what you've been doing?"

"I walked away from my home, my career, the only serious relationship I've had my whole life, just a few months ago—my career. And then you came into my life and I wasn't ready. I'm *not* ready."

"So, you saying I came on like gangbusters?" He asked, defensively.

"I'm saying that before you fall in love with a woman, you need to know who she is. And how can you know if she can't even answer that question for herself? I'm still figuring it out, Nick. Before I get involved with anyone, I need to know."

NICK DIDN'T GO the lake. He didn't want to go back to New Orleans. Nick ended up in the last place he expected... at Luther's.

THE WRECKAGE

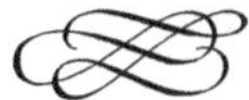

Nick texted, asking Luther if he could stop by. Luther stared at it, debating on if he should even respond.

"Come on through." He reluctantly texted back, before taking a couple of shots of gin to settle his nerves.

❧

LUTHER'S STOMACH ached at the thought of seeing his kid. The fact that Nick was in town meant that he'd come to see Terri. There was no telling what state of mind Nick would be in when he made it to Luther's. The best he could do, was brace himself.

Despite his best efforts, he hadn't been able to get Terri out of his mind. Luther felt like shit about what happened between the two of them the other night. He'd loved every second he'd spent with her, then put her out like she was just another lay, and nothing could've been farther from the truth. That was the problem.

Ten minutes passed when he heard a tapping against his door.

"Good to see you, son," he said, studying Nick's face for some kind of indication of where his head was.

"Yeah, you too," he replied with a slight nod.

His son made himself at home on the sofa, but Luther couldn't read him.

"You want a beer?" He asked on his way to the refrigerator.

"Sure. I'll take one."

That knot in his gut was starting to feel lethal. Luther resisted the urge to make small talk. That really wasn't their way. Luther handed Nick a beer, then sat in the chair across from him.

"When'd you get in town?" he eventually asked.

"About an hour ago."

Long enough to see her. Luther didn't believe she'd tell Nick what happened between the two of them, but guilt ate at him, convincing him that maybe, Nick could somehow figure it out just by looking at her… at Luther.

"How long you staying?"

Nick shrugged. "Not long. I'm headed back now. Just thought I'd swing through, first."

There was something in Nick's eyes, in his tone that signaled a problem. Luther wouldn't ask. Not directly.

"You going to see your lady friend?" He asked, reservedly.

Nick averted his gaze, took a sip of beer and shrugged. "She was busy," he explained with hesitation.

Luther nodded and decided not to push the issue.

"So, I hear you're working with Miss Mavis and Lucy again on this theater thing?" Nick asked, feigning enthusiasm.

"Yeah." Luther half smiled. "Those two are full of surprises and I mean that in a good way."

Nick chuckled. "Can't wait to hear what you come up with."

"Terri's contributing some time too," he dared to mention.

Had she spoken to Nick? Had Terri done the right thing and ended their relationship? Nick's vibe sent a message that maybe she had, but Luther needed to know.

"Yeah. I know." Nick looked down at the beer bottle in his hands and sighed. "Can I ask you a question?"

Luther's heart drummed. "Of course."

"Is mom the only woman you ever loved?" He shifted his gaze to Luther.

"Yes."

Nick turned contemplative for a few moments, before continuing. "Y'all were young when you got married."

"We were. I was almost nineteen. She was fresh out of high school, seventeen."

His son sighed, "How did you know, *that* young, that you loved her?"

All this talk of love—was Nick actually in love with Terri?

Luther gave his answer some thought. "The truth? Sometimes I wonder if we really *knew* or if we just *thought* we loved each other. We were kids, Nick. How do you know something like that, for real, at that age?"

"But you said she was the only woman you've ever loved."

"And she was. But I'm not a hundred percent convinced if what we felt was real love that young, or if we were two kids who thought we were." Luther paused. "I do know that whatever it was we felt, grew until it became exactly what we believed it always was. If that makes sense."

Again, silence drifted between them for several minutes.

"Why'd you stay gone?" Nick finally asked, looking at his father. "Especially when she kept getting sick. Why didn't you just come home?"

Nick had spent a lot of years living in angry speculation of his idea of who and what Luther was, but he'd never asked, until now.

"I came home, Nick," he confessed. "The first time she got sick, I came home and stayed."

"I don't remember."

He shook his head. "No, you were young. Two, three years old," he explained. "I worked at Roscoe's fixing cars."

Nick laughed, "*You* fixed cars?"

"I *tried* fixing cars," Luther corrected himself.

"Mom was sick when I was that young?"

Luther turned introspective. "Off and on," he explained. "It wasn't so bad in the beginning. Ava was young and strong and she would beat it, but, we were fuckin' broke. Broker than broke to the point that they were threatening to take the house and she wasn't having that."

"So, you went back to playing?"

Luther shrugged. "Had to. It was good, quick money, and we managed to stave off bill collectors long enough for me to catch up on some things. But it meant, hitting the road again."

For years, things were fine for them. Better than fine. The money rolled in while Luther rolled on, in and out of cities, states and countries, sending back almost everything he made to Ava.

"Were you faithful?" Nick asked.

Luther looked at him and swallowed. He knew. He knew about Terri.

"Did you cheat on Mom?" he asked again.

Luther shook his head. "Never. I thought about it," he admitted. "Came close, but—I couldn't."

He expected Nick to say her name and to ask what went down between Luther and Terri.

"I'm thirty-five and I've never, truly loved a woman," he said. "But I think I could love her."

Luther's heart sank to his stomach. What had he done to his boy?

"So, what are you telling me, son?"

Nick took a long drink from his beer. "Nothing. I was just wondering if falling in love feels like getting hit in the chest with lightening or something else definitive." He laughed.

"Not necessarily. But I guess it's different for different people."

"She's not feeling me like that, though," Nick eventually admitted, his disappointment coming through loud and clear.

"You sure about that?" A hint of relief seeped in. Maybe she had done the right thing and ended things with Nick.

"Yeah." Nick's gaze fell to the beer in his hands.

"You good?"

Nick shrugged. "I mean I have to be. Terri's dealing with some things that ain't got nothing to do with me, so..."

"The right one is out there, Nick," Luther offered, feeling a hint of relief that she'd kept her word. "You ain't chopped liver, man."

Nick bobbed his head and looked at Luther. "You're right. I ain't."

❧

HALF AN HOUR AFTER NICK LEFT, Luther stood at the window staring out at the tree lined street below, relieved, that maybe, just maybe, all of them could walk away from this thing unscathed. He and Terri had momentarily gotten caught up in—whatever it was. Luther certainly couldn't name it. Pretty woman, but the world was full of those. Luther reasoned that his attraction to her was rooted in a moment of weakness, maybe even chemistry. Another time, another place, nothing about what he and Terri had done would've been wrong. But timing had never been kind to Luther.

His phone rang. "Mavis, what can I do for you?"

"Can you swing by tomorrow at around two?" she asked.

"For you, of course I can," he smiled.

"Oh, thank you, Luther. We're having an emergency meeting with the planning committee and we need your input."

"Will everyone be there?" he asked, not mentioning Terri's name.

"Yes, thank goodness. Oh, all but Ms. Dawson. She's swinging by earlier to drop off a few scripts. She mentioned not feeling well and won't be able to make it."

Disappointment. Relief. Luther was filled with both.

"I'll be there," he assured her before hanging up.

It was over before it began and that was a good thing. Terri was a fantasy; the object of a wish Luther had denied himself too long. It wasn't about her, but rather, what she represented. He was tired of being alone. Luther and Nick were on the same quest and for a moment, with the same woman. Which was fuckin' crazy. Spending time with Terri had been a mistake, but in retrospect, it had only been a mistake because Nick was involved. There was nothing Luther wouldn't do for that boy. But what he'd done *to* him, was another unforgiveable mistake.

BESIDES

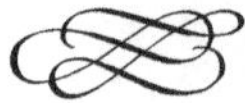

"Hear me out before you hang up," Roxy demanded.

"What is it with you calling me at dawn's ass crack," Terri grumbled, putting Roxy on speaker and squinting to try and see the time on the phone. "It's six in the morning, Roxy," she protested. "*My* time."

"I know," Roxy sighed. "I'm in Cali, T. So, yeah. My ass is up way too early. But I woke up to a text that could change your life, sis. Seriously."

Two things happened at the sound of those words; Terri's heart jumped into her throat, threatening to come out her mouth in the form of a scream. But then it immediately, dropped to her stomach like a rock, making her feel like she was going to vomit.

"What?"

Roxy laughed, "Desmond Williams is starting to cast for his new film, a period piece set in the early seventies, called *On the Point*, and there's a character I think you'd be perfect for."

Terri came out of her kitchen and sank down into her sofa. Six months ago, she'd have turned a somersault hearing news like this. But Terri had given up acting. She'd walked away from the anxiety and depression that came from hoping, wishing, wanting something like this to happen, only to be disappointed time and time again. Of course, in the time she'd done all that retiring and setting out to try and find herself, she'd slept with a father and son. A move too damn foul for words. Going back into acting would mean leaving town and putting all this mess behind her. And it needed to happen.

"You there?" Roxy asked.

"I'm here," Terri swallowed. "So, tell me about it."

She didn't want to know, but she did. She didn't want to want this, but—she did?

"It's a lead role, Terri," she explained. "The character's name is Irene. She's a single mother who works at a bank, struggling to make ends meet and raise a teenage daughter. The daughter is seduced by an older man who kidnaps her and traffics her for sex. The police aren't helping so Irene takes matters into her own hands and solicits the help of an ex-con-slash-killer for help. Ryan Jacobs has signed on to play the male lead."

Ryan Jacobs was as 'A' list as it came in the film industry.

"And you want to hear the best news?" Roxy continued?

Terri pushed back a familiar wave of excitement and shrugged. "Sure."

"Desmond called me, Terri, asking for you. *He wants to fly you in as soon as possible,*" Roxy had told her. "Limo. A five-star hotel in Beverly Hills, all expenses paid, girl. Four days, three nights, A-list treatment. So, pack a bag, girl. You're going back to Hollywood."

Terri sat up and leaned against the back of the couch. No, she wasn't going to do this—get all crazy overjoyed at the thought of finally landing the kind of role she'd always dreamed of. Terri wasn't going to let herself be pulled into that trap again, losing herself in a cloud of hope thick enough to cut with a butter knife.

But a five-star hotel? A limo and time away from this town and the greasy mess she'd been bathing in?

"I could use the trip," she admitted. "Getting the hell out of Dodge sounds really good, right about now, but I'm not getting my hopes up. I've been here too many times to count, Roxy."

"The director of this film asked for you, specifically," she reminded Terri. "Don't claim defeat before you've even given this a chance."

"I'm not," she responded. "But I'm being realistic. I know you don't believe it, but I'd retired, Rox. I was done. That's why I moved here, and I was just starting to make peace with that. You just haven't been listening."

Weighted silence hung between them. "I ran into David Randall at a party a few nights ago," Roxy continued. "He wants you to come back to the show."

"He said that?" Terri asked, stunned.

"He's called a couple of times," Roxy admitted. "We've been conveniently playing phone tag. I like the idea of him sweating. And he is."

"Like I'd ever go back to that show."

"If you went back, Terri, it'd be on our terms, and they'd be steep. His audience has put a fire under his ass to get you back on that show, T. The ball's in our court, sis. Reality television has won you a whole new fan base, Terri. I know you hated it, but it was a game changer."

And just like that, she went from being a has been to a hot catch? That was the nature of this beast. From hot to cold, just like that, or vice versa. It was exhilarating. It was heartbreaking.

"So, what happens next?" she finally asked.

"Desmond's assistant has booked you a flight to California tomorrow night. Spend a few days chilling, relaxing, sight-seeing, whatever. Audition a few days later. It's not a lot of time to prepare, but they want to make a decision on the cast as soon as possible and start production."

"Where's filming going to be?"

"On location in Denver," she responded.

"*If* I get the role," Terri reminded her.

"You practically have it, Terri. What Desmond wants, Desmond usually gets."

What was that—that feeling? Was Terri actually feeling hyped about this? A little?

"I don't have the part but, my mind is all over the place, Rox. My emotions are crazy. I don't know if I should be happy or scared or—"

"It's your dream, Terri," Roxy said. "It's always been your dream and it always will be. You know this."

She knew it. Damn, she knew it better than she knew her own name.

"Maybe it's time to stop licking my wounds," Terri admitted with a sigh. "And get back to business."

All this nonsense with her, Nick and Luther was the wake-up call she needed. Terri had no business in a predicament like that or in a town like this. But for a time, it had been a pretty decent place to hide.

"All right," she sighed. "I guess I'm getting on a plane."

"I'll see you in Cali," Roxy promised before hanging up.

SINKING SHIPS

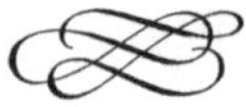

Terri pulled into the theater parking lot a little after eleven in the morning, carrying an armload of scripts and her travel mug full of coffee.

Mavis saw her coming and greeted her at the door of the theater. "Hello, love," she said, her cornflower blue eyes sparkling. Mavis and Terri exchanged air kisses on each cheek before Terri followed her down the hall to the office.

Mavis' style reminded Terri of a gypsy. The woman was always draped in flowing fabrics of vibrant colors. Turquoise rings and silver bangles adorned her wrists, neck and ears, and from time to time, silver haired Mavis had nerve to wear colorful, wax cloth head wraps better than Terri ever could.

"Did you finish reading all of them?" Mavis asked, taking a seat behind her desk.

Terri sat across from her. "I did," she said, with much reservation.

Mavis laughed, "That bad, huh?"

Terri offered a smile and hesitant shrug.

"Well, so far, we've decided four, one-acts and one other two-act production," she explained. "Not enough to fill a week, but we've got another sixty of these things to go through." She stared at Terri with pleading eyes.

"I'm going to be out of town for a while, Mavis," Terri, hastily, reminded her.

Mavis leaned back and smiled. "I know. But you'll be back. Won't you? Even if you get the part?"

Would she?

The plan was to drop off scripts to Mavis, drive to the airport in Baton Rouge and fly to Los Angeles. She desperately needed to get away and planned on staying a few extra days, depending on how the audition went. If it soured, she'd need time to deal with it. If it went great, she'd need time to deal with that, too. Time away from this place would help clear her mind, body and soul of the sordid mess she'd become immersed in.

The more she thought back to that evening, the more disgusted she felt. Terri was not *that* woman. A woman on the verge of getting serious with one man, then slathering herself all over another one. And she damn sure wasn't the kind of woman who spread her love among family members. More than any of that, Terri absolutely, wasn't the kind of woman, who, after a bout of hot and heated sex with her lover's father, slithered out the back door of a man's apartment in the middle of the night, tiptoeing to her car, and driving home wallowing in regret and shame. Nope. She was not that chick.

"Well, I do have a house here," was the best answer Terri could muster.

"It sounds so exciting," Mavis said, looking and sounding dreamy. "Flying off to Hollywood to audition for an actual role in an actual movie."

Terri turned introspective. There was a time when it was exciting. Terri would get a call like this and not sleep for days before or after. And nothing, absolutely nothing, was better than getting the call with those magic words, *"Congratulations, Ms. Dawson. You got the part."*

"Are you nervous?" Mavis asked.

Terri was surprised by the fact that she wasn't. "I've been doing this a long time, Mavis, so" —she shrugged— "Not as nervous as I used to get."

"Can I tell you a secret?" Mavis asked, leaning forward.

"Sure," Terri leaned forward too.

"Lucy and I were talking and we both had hoped that maybe— "

Terri knew what the woman was going to say even before she said it.

"Would you ever consider playing a part in a lowly community theater production?"

Terri had actually *not* considered taking on a role in the theater festival, but she was moved that Mavis actually asked.

"If it weren't for this audition, Mavis, I might." She sort of lied. But only because she liked Mavis and didn't want to hurt her feelings. "This year, however, I'm fine with reading scripts and hosting the opening and closing nights," she added, because she felt bad about the lie.

"Fair enough," Mavis said, resting her hand on the stack of scripts in front of her.

"Well, I'm going to go," Terri said, standing to leave. "I've still got to pack, and I want to get to the airport early."

Mavis escorted her to the door. "You have a safe trip, dear." She hugged Terri. "We'll see you when you get back. Break a leg."

The last thing, or rather, person, Terri expected to see walking back to her car was Luther Hunt leaning against it. Terri slowed her approach, then glanced back to see if Mavis was still at the door. Thankfully, she wasn't.

Tall, debonair and asshole Luther had the nerve to smile. "How you doing, Terri?"

She stopped about six feet away. "Fine. I'll be even better if you get away from my car."

It wasn't even Luther that she was pissed at. Terri was angry with herself for getting caught up like some clueless groupie.

He graciously moved, but closer to her. "I wanted to apologize."

Terri rolled her eyes, circled a wide arc around him and made her way to the driver's side of her car. "No need."

It was as if the man had a powerful electric charge for an aura radiating like sun rays. Terri felt from ten feet away.

Luther turned to her. "There *is* a need," he continued. "I made a move and I shouldn't have. I came on to you and that was wrong."

Terri opened her door and stopped short of climbing inside. "Luther," she sighed, poised on the door between them. "What happened, happened. We both know it was wrong. And we both know that it won't happen again. End of story."

"I saw Nick yesterday."

"So, did I. And it's over between me and Nick."

"You were clear on that?"

She narrowed her gaze at him. "Not that it's *actually* any of your business. I'm a grown woman and I don't need you telling me how to handle my relationships. I didn't break it off with him because you asked me to. I did it because it was the right thing to do."

"Apologies. Again, I'm out of line. And I was out of line for how I ended things that night with you."

Terri studied him for a few moments. He had sincerity written all over him, which eased the tension a bit.

"I would never, ever want to come between you and your son," she admitted. "But I can't lie. If I could go back to the first day I moved into this town, I'd have preferred for you to ask me out first."

Luther grinned and scratched his head. "I'd intended on asking you out," he confessed. "But then you twisted your ankle, and Nick rushed in and swept you off your feet."

She smiled. "Well, my timing has always been a little off."

He nodded. "Same here." Luther shoved his hands deep into his pockets. "I hear you're taking off."

"Got an audition in L. A."

He leaned his head to one side. "You excited?"

Terri thought before answering. "I've gotten so used to being disappointed, I don't remember how to be excited about stuff like this anymore."

It was the sad truth.

"Don't do that," he told her.

"What?"

"Don't let go, especially emotionally, of what you love."

Unexpected tears stung her eyes and a big, old lump swelled in her throat, threatening to release an earth-quaking sob.

"Just remember why you love it, Terri. Not the let downs and disappointments." Luther came closer to her. "Remember how it makes you feel when all the planets are aligned, you're in your zone, and nothing or nobody can derail you. And then remember, that it's you who brings the magic to the craft. Not the other way around."

Luther stood on the other side of her opened car door, too damn close. Terri blinked up at him, and there it was again. That pull, magnetic and electric, drawing her to him, almost too powerful to resist.

He noticed it too, and Luther took a hesitant step back, took a deep breath and blew air, forcefully passed his pursed lips.

"You be careful out there," he told her. "And, you got this, baby girl. Break a leg, or hell, break both of them."

Luther turned and headed inside the theater, stopping at the door long enough to see Terri climb into her car and drive away.

DON'T TURN AROUND

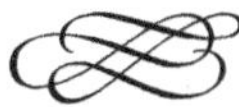

Riding in the back of the limo from LAX on the way to her hotel, Terri felt like she'd awakened from a fog, or walked off a movie set that was Devastation, Louisiana, and back into the real world. Traveling bumper to bumper on the 110 heading to Beverly Hills, Terri felt like a fish swimming around her part of the ocean. She was in her element, and yeah, she'd missed it.

"Hey," her best friend, Nona, answered, flustered, sounding like she was in the middle of a construction zone. "Bout damn time you called me. What's it been? A month?"

Terri laughed, "You'll never guess where I am?"

"On the highway, headed here to my place?"

"I'm on a highway in L.A. I've been flown in to audition for a lead role."

Nona's silence spoke directly to Terri's spirit.

"Is that a good thing?"

Terri sighed, "I'm not sure, but the role was too good to pass on, so…" She shrugged.

"I get it," Nona said, warmly. "Well, you know I want nothing but the best for you, girl."

"I know." She smiled.

"Let me know how it goes."

"I will," Terri assured her. "I'll let you go. Sounds like walls are coming down around you."

"Girl, that's not far from the truth. We're opening up the workspace here at the offices. I'm not even supposed to be here, but I needed to pick up some things. I'm on my way home, though. But, you be safe, and let me know how it goes. Promise?" she asked

"Promise."

The Peninsula Beverly Hills hotel put the "C" in charming and the "E" in cost a whole lot of damn money, expensive. Since stepping off the plane, Terri felt like an actual upper echelon celebrity, which was all she needed to snap out of that visceral trance she'd been wading through since before leaving Atlanta.

Terri sat on the side of the king sized bed, kicked off her shoes and sighed. The beautiful view from her window, framed by pink and blue floral curtains, reminded her of a fantasy.

"Eight-hundred-dollars a night," she murmured in disbelief.

Yeah, she'd been ghetto and looked up the cost in the Baton Rouge airport. Someone in Hollywood actually believed that she was worth spending $800 a night on a hotel room for. Terri choked up over the thought. Six months ago, she was barely treading water in her career, and now she was here. The pendulum had swung so far, the opposite way in her career, she felt like she was hanging on to it for dear life.

Terri's phone vibrated on the bed. It was her agent.

Meet me in the bar in an hour. I'll buy you a drink.

Terri texted a thumbs up.

"How's the room?" Roxy asked, embracing Terri in the hotel's bar.

"Elaborate," Terri responded with a smile, raising her glass in a toast.

You don't stay in a five-star hotel in the Hills and meet your agent in the bar in jeans and a tee shirt. Terri had paid a nice, little chunk of change for this dress and had only worn it once. The shoes hurt like hell but were cute as fuck, and she noticed a few heads turning as she crossed the room and made her way over to Roxy.

"You look amazing, sis," Roxy told her.

"You too." And she did. Roxy's long, dark wavy tresses hung past her shoulders. Her athletic form was draped in a white, silk, jumpsuit with a plunging neckline, and the sister's full lips were the most perfect shade of red Terri had ever seen.

She didn't need to see everybody in the room staring at the two of them, to know they were.

"So, where the fuck is Devastation? I tried to find it on a map and couldn't," Roxy laughed.

Terri toyed with the napkin under her glass. "Got jokes, I see."

"Enough to open a late night talk show."

Terri laughed, "Don't knock small town living until you've tried it, Roxy."

Roxy turned her head slightly and studied Terri. "Well, apparently it's been damn good for you." Her sarcasm wasn't lost on Terri. "Details, T. I'm getting in *all* of your business."

Her face flushed warm. Terri folded her arms across her chest. "I don't want to talk about it."

Roxy cocked a perfectly arched brow. "Why not?" She studied Terri for a moment. "Don't you dare tell me you're embarrassed."

Terri just looked at her.

Roxy reared back. "Girl," she said, smacking her lips.

"Roxy, can we not?" she asked, exasperated.

"Fine." Roxy raised her hands in surrender. "I just want to make one comment and then I'll leave it alone." She paused, but Terri didn't protest. "You're a grown woman, T. A beautiful woman and free to be all the single woman you want to be."

Terri grimaced. "What I did was shady."

Roxy returned a see-saw nod. "Some might say that. However, it's done. And—you broke up with the good doctor?"

"Of course, I did."

"He doesn't know?"

"Of course not. He doesn't know and he never will if I have anything to do with it."

"No harm, no foul, T." Roxy leaned back, raised her glass in a toast and waited for Terri to raise hers too. "It's done."

Roxy was wrong. There was plenty harm and plenty foul, but she was right about one thing. The whole ordeal was over.

"So, when you book this role, are you moving back to civilization?"

"Hell, if I know," Terri huffed, chuckling. "But for the last six months, I haven't missed this. I haven't flipped through pages of *Variety* to find out who was doing what in this industry. I haven't kept my cell phone in the pocket of my bathrobe, waiting for you to call telling me about the part of a lifetime, getting flown out to Hollywood, and being set up in a five-star hotel by a big-named producer" — she waved her hand— "only to go to bed feeling pitiful, because that call never came."

"I get it," Roxy eventually said. "It's feast or famine in this business and it's not for the faint of heart, but it isn't over for you, Terri. I never thought it was. I promised you that I'd keep looking for the right project for you and that's what I've been doing. You're the only one who's given up on you, sis. Not me."

Terri smiled warmly at her friend. "Thanks, Rox. You have no idea how much I appreciate you."

"So, you nervous about the audition?"

"No," Terri said, waiting for the butterflies to fill her stomach and make a liar out of her. It didn't happen. "It's odd, but I don't feel anything. I'm excited to be back in L. A. because I've missed it. I loved the limo ride from the airport, and this hotel is magical."

"They want you for this," Roxy reminded her. "I hope you want it, too."

Terri honestly wasn't sure if she did, anymore.

TERRI SPENT the next few days rehearsing the lines for her audition. The script had been picked up by a major movie network and Terri's face would be on the movie's poster. So, why wasn't she jumping through hoops over this? Why was she sitting in this posh, Beverly Hills hotel, sipping hot tea and staring out the window as if her whole life wouldn't be changed in an instant if she actually landed this role?

Terri's phone vibrated. She glanced at the screen and saw Nick's name. God! She did not need this right now. Terri let it ring until it stopped. A few moments later, she saw that he'd left a voicemail and Terri decided to listen to it.

"Hey. I know you're probably busy hobnobbing with those Hollywood producers and all, but I wanted to—I don't know..." his voice trailed off. "I probably shouldn't have called. Good luck, Terri. I hope —I hope you get what you need from this."

Terri loathed herself for what she'd done to him. Nick deserved a whole lot more than what she'd brought to the table. Terri had let him down as gently as she could. Nick was on his way to something serious with a woman, love, marriage, and kids. But from the beginning, despite her best efforts, she couldn't really see herself being that woman.

Time, she thought, could've changed her mind. Patience would've been required on his part, though. She really was trying to find herself, as cliché as it sounded, and until she did, the Dr. Nicks of the world would have to take a back seat. What kind of woman would she have been to get into a serious relationship using the "L" word if she had only a vague notion of herself?

A little voice whispered to her, *"So, what about Luther?"*

Terri rolled her eyes and groaned, "Shut up."

She didn't feel any way about Luther. The two of them just spoke the same language. That's all. Both were entertainers and creatives and without having to say it, they connected on a cosmic, spiritual level that didn't need to be spoken.

The night she and Nick watched Luther perform in New Orleans, Nick's eyes were wide with admiration of his father playing on that stage. Terri's soul was lit up at the joy emanating from the man immersed in the heart and soul of his passion, his art. Luther shone like a beacon, in his element, living his purpose. She knew that feeling. Terri felt it with him and for him that night. She envied him.

So, here she was, sitting smack down in the middle of an opportunity to have her own soul immersive moment, and Terri had been searching long and hard for her own light. It was like the damn thing had blown a fuse or something. She couldn't find it, and if she was going to give the audition of her lifetime, she desperately needed it.

Terri picked up the script and stared at the words. She loved acting because through it, she could be everyone and anyone, but in doing so, she'd never learned to be who she was. She'd always believed that to be a good actress, she had to sacrifice her whole self for it, but maybe that had been the problem.

As if on cue, Luther's words came back to her.

"Don't let go, even emotionally, of what you love. ...remember why you love it, Terri."

Did she still love it? Did she still need it?

SWEET DREAMS

"Terri! Wow," Desmond Williams gushed when Terri entered the audition room. The handsome producer made his way across the room to Terri, took hold of her hands and kissed her cheek. "I would never have thought it possible, but you're even more beautiful than I remember."

Terri blushed. "And you are absolutely kind and generous with your compliments, Desmond." She leaned back and smiled. "Thank you so very much for this opportunity."

"Please," he said, lighting his fingers to his chest. "I'm so happy you agreed to come and do this. When I first read this script, I thought of you and only you for the part of Irene."

Terri squeezed his hands in appreciation. "I don't mean to put your feet to the fire, but why me?"

He raised his brows in surprise. "You serious? I mean, you're one of the best and most underrated actresses in the business, Terri."

He said it like he meant it. He said it so that she had no choice but to believe him.

"This role is perfect for you."

He was right. After reading the script, Terri felt like the role was written just for her. Being here now, Terri was starting to feel what she'd been waiting to feel for days. A sense of purpose and belonging. A spark of excitement and even trepidation, nerves, the way she used to get before every audition. Adrenaline, fired in her veins and, like always, she drew strength from it.

"I think it's the most compelling role I've ever auditioned for," she agreed.

He smiled, then took her over to meet the rest of the team, including Roxy and the actors she'd be doing a scene with.

"Ready when you are, Terri," Desmond announced after everyone had settled down.

The scene was particularly gripping, where Irene, desperate to find her child, confronts an ex-convict who'd spent twenty years in prison for third-degree murder.

Terri took several deep breaths, before magically and instantly becoming Irene, challenging a man feared by everyone in the neighborhood.

"I don't care who you are or what you've done," she began, gathering her courage, the courage needed to face this dangerous man and save her child. "I don't give a damn who you are, or what you've done." Her voice cracked. "I need your help."

Terri pursed her lips, curled her fists and glared at this beast of a man, portrayed by a young actor, reading from the script.

"Why the hell would I help you? You don't mean shit to me and neither does your kid, lady."

He turned his back to her and began to walk away. Terri aggressively grabbed his arm and circled to the front of him.

"What if she was yours?" Terri blurted out in fearless passion, pointing her finger at the man. "Your baby girl out there, snatched off the street, out of her life by people who only see a body and money and not some terrified, little girl?"

"But she ain't mine, and I'm going to keep on minding my damn business, lady… and leave you to yours," he said dismissively.

"I read about you," she told him. "That you'd been set up or wrongly convicted. That you spent time in prison for a crime you didn't commit."

He huffed and turned back to her. "Don't believe everything you read."

Tears streamed down her cheeks. "No one helped you."

"Lady—" he said, exasperated.

"No one came to your rescue, or heard you, or gave a damn about you."

"It's not the same thing," he argued. "What happened to your kid is not—"

"It's exactly the same," she yelled. "It's the fuckin' same because, just like my baby, you were invisible too. What if just one person had listened? What if just one person had said, I believe you, fought like hell to save you?"

"Yeah, well I didn't need saving."

"She does," she said with compassion. "I can't do this alone." Real tears stung her eyes. "I'm asking—no, begging you to be that one person for my baby."

"She's got you."

"I'm not enough," she snapped, a tear rolling dramatically down her cheek. Terri quickly wiped it away. "Please," she gave in to the desperation this character was feeling. "I need to save her, and I need you to help me because there is no one else for her, for me. Please."

Applause erupted and everyone in the room who wasn't standing, bolted to their feet.

"Remember how it makes you feel when all the planets are aligned, you're in your zone, and nothing or nobody can derail you. And then remember, that it's you who brings the magic to the craft. Not the other way around."

She remembered.

HALF AN HOUR LATER, Terri and Roxy huddled together in the corner of the room.

"Oh my God, Terri," Roxy exclaimed, wrapping her arms around her. "You were amazing, girl."

"It felt good, Rox," Terri beamed. "Felt so right. Bringing a character like that to life has been what I've dreamed of doing my whole life."

"It's *your* role, Terri. No one else can play Irene but you. If Desmond and everyone else in that room weren't convinced before. They're convinced now."

She had been so silly to think that she could walk away from all of this. These were her people. This was her world, and only Terri had the magic to bring Irene to life. Not anyone else.

Terri went to the bathroom, while Roxy headed to the lobby. On her, she caught a glimpse of a familiar face; A-lister Joy Graham, chatting it up with Desmond in the audition room. Terri stopped. The woman glanced dismissively at Terri over Desmond's shoulder, then shifted her focus back to the producer.

The question punched Terri hard in the gut. What was Joy doing here? The woman had several Emmy's under her belt and even an Oscar nomination. In an instant, Terri fell into the old trap of negativity. The feeling of losing before she'd had a chance to win, soured in her gut.

❧

"Is that Joyce Graham I just saw?" she asked Roxy, standing outside.

"Yes," Roxy acknowledged. "She and Desmond are old friends. I hear she's interested in co-producing a new project with him."

Terri breathed a subtle sigh of relief.

Roxy chuckled. "I know what you're thinking, and you have nothing to worry about, Terri. The role is yours. Desmond's assistant promised to send the contract to me by the end of the month, lady." Roxy held the door open for Terri. "It's all good."

❧

TERRI HAD a few days left in L.A. She lounged by the pool, reclining on a chaise with her eyes closed, nursing a glass of Riesling and wearing a two piece, her mind reeling with thoughts of her next move. Since leaving Atlanta, she'd put on a good ten pounds, but she wasn't worried. Terri would get the weight off in plenty of time to start filming.

One thing she knew for certain. It was time to leave Devastation. Terri would put the house on the market and find a small condo—where? L. A.? Atlanta? New York? No. Not New York. And not L. A.

Devastation had given her a taste of small town living that she found surprisingly addictive. So, maybe she'd find a place in the Valley or in Northern California.

Landing this role had not only resurrected her career, but it brought life back to her spirit. Fuck finding herself. Terri knew who she was, and what she was, and what she wanted. It had never changed. She was Terri Dawson, actress… and a damn good one.

Getting this part snapped her out of that emotional coma she'd been in, which was probably the reason she'd become involved in that fiasco with Nick and Luther. Only a clueless woman would wind up in a mess like that, a woman who had no sense of self or purpose. A woman without goals, ambitions, and laser sharp focus on what her next move would be.

Terri hadn't felt this in tune with who she was in ages. Getting fired from that reality show had been a blessing. The time away from the industry had been time she needed to rejuvenate. The role of Irene could very well land Terri that coveted Emmy nomination she'd always dreamed of.

A WOMAN LIKE ME

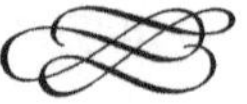

Nearly two weeks had passed since Terri's audition and her feet still hadn't touched the ground. She'd forgotten what it was like to feel this excited, to be this hopeful about the future of her career. A role like this was the kind of launching pad she needed to take her to the next level. After she hit forty, Terri began to hear her biological clock ticking. Not the kind warning her that time was running out to have a kid, but that her time as an actress, in an industry where youth and beauty were everything, was coming to an end. Sure, there were exceptions. Viola Davis could get any role she wanted, but Terri was no Viola. Halle was still Halle. They were the exceptions and not the rule, though. Terri wanted to be an exception.

Since returning home, her mind had been swirling with what to do next. Terri was going to have to move. Maybe not immediately, but eventually she needed to put herself a taxi ride away from the next audition. She'd grown fond of this little town. Devastation had wrapped around her like a blanket, and surprisingly, she'd made herself comfortable here, until Luther happened. But since ending her relationship with Nick and promising herself never to stand within five feet of Luther, Terri felt like she was standing on solid ground again.

Fate was sending her all kinds of signs that it was time to go, though. That major "uh-oh" with Luther was a blaring red flag that she needed to move on. How she'd managed to let herself go "there" still baffled Terri, especially considering how great Nick was. They'd spent months together and Teri could not pin down one negative thing about the man. He was ideal in every single way, except— Except nothing.

The October sun hung low in the air this Saturday afternoon. Terri decided to get out of the house… and her head, and spend some time at a local farmer's market. She had put on some fluff since leaving Atlanta, and it was past time for her to get back down to her fighting weight. Fresh fruits and vegetables were back on the menu.

People in town still smiled politely, passing her, recognizing her as the celebrity who'd bought that old place on Dupelo. Every now and then, Terri would catch someone standing off in the distance snapping photos of her, but she'd pretend to be oblivious. Truthfully, it was all rather charming and she was definitely going to miss the attention.

TERRI STOPPED at a display of fresh pears. She was examining them when the sound of singing and music captured her attention. It was beautiful, bluesy and rich, drawing a crowd to a large tree across the park. Terri strolled over to the gathering and fell in with the crowd, captivated by the haunting sound of this Pied Piper calling to them.

The sounds of bongos, a flute and guitar wafted through the air, as Terri weeded her way through the crowd, making her way close enough to the front to see Luther, another old man, and two younger men, creating this warm, enveloping, and comforting song, in the middle of a crowded park.

The old man hummed and sang in a ragged, whiskey-tinged voice. Another man knelt beside him playing the flute, while the other, sitting next to Luther, tapped his fingertips on the tops of bongos. Luther, of course, expertly strummed an acoustic guitar, and then surprised everyone when he sang too, harmonizing with the old man like they'd been doing this for years.

It was a folk song, something local and homegrown, charming in its unevenness, unpolished. Terri stared, mesmerized at Luther, looking unimpressed by the spell he and the other men wove underneath that tree. The old man led the group down a rabbit hole of history, riddled with pain and heartbreak. Luther and the others followed close behind him, and the crowd gathered around, trailed behind.

Terri was transfixed by Luther. A strong, sad, and lonely man, unaware of the impact he had on her that even Terri couldn't explain. Luther had built a moat around himself. One that he was desperate to cross but refused to. He'd let her cross it, though, to get to him. She'd been telling herself that their encounter had just been about sex. But it wasn't. Not for her. And she suspected it hadn't been that for him either, though, he'd go to his grave before admitting it… because of Nick.

She wanted more of Luther. Not just intimately. Terri wanted to know him, all of him in ways she'd never been interested in knowing another human being. There was something rich about his energy that was a magnet for hers. There were stories in him she instinctively knew could capture and hold her attention for hours, listening to them unravel in his telling.

Terri was so fixated on Luther that she didn't feel arms slip around her waist until it was too late. Luther looked up, his eyes met hers, in time to see Nick slip up behind her.

"Hey, you," Nick whispered.

Terri's heart sank to her stomach as she turned to him. "Nick."

He smiled. "Don't you look pretty."

Terri returned a curt smile, then turned her attention back to the musicians, avoiding Luther's passing glances. She desperately wanted to leave, but for some reason, Terri stood planted between Nick and Luther.

Five minutes later, Luther and the others finished playing and the crowd around them erupted in applause. Nick looked over her head at his father, grinned and acknowledged him with a nod. Terri looked to Luther, who briefly made eye contact with her, before dapping the old man he'd been performing with, and getting up and making his way over to the two of them. Leaving now would make it obvious. Wouldn't it? Would Nick put the pieces of the puzzle together and realize that something had happened between Terri and his dad?

"When'd you get to town?" Luther asked, looking at Nick.

"Not too long ago. Heard you were out here, so" —he shrugged— "thought I'd swing by and look who I found." He looked down at Terri and smiled.

Terri swallowed. "It sounded great," she said to Luther.

If Nick saw the look in Luther's eyes, did he know what to make of it? Terri saw it and without saying a word, understood everything the man fought to keep to himself.

"Thanks, Terri." Luther turned his attention back to Nick. "It's good to see you, by the way."

"You too," she nodded.

"Hey, I got to get back to the bar," Luther explained. "You swinging through before you go?" he asked Nick.

"Yeah, I'll swing by," Nick assured him. "What's the special?"

"I don't know, man," Luther joked. "They don't tell me nothing. I find out like everybody else when I read it on the chalkboard."

Nick laughed. Terri pretended to adjust her skirt and eased out of his grasp, miffed by how forward he was. What part of I-need-space-it's-not-you-it's-me didn't Nick understand?

"Just so you know," Nick added, "I sing a little too, Pop." He glanced at Terri. "Just in case somebody listening might be impressed by crooners."

"I don't know about crooning," Luther laughed. "More like crowing if you ask me. I can carry a tune, but not far."

"You did great," Terri added.

Luther returned a slight bow. "Appreciate it."

"I'm going to finish my shopping," Terri said, turning to leave.

"Okay, baby. I'm right behind you." Nick said.

Baby? Really? He had to "baby" her now?

Terri had hurried and bought spinach, tomatoes, and blueberries, and hoped to make a mad dash to her car before Nick caught up with her.

"Why don't you slow down and tell me how the audition went," he said, jogging up behind her.

"Fine."

"Fine," he repeated. "Just fine?"

Terri stopped. "It went well, Nick. Fine."

"You get the part?"

Terri nodded. "I had it before I got off the plane."

"Good," he said, taking hold of one of her hands. "So, what does that mean? You'll be gone for a while?"

"Yeah. Filming starts soon."

She had no idea when filming started, but Terri decided that there was no better excuse in the world to end a relationship than not having time for one.

The expression on his face, disappointment, regret—whatever it was, pulled at her heart. But Nick quickly composed himself.

"Well, at least have dinner with me tonight."

"Nick—"

"Come on, Terri. It's just food," he cocked a brow and smirked.

"I told you, I'm not ready for a relationship," she said as politely as she could.

"It's not a relationship," he clarified. "It's a meal."

"It's sending the wrong message," she clarified. "You're sending a message that you want more than that."

"Of course I do," he admitted. "But the conversation was always good between us." Nick shifted his weight from one foot to the other. "Look, I'm not dense, and I'm not stalking you. I can't stop caring about you, though. I can't just turn it off, Terri."

"You should."

"And I will. In time. I had no intention of seeing you today, but when I did— I know it's over," he said, disappointment shadowing his expression. "Friends. We can't do just do that? Friends over some ribs or catfish?" He smirked.

Terri couldn't help it. Hell, she was on her way out of this town anyway, sooner rather than later. Terri had made her point with Nick. Their romantic relationship had come to an end. Their friendship could, maybe suffer through dinner, but she was ghosting Devastation, Louisiana and everyone in it.

"I'll pick you up at six?" he asked.

Terri shook her head, brushed passed him and waived her hand. "Six is fine."

SALT ON MY WOUNDS

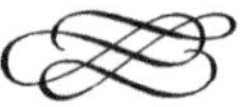

"What the hell are you doing, Terri?" Luther blurted out as soon as she answered the phone.

"Luther? What—"

Luther raked his hand across his head and stopped pacing. "We agreed you'd break it off with Nick."

"I did break it off, Luther," she snapped.

"That's not what I saw today."

"I didn't expect for him to be there," Terri responded. "I haven't seen Nick since before I left for California."

"But you've spoken to him."

What the hell was she doing? Luther had been trying to make sense of that encounter in the park since it happened, and none of it added up.

"He's called a couple of times, but I haven't spoken to him until today," she explained.

Luther sat down and groaned.

"I told Nick that it was over," she reiterated. "I told him that I needed to get myself together before I could be with him or anyone else."

Woman talk for *"It's over but not really."* No wonder Nick was confused.

Luther leaned back in his chair. "Terri, you can't half ass end it," he explained. "You needed to fuckin' tell him it was over."

"I did," she retorted. "Look, Luther, I'm handling it. I'm not seeing Nick. I told you that, but that's all I'm telling you because it's none of your business"

Luther sat up. "No. Ever since you fucked with me, it's *our* business. You being with my son is all kinds of wrong."

"You don't have to remind me of that," she exclaimed.

He'd done some pretty low-down shit in his day, but nothing, absolutely nothing, could compare with what went on between him and Terri in this apartment. The fact that she was worried about being rude or was more concerned with letting Nick down easy was fuckin' ridiculous as far as Luther was concerned.

"You think I don't have a conscience? I didn't invite him to the park, Luther. Nick took it upon himself to—"

"Read between the lines?" He interrupted. "Ignore mixed signals?"

"I'm not sending mixed signals."

"They sound pretty mixed to me, Terri, and if I can't make sense of them, how the hell do you expect him to."

"Why are you attacking me?" She shot back. "Why are you acting like I'm the only one here who's guilty, Luther."

"That's not what I'm doing, and you know it."

"Look," she huffed. "It's over between Nick and I and that's all you need to know. I'm moving on with my life and putting Nick, you, and this damn town behind me. Trust that if you don't trust anything else."

Finality weighted her tone. Terri was finished, in more ways than one, and a part of him, one he shamefully turned his back to, hated the fact that his name was one she'd just as soon forget.

"We both played a part in this," he reasoned. "We both need to make sure he doesn't get hurt."

"It was never my intention to hurt him," she eventually admitted.

"Then you need to make it clear to him, Terri," he reminded her.

"He doesn't deserve this. Nick still sees opportunity. He's not convinced the door is closed."

"How do you know what he's thinking?"

Luther leaned back. "He doesn't believe it's over because he doesn't want to."

If the situation were reversed, and he was the one Terri had broken it off with, he wouldn't want to accept it either.

"It's because I care about him, Luther. That's what makes this so hard. He was starting to believe—"

"That he loved you."

"That he could."

Naturally, Nick could love her. That was the problem. The longer she dragged this out, the harder it would be. Terri had to know that, and for the life of him, Luther couldn't understand her reasons behind stringing Nick along.

Nick hadn't come right out and said it, but before all of this happened, he came dangerously close to admitting to Luther that he was in love with Terri.

"He cares for me and I don't want to be brutal."

"Brutal?" he said, surprised by this twisted sense of resentment ballooning inside him. "You fucked me, Terri. That's brutal."

"Don't you dare," she threatened. "You be careful how you talk to me, Luther."

"All I'm saying is for you to do what needs to be done. To hell with love or letting him down easy. My son can't be with a woman who—"

"A woman who what?"

Goddamnit, Luther! Easy.

"You know what I mean."

"I do. And I'm sorry that I do. You can kiss my ass, Luther."

Terri hung up before he could say another word. Putting all the blame on her was never his intention. She'd cheated on Nick with another man, who happened to have been him. *That part.* His son deserved a woman who would never in a million years do some shit like that. And he deserved a father who wasn't Luther. He couldn't change the latter, but Terri could fix the part that involved her.

Recalling his son's face earlier today when he looked at the woman, filled Luther with a deep, resounding kind of agony that broke his heart. Something else resonated with him, as well, the greasy, ugly feeling of jealousy he hadn't expected. He hated himself for it.

"Shit," he blurted out, closing his eyes.

Luther had been a fuck up for most of his life. On the outside looking in, he shined like a gold coin. Luther Hunt, one of the most sought after guitarists in the music industry, was a fuckin' failure at the things that mattered most.

When Ava told him to keep playing, convincing him she was fine and that she was getting better, always getting better, he believed it, because he didn't want to come home. Luther was living his dream, while she suffered in silence, letting him. When she said she was fine, he convinced himself that she was. When he spoke to Nick on the phone and the boy told him that his mom was still in bed, Luther convinced himself that she was tired. Those times when he did come home, he came bearing expensive gifts and stories from his escapades on the road, ignoring her weight loss, the circles under her eyes, and the darkness in Nick's whenever he looked at Luther.

By the time Luther decided to stop running from reality and face it, he was too late. Lupus had done its damage, and Ava was never going to be alright again. He lost her, but he'd lost his son long before that. It had only been in the last year that Nick had started opening a space just big enough for Luther to slip through, barely, to build a relationship with his son for the first time in the boy's whole life... and then this shit happened.

Nick was everything. Luther was still fighting for his redemption with his son, and this trespass would be absolutely unforgivable if Nick ever found out. Luther couldn't let that happen. A woman would not be the reason he lost his son, again.

THE TRAIN

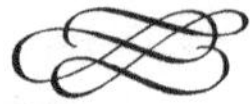

Terri's apprehension was as thick as molasses. She sat next to him in the car like he had the plague or something, but she hadn't bailed on him. She should've. Pride had fucked that up, though. He'd pulled up to her place, but before he could even get out of the car, Terri came out, locked the door behind her and climbed into the passenger seat.

"Hey," was all she said, glancing quickly at him.

Nick leaned over and kissed her cheek. "You look pretty."

Terri smiled.

"I'm not used to this," he admitted.

"I'm sorry?" She finally looked at the man. "What?"

He felt silly saying it, but it was the truth, "I'm not used to women not wanting to be—to being dumped."

God! That sounded beyond desperate and definitely egotistical. More silence and then both of them burst out laughing at the same time.

"First time, huh?" Terri composed herself and asked.

Nick laughed too. "Yes! Until you, I didn't even think it was possible."

"A new Italian place opened up a few blocks from the theater," she offered. "You want to try it?"

"Aw, I kind of promised Luther we'd swing through. Maybe next time?" He asked, hopeful that there might actually be a next time, taking hold of her hand and kissing it.

Terri returned a subtle nod, which didn't give him a whole lot of hope for another date, but the night was still young.

BUSINESS WAS BOOMING. Luther's place was packed, but he'd been sure to reserve the best table for Nick and Terri. A curvy redhead, sounding like Joni Mitchell sang, accompanied by a Hispanic dude on guitar and a brotha on the bongos. The music was good, mellow and easy. Luther came by and said a quick hello but spent most of the night working the room, stepping up as MC when needed, and hurrying back to behind the bar to fill drink orders.

They shared the ribs, with sides of greens, Mac n' cheese, and pickled onions. Small talk filled the space between them. He had a feeling that Terri might've been fine with that, but he couldn't be.

"So, now that you got that part, what's your next move?"

"Well, we'll work through the details of the contract," she explained. "Probably start filming shortly after that."

"You'll be gone awhile, then."

"Couple of months, maybe." She shrugged.

"But you plan on coming back?"

The look on her face answered the question, as far as Nick was concerned. "If I do, it won't be for long, Nick. I plan on moving back to Cali. If this movie does what I think it will for my career, I need to be where the action is, so to speak."

"Is that why you want to end our relationship?" he asked. "You knew you'd be leaving?"

"That's a big part of it," she responded with a hint of reluctance.

Relief set in and Nick suddenly gave in to optimism. "If it's just a distance thing, Terri," he reasoned. "That's not a big deal. I mean, we're doing that already. And I, personally, think it works. We work."

"You're a few hours away, Nick. I'll be a few states away. It's not the same."

"It's not, but if people want to make a relationship work then they do," Nick argued. But then another thought occurred to him. "Unless…"

"Unless?"

Nick was anything but insecure, but this woman had him feeing like a science nerd in love with the head cheerleader. "You're just not interested in a small town doctor. Is that it?"

She smiled. "You work in New Orleans. That's hardly a small town."

"Compared to L.A," he shot back, "that's all it is. But is that it? You heading to Hollywood and this" — he motioned between them— "doesn't fit the image?"

"Hey, you two," Luther interrupted, standing over Nick. "How's the food?"

"Delicious," she responded with a soft smile and casual glance at his father. "I'm stuffed."

"Why don't you sit for a minute," Nick offered, motioning to the empty space next to Terri.

Luther glanced around the room before taking Nick up on his offer. "How's doctoring?"

Nick shrugged. "Never dull."

"The band's really good." Terri toyed with her straw in her drink.

"Yeah," Luther acknowledges. "Came from Nashville."

"Mom would've loved them." His mother was eclectic and loved everything not quite the status quo.

"She would've." Luther smiled.

"So, you hear the news?" Nick asked.

Luther raised a brow. "News?"

He looked at Terri. "About Miss Terri, here."

Luther looked perplexed.

"Come on, Pop. People in this town can't change their underwear without everybody knowing about it. So, you can't tell me you don't know about this."

"Nick," she softly protested.

"Seriously?" Nick asked, surprised. "You're being bashful?"

"What news?"

Nick stared at her, waiting for her to share it.

"I got an acting role."

"A lead," Nick added.

"Congratulations, Terri," Luther grinned. "That's outstanding."

"Thanks."

Was it Nick's imagination or were these two a little stiff with each other?

"Hey, Nick," Yolanda said, coming over and sitting down next to him. "Terri. Congratulations. I heard you got a part in a film."

Nick looked at Luther. "Now, how'd she hear about it and you didn't?"

"I ain't nosey." He looked at Yolanda when he said it.

Yolanda wrinkled her nose. "I ain't either. But I'm astute and I'm a fan." She smiled at Terri.

"Thank you, so much," Terri responded.

"There you are," a lovely, polished, and curvaceous woman said, placing a hand on Luther's shoulder, leaning down, and kissing him on the cheek.

Nick and Yolanda looked at each other, as to both be thinking, "Who the hell is that?"

"Told you I'd swing through," she said, running her hand along his back between his shoulders. "Bet you never thought you'd see this day coming."

Luther immediately stood. "I'd given up on you, woman."

She chuckled, wrapped her arms around him and leaned into him.

"Angie," Luther said. "This is my son, Nick. Our friends, Yolanda, and Terri Dawson."

Angie wrapped both arms around Luther and squeezed. "Nice to meet y'all." She leaned back and smiled up at Luther. "The place looks good. The fact that it's so packed tells me the food must damn good."

"Eh, it's all right." Luther smirked.

"I'm telling Stella you said that," Yolanda warned.

"Do it, and you're fired," he threatened.

"I'm so sorry," Angie said, looking back and forth between Luther and Terri. "I didn't mean to interrupt your date."

Luther looked at Terri, "No, we—"

"We're not together," Terri chimed in.

"She's *my* date," Nick clarified.

"I thought—" Angie looked at Yolanda.

"Nope." Yolanda grimaced. "I wouldn't date Nick's ugly ass if you paid me."

Nick breathed a sigh of relief. "Thank goodness."

"Come on," Luther told the woman, leading her to the bar. "Let me buy you a drink."

"Y'all enjoy your evening," she called back over her shoulder. "And it was nice meeting you."

As soon as they were out of earshot, Nick looked at Yolanda. "Who dat?"

She shrugged. "Your guess is as good as mine."

"I thought you said you were astute," he challenged.

"Your daddy's sneaky," Yolanda declared, getting up to leave.

Luther was full of surprises. That was becoming more and more obvious.

"Can we go?" Terri abruptly said.

His father and Angie returned to the table. Luther sat a pitcher down and filled four glasses.

"You know how Lou is," Angie said, carrying on with whatever conversation the two were immersed in.

"Hardheaded. Stubborn. Mean?" Luther asked.

"Well." She scratched her head. "Yeah. Then there's that," she laughed.

"Here's to losing your virginity," Luther said, raising his glass in a toast.

"Here's to the sorry son of a bitch who beat ya to it," Angie responded.

"Uh," Nick said, giving Terri the side eye and raising his glass. "Cheers?"

Nick eagerly contributed to the banter, enjoying this casual vibe with his dad and Angie.

"Angie wasn't a musician," Luther explained, finishing his drink. "But she was one hell of a groupie."

"Actually," she corrected him, rolling her eyes. "I wasn't a groupie. I was a stagehand-slash-assistant equipment manager."

Nick drew back. "There's such a thing?"

Luther squinted at Angie. "Right? You made that shit up."

"I got a paycheck."

"So, you say."

"Asshole," she snapped, tossing a paper napkin at him. "I had a real job. One above and beyond sniffing around you trying to get your attention."

"I just played guitar, Angie," he reminded her. "Nobody wanted my attention."

She laughed and raised her glass to her lips. "Uh-huh."

An hour later, Nick and Terri were saying their goodbyes.

"Have a safe trip back to New Orleans," Angie told Nick. "And great meeting you, Terri. Congrats on that new part. Can't wait to see the movie."

"Thanks, Angie. It was nice meeting you too."

Terri smiled, but Nick had a feeling that he wasn't the only one who didn't feel the sincerity.

TOMORROW

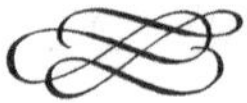

Absurd.

Terri rode in silence next to Nick on the drive home, with that word resonating in her mind. The whole evening had been absurd. Nick, refusing to be let down easy and accept that the two of them would never be a couple. Luther and yet, another woman pining all over him. And that Angie broad with her snide remarks that dude brains were incapable of detecting.

"You're an actress?" She smiled when Nick told her. *"What films have you stared in that I may have seen you in."*

Then Nick rattled off a few of Terri's accomplishments, rather clumsily, and a strange look filled the woman's eyes with knowing as they locked on to Terri's.

"Wow. Sounds like you've got skills. Acting, skills." The woman's eyes lingered on Terri's a bit longer than necessary, before shifting it to Luther.

Like, what the fuck did she mean by that? A dig? And what was that look?

The woman looked to Nick, and then back to Luther. "Speaking of groupies... I assume the two of you have seen all of the roles Miss Terri has played?"

Angie winked at Terri.

The woman knew. The implication of her snide, little comments seemed to be lost on Nick, but Luther's subtly averted gaze spoke directly to Terri.

"I hope you had a good time," Nick said, interrupting her thoughts.

"It was nice," Terri replied.

After a few moments of silence, Nick made a statement that shook her. "You're not feeling Luther. Are you?"

"Why would you say that?" She asked, surprised.

Terri had made it a point not to let any feelings for Luther, good or —whatever show. He'd done the same. She was pretty sure they'd been convincing, at least to Nick. That Angie on the other hand...

"You get quiet when he's around," Nick commented.

"I don't— I'm fine with him, Nick."

"Yeah, okay."

Let it go, Terri. Let it all go. Devastation. Nick. Luther and his sad, sob story about his noble, dead wife, his estranged-on-the-mend relationship with his wounded son, and her own jealousy over seeing Luther with any other woman who isn't her, even though she had no desire to spend one more minute with the man.

"People have long distances relationships all the time, Terri."

Nick's voice cut into her thoughts. "What?"

He slowed and finally stopped in front of her house and turned off the engine. "I think we can make it work. Look, I get that your career takes precedence right now and that's cool, but we're good together. You don't have to say anything right now. Just think about it."

"Nick, I'm going to be so busy," she began explaining, "too busy to even think about a relationship."

"I get it, but, I'm not in a hurry, Terri. You do what you got to do, and I'll be here when you're done, and we can pick up—"

"We're not going to pick up anything," she snapped, feeling like shit as soon as she said it. She didn't want to hurt him, but damn. "I'm moving, Nick. Leaving and going back to the life I know. The life I love. This film is everything to me. My whole career will turn around because of it and that's all I care about. That's all I've ever cared about. I just ended up here because the business broke my heart."

"Wow," he said, with an introspective nod. "So, that's it? That's it. For real?"

"I never meant to—"

Nick groaned and waived her off. "Don't—not the clichés. Please. I don't need it and you don't need to recite it like you're reading from some handbook."

Terri really never meant to hurt him. She never meant to have sex with his father. She never meant to care more about her career than him. Nick Hunt was a brilliant and beautiful man, and he deserved a woman smart enough to appreciate that.

"I am sorry, Nick."

He sighed. "Goodnight, Terri…and take care of yourself."

HALF AN HOUR LATER, Terri sat on the sofa sipping on a cup of hot tea. Months ago, she'd left Atlanta and landed here. Somehow, Terri now found herself starring in her own shitty reality show, smack dab in between two men—relatives, father and son, for crying out loud. Maybe someday, she could've loved Nick. He was exceptional. The part that blew her mind, though, was how enamored she'd been with Luther, the slut. Who the hell wasn't he fucking? That singer in New Orleans, the woman tonight, and maybe even that little bartender working for him. Oh, and of course, there was Terri's smitten ass. Luther Hunt, feigning guilt for leaving behind a sick wife, who insisted he didn't bring his cheating ass home even when she knew she was dying. Ava wasn't stupid. Her husband was out there, and she wasn't blind to it. It didn't take a rocket scientist to figure why the woman didn't want him to come home.

But whatever. Terri's life was bigger than the Luthers of the world. She was moving on and into the life she'd always dreamed of having. Pride swelled in her chest. She'd more than nailed that audition. Terri owned the part, but the truth of the matter was, she'd gotten it even before she auditioned. Studio execs wouldn't have paid for her to come to California if they hadn't made the decision to give her the role.

Devastation was never meant to be permanent. Terri knew that now. And destiny never abandoned her. It had taken a detour. That's all. Finally, what was meant for her found her. Until she'd gotten the call from Roxy about that role, Terri didn't realize just how happy she was that it had.

She sighed, finished her tea and made her way to the bedroom. Small towns and their drama. This place was like that soap opera she'd played in. Terri chuckled at the comparison, but she'd managed to get herself ensnared in some of her own.

She'd learned some things about herself since moving here. Other than the fact that she could actually cheat on her boyfriend, which she swore she could never do in life, because she wasn't the type, though, technically, Nick wasn't her boyfriend. Yeah. No. It really didn't count.

Her career being the most important thing in her life—more important than the Dr. Nicks of the world no matter how outstanding they were. But, as important as it was, she could never, ever let acting be *all* that she was. Not anymore. The time she'd spent here, Terri had taken the blinders off and saw that there was too much going on in the world around her to live and breathe just one thing.

She'd found simple release and even joy doing mundane things like mowing her grass or suffering through reading terrible scripts for the community theater festival. As strange as it was, Terri had found connection in ways she would never have found if she hadn't, even temporarily, quit acting.

There were the quirky and surprisingly creative theater mavens, Lucy and Mavis, who's company she truly enjoyed. Even Lanette, with her weird, overbearing, inconsiderate and burdensome self, offered a kind of magic all her own, opening Terri's eyes to the very real fact even if it looks like a duck, quacks like a duck, stand back—it might just be a Lanette.

Nick had shown her what it was like to be courted, the old-fashioned way, and she liked it. He really was too good for her. One day, he'd see it. One day, he'd find a gorgeous twenty or thirty-something-year-old who worshipped the ground he walked on, because he deserved that.

And Luther? Terry leaned back onto her pillow, closed her eyes, stretched, and moaned at the memory of that, whorish, delectable, brooding, lying man smothering her with kisses, rippling muscles, and low, satisfying moans, filling her soul. He'd shown her a passion she'd never felt before, and in that single encounter... for the time, Terri had given *all* of herself to a man, mind, body, and soul. Deep down she knew... she'd never *really* regret it.

THROUGH THE FIRE

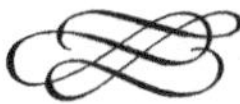

The fact that Lanette Dole was recovering from a recent suicide attempt didn't seem to bother her in the least.

"You good, sugah?" Luther asked, setting a bowl of nachos with extra Jalapenos on the table in front of her.

Lanette chair danced with gusto as the band he'd brought in from Nashville jammed with the Boys to Men's Motown Philly.

She looked up at him with a bright, wide smile and gorgeous, sparkling eyes, filled with her own brand of happiness. "I'm great. Thanks, Luther. I love this group," she shouted over the sound of the music.

He nodded and left her to her own, private party.

The place was packed. The cover band, *Miss Jenkin's Boys*, was a local favorite and filled the place every time they came through. Night's like this, Luther stepped up to help waiting tables and mixing drinks. He didn't mind. In fact, he actually enjoyed helping out. It was his business, after all, and any night when the joint was on and popping, Luther had no problem expressing his gratitude by putting in a little extra work.

During intermission, he decided to step outside to get some air.

Luther checked his phone and saw a text from Lisa, a realtor he'd been working with for the last six months.

"Hey, you," she texted. *"Got time to chat?"*

Her message had come through half an hour ago, but Luther hadn't had time to call her until now.

"Hi," she answered.

"This a bad time?"

"No, I'm just sitting here in my pajamas and fuzzy slippers going over some blueprints."

"Sounds sexy," he teased.

"My pajamas or the blueprints?"

"Both."

She chuckled. "What are you doing?"

"Taking a break right now. I got a full house and I've been helping out the wait staff and bartenders to help keep the food coming and the booze flowing."

"Nice. So, you still interested in coming out this weekend? I have something I want to show you."

"Definitely. Whatcha got?"

"It's an old saloon," she told him.

He laughed, "Seriously?"

"Dead serious. It's been updated a few times, but not recently and it's in desperate need of a remodel. Since you mentioned expanding your business, I thought it'd be something worth showing you."

Luther nodded, slightly. "Nice. Then, I can't wait to see it."

Nights like tonight made him think he was crazy for even thinking about opening another spot, but, Luther's business was doing well, and more and more, he'd been thinking about expanding.

"It's even got a few rooms out above the bar that can be rented out."

"Interesting," he responded.

"I'm going to ask you one more time," she paused. "Are you sure you want another restaurant, Luther. You're doing good where you're at, but—you know the risks."

He sighed. "I know the risks."

They spoke a little longer and then said their goodbyes. Luther had become an expert at staying busy. He needed another business like he needed a hole in the head, but he needed extra time on his hands, even less.

He hadn't heard from Nick or Terri since they'd come through a few days ago. The fact that Terri hadn't *convincingly* broken it off with his son after what'd happened between her and Luther was ludicrous. He'd called Nick a day ago to try and get a feel for where his head was, but he was busy with a patient. He promised to call Luther back and never did.

Luther had left several messages for Terri, but of course, she wasn't answering. He was certain that Nick still had no idea what had happened. If he did, he'd have shown up at Luther's delivering a fist to his face.

"Who you hiding from?" Lanette asked, coming outside.

"Not hiding. Just getting some air."

The colorful braids she'd worn when he saw her at the hospital were gone. In their place, bone straight, sandy blond hair, parted in the middle and hanging down her back. He'd heard that her mother was white, her father black. Lanette had a family full of white folks in town that didn't seem to want anything to do with her, and a family of black folks somewhere else, who might not have even known she existed.

"You seen Terri?"

Luther was caught off guard by the question but didn't show it. "Not lately."

"Me either," she said, her gaze drifting away in introspection.

Luther braced himself whenever he had a conversation with Lanette. You never could tell what kind of nonsense was going to come out of her mouth.

"Her car is at the house," she continued. "I knocked but nobody answered."

Terri probably saw that it was Lanette on the other side of her door and ignored her.

"Heard she had some big audition in Hollywood about a month ago," she said, looking at him.

"Yeah, I'd heard that."

"Think she got the part?"

He shrugged. "I heard she did."

"Really?" Her whole face lit up. "That girl lied and said she'd quit acting." Lanette shook her head. "You think she's moving to Hollywood?"

"I'd imagine."

Luther hadn't really considered the possibility until now, but Terri might very well leave now that she'd gotten that role.

Lanette gave him a side eye look like she didn't believe him. "I know you like her."

Luther sighed. "She's a nice woman."

"No, I mean, you *really* like her." Lanette nudged him in the side with her elbow. "She's cute and all, but—"

As far as he was concerned, Luther was done with this conversation. "I need to get back inside."

"You might can handle those celebrity types, since you are one, but Nick can't."

Luther kept walking.

"She likes you, too." Her crazy ass blurted out. "And Nick."

He stopped and turned.

A wicked smile spread her thick lips and she folded her arms. "I ain't even mad at her."

Had Terri actually had that conversation with this woman or was Lanette psychic? Either way, Luther wasn't volunteering anything.

"You get home safe, now," he offered, before going inside.

"I think she should pick you, though," she shouted. "Nick's way too—"

Luther let the door close behind him before he heard the rest of the nonsense spurring from the woman.

The door opened behind him. "Young," Lanette finished, the door closed again.

A FEW DAYS LATER, Luther received a call from Lucy, at the theater.

"Have you spoken to Terri?" She asked, concerned.

Why the hell did everyone seem to think he had the Terri Dawson watch? The two of them had masterfully avoided colliding for the last month and he couldn't be happier.

"I haven't, Lucy."

"Mavis and I stopped by her house to see if she was still willing to help out with the festival. Her car is there, but there was no answer."

"You tried calling?"

"Several times. It goes straight to voicemail."

"Well, maybe she's not in town, Lucy. She could've taken a cab to the airport."

"The airport in Baton Rouge?" she asked, sarcastically.

The Baton Rouge airport was over fifty miles away.

He sighed, "I don't know where she is."

"We went by her place the other night and saw a light on. It went off as soon as we pulled up in front of the house."

Now, Luther was concerned. It was one thing for Terri to dis Lanette, but things were beginning to sound strange. Strange enough for him to conclude that maybe he did need to swing by her place and check on her.

"TERRI?" Luther called out after ringing her doorbell and knocking. "It's Luther." He waited and listened. "Terri?"

All of a sudden, the door swung open. "That sonofabitch gave my part to that fuckin' cow!"

Terri's wild, swollen bloodshot eyes bore into his. She wore an oversized tee shirt, socks and clutched a bottle of wine by the neck like she was trying to strangle it. Terri spun, turned up that bottle and left Luther standing, mouth gaped open, on the other side of her screen door.

Reluctantly, he stepped inside. The kitchen counter was covered with opened boxes of cereal, bowls stacked together, and an open bag of chips.

"What happened?" He dared to ask.

She drew the back of her hand across her mouth and started talking so fast he could hardly keep up.

"He told me the role was mine," she said, walking around the small room, pacing like a tiger in a cage. "Sent my agent a goddamned contract." She stopped and stared at Luther. "A whole fuckin' contract, talking about, 'Whatever you want, Terri. Just ask and we'll get it in the contract.'"

Terri started crying and pacing again.

"I saw her that day, and I knew." She paused and took another drink. "I knew in my soul, even though I tried telling myself that it wasn't true. I knew that it was. I knew she'd come to take my part. Roxy told me, 'No, Terri. That role is yours. You were hand-picked for the part. She's just his friend. They're working together on something else together,' but that greedy pig of a woman looked right at me." She stopped and glared at him. "Looked me dead in the eyes and acted like she didn't know who the hell I was or why I was there. But that bitch knew." She grimaced. "And she knew that'd she'd get the role that was written for me."

Luther was speechless, and watched Terri turn up that bottle again.

"And then his punk-ass had the nerve to call Roxy and tell her that it wasn't his decision. That the studios wanted her because her playing the role guaranteed a broader reach. More people will watch with her as the star of the film and not me because she's more recognizable."

Terri planted her hand on her hip.

"Damn," was the best he could come up with.

"Then the mother fucker had the nerve to offer me the role of the sorry ass detective." She continued, glaring at Luther like he was that director. "Can you believe that shit?" Tears streamed down her cheeks. "It was my part, Luther. I kicked ass on that audition and everybody in the room knew it. I knew it. But that bitch walks in and all of a sudden, it's not my role anymore. She got wind of the film, showed up out of the blue and gets *my* part. What kind of shit is that?" Terri broke down in a full-on cry.

He didn't know what else to do. Luther gathered her in his arms and held her.

Terri let him.

BABY BIRD

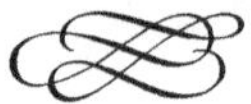

Terri sat with her feet tucked beneath her in the chair across from the sofa, where Luther was sitting. Her throat was aching from breaking down and sobbing like a baby in his arms, which mercifully ended after a good ten minutes.

"This last week has been surreal," she began, staring across the room through the window. "I came back from L.A. and started looking for places to stay in Detroit," she sniffed. "That's where we were going to be filming. I'd even started packing—ordered a bunch of boxes and tape."

Terri reached for the bottle on the table, then set it back down without taking a drink.

"You sure the role went to someone else?" he asked, probably for lack of not knowing what else to say.

"I had the part, Luther. Biggest part of my entire career. A role that would've changed everything," she reminded him. "Last week, Roxy called, apologizing profusely, before telling me that Joy Graham's agent had gotten wind of the part, called the studios and told them that she was interested in playing Irene."

Terri blinked away tears. "She's a bigger name than me," Terri continued. "The studio execs salivated over the fact that she wanted the part, and they gave it to her. Then, offered me the role of the detective." She rolled her eyes in disgust. "A bit part character that nobody will ever fuckin' remember, not even the actor playing it."

She felt like such a fool. Like fate, the universe, all those people she'd auditioned in front of, even God, were all laughing at her.

"I've worked so long and so hard for an opportunity like this, Luther. I thought, finally, all the sacrifices, tears and faith that I've always had in myself, in what I do, had paid off."

There was no hope left in Terri. Roxy had been blowing up her phone, but Terri refused to take her calls. It wasn't that she blamed her agent. Roxy would undoubtedly, bend over backwards trying to reassure Terri, promising her that the role she was meant to play, the one written just for her, was out there, and Roxy would find it. Terri wasn't interested.

She had no idea how much time had passed before she realized that he had hardly said a word. Luther was in the kitchen filling two cups with hot water. A few more minutes passed, and Luther showed up standing next to her like some, tall, dark, handsome genie handing her a hot cup of tea.

"I have tea?" she asked.

He sat back down, took a sip from his cup and shrugged. "Surprised the hell out of me."

Terri managed to smile. "I was doing just fine before this happened." Terri pursed her lips and blew steam from her cup. "I was working my way toward making peace with my retirement and actually getting excited to be part of the Devastation Annual Theater Festival."

"Yeah, I could tell you were really into that," he teased.

Terri's brief laughter was quickly followed by rogue tears. "I really am done this time. No more auditions," she sobbed. "Nobody knows—nobody understands wha—"

Next thing she knew, Terri was airborne, scooped up in Luther's arms, then lowered himself into the chair she'd been sitting in with her in his lap. Terri rested her head on his shoulder until this new stream of tears stopped flowing.

"Can I ask you something?" he said, his lips inches away from hers.

She was feeling vulnerable and vulnerability mixed with a handsome dude coming to her rescue could, in their case, lead to something neither of them wanted.

"Of course," she answered with reluctance.

"How do you eat like that" — he glanced over his shoulder at the kitchen— "and not get big as a house?"

Terri looked over at all the cereal boxes on the countertop, then turned back to him. "I've put on ten pounds since I moved here."

"Only ten?"

"So far," she answered, eyeing him suspiciously. Was he giving her a backhanded compliment? Or no?

"Mavis has more scripts she wants you to read."

Terri grimaced. "Have you not heard me? Do I look like I'm in any frame of mind to read more bad plays?"

"No," he said, matter-of-factly. "You don't, Terri. What they did to you was shitty, baby. But what they did does not define who you are."

"Don't start, Luther. Don't sit here trying to cheer me up and make me feel better about myself. I feel like a sucker. Let me sit here and feel like a sucker."

He laughed, "My bad. Forgive me for trying to shine light on your beautiful, magical ass."

"Thank you. I don't want to feel beautiful and magical right now."

"Noted."

Terri's nether parts were starting to tingle. Her body melted into his like warm, gooey caramel, and more than anything right now, she wanted to close her eyes, wrap all of her around all of him, and make the whole world vanish. But she'd sworn off Luther long ago and the last thing she needed was to pile more regret on top of the shitty pile she already had.

"You should leave," she told him instead, pushing away from him..

"I should," Luther agreed, staring deeply into her eyes, and tightening his grip.

"I'm an emotional wreck, Luther, riddled with bad judgment, toxic emotions and busted pride running on turbo."

"I know."

He said it, but Terri wasn't convinced that he really did *know* that this moment was heating to a rolling boil. A part of her wanted to escape in it, in him and dissolve into this man until they were one cohesive blob. But messy was becoming far too relevant in her life now, and the last thing she needed was more of it.

"We said this wouldn't happen again Luther. I made it clear to Nick that it was over between us, but we need to stop—now."

Luther was silent. That dreaded vulnerability slithered up her spine though, threatening to overtake what remained of her fragile self. With everything else she'd been through, Terri needed him to answer the question plaguing her since the two of them had, had sex.

"You felt it too, right?" She swallowed. "When we were together." A lump swelled in her throat, reminding her that more tears were just one wrong answer away. "I wasn't just another booty call?"

She felt as pitiful as she sounded, and Terri wished those words had never passed her lips.

"I *feel* it, sweetheart," he replied, warmly and with enough sincerity to be believed. "You were not a booty call, Terri. You were not a conquest or an accident." Luther paused, bobbing his head, slightly in introspection. "You and me are victims of bad timing." He smiled. "And worst luck. That's all."

Terri allowed herself to ease into the comfort of his words, misguided or not, right or wrong. What he said, mattered. She released a subtle sigh, then rested her head against his shoulder, again. "I've decided to move to Houston."

"Is that really what you want to do?" he asked.

"I'm in a terrible place, right now, Luther. Good judgement is not on my side, but I'm sitting here with you, knowing that if you don't leave soon, we'll... and I want to," she admitted. "I desperately do."

Terri wanted more of him without feeling like shit for indulging. She wanted to make him forget about all his other girlfriends and convince him that he couldn't live without her. Terri wanted to pretend, that she was exceptional and desirable and more special than any other woman in the world. Idealistic shit like that was so uncharacteristically her that it set off a quiet panic inside her.

"I can try to pretend that I don't want you, Terri, but I'd be lying," Luther admitted. "I'm trying to do the right thing, by Nick, by you. But the right thing for me, *is* you, no matter how much I keep denying it, honey."

"Maybe it's just sex—for both of us," she reasoned, looking up at him.

Deep down, Terri hoped that the attraction between them was purely sexual, because that would be easy to deal with, like as simple as taking a pill or something and all of a sudden being cured.

"You believe that?" he challenged, raising a brow. "Is that all it was for you?"

He posed the question like he already knew the answer, so Terri didn't bother with a response.

"I've been pent up, emotionally for a long time, afraid to connect to another woman because I didn't feel I deserved to. I didn't even know if I could love another woman after Ava."

"Wait. Love?" She shot up a brow.

"What? No. Did I say that?"

"You did. You love me?"

After a long pause, Luther responded. "If I got out of my own way, I could let myself go there, but—"

Did she love him? Could she? All she knew was that he was the only person she'd let into her house after getting back from L. A. She trusted him with her pain in a way she didn't even trust Roxy or Nona. Was that love? Potentially?

Without thinking, Terri pressed her hand against the side of his face and pulled his lips to hers. The image of Nick's face jolted her thoughts like an electric shock. Terri squeezed her eyes shut tighter, and held on to Luther with every ounce of strength she had. Yes. She was going to have to leave this town. There was no way she could live this close to him and deny herself Luther Hunt.

"Terri," he said, easing back and breaking the seal of their kiss. "We can't do this."

“Yeah,” she said, hastily climbing off his lap. “You’re right. Thanks for stopping by.”

Bullet dodged!

Terri rigidly held herself together as she followed him to the door, replacing thoughts of regret with ones of packing and of calling Nona to let her know that she’d be in Houston at the end of the month. The sooner the better, and this time, Terri really would bury her head in the sand and fade from the public eye forever. She nearly bumped into him when he abruptly stopped, filling nearly every square inch of her doorway, blocking out the afternoon sun. She was just about to give him a good, hard shove, when he turned, wrapped one long, strong around her waist, lifted her off the ground and filled her mouth with his tongue.

Terri wrapped both legs around his waist, feeling as if she was sailing from the living room to the bedroom. This would be the last time, so shit. Why not?

GROWN FOLKS BUSINESS

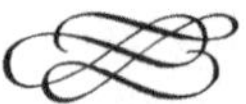

Luther refused to leave this encounter with Terri abbreviated like before. She'd made up her mind to leave Devastation, and he agreed that her moving away was the only answer. If she stayed, so would temptation, and Luther wasn't strong enough to resist her. If she was leaving, then now, this moment was all he cared about. Was it a lame excuse to cross that line with her again? Absolutely. It was certainly a selfish one, but there was no turning back.

What if he let it all go? The guilt? Regret? Punishing himself for not being there for his wife and son when they needed him most? What if, for now, he surrendered to the fantasy of this woman and make her his, and create an alternate universe where there was just her and him?

Luther stood, braced against the side of the bed between Terri's thighs, and took off his shirt. His gaze locked into the eyes of this beautiful woman, seeing possibilities he'd denied himself access to from the moment he'd first laid eyes on her. Terri sat up and began unbuckling his belt. The world outside the intimate gathering of *them* disappeared in a vacuum and inhibitions, regret, guilt, faded with them.

Terri freed him from his jeans, and it took every ounce of restraint he had not to drive himself into her. Luther refused to rush this… this precious and last time the two of them would have together.

He lowered his mouth to hers, then coaxed her onto her back. Terri's legs spread wide, accommodating him, but Luther held back, making love to her mouth, sexing her tongue with his. Fuck! When was the last time he'd kissed a woman like this? When was the last time he'd wanted to?

She dug her fingers into his back, tugged on his lips with her teeth, drew her knees higher, coaxing him to ease into her. Luther's dick bucked in protest of his defiance and his determination to make this last as long as he could. He eased back and slid the hem of her shirt over her breasts and hungrily engulfed one beautiful, dark and erect nipple, and then the other. Terri arched her back, moaned her response, and whispered something—something he—

It didn't matter what she'd said. Luther was driving.

Luther lowered his mouth to the soft folds of her pussy and inhaled, savoring her scent, slipping his tongue between the folds of her sex, grazing his tongue lightly over her thick, sensitive clit. Terri cried out, clutching Luther by the head, trembling against him. He ached to be inside her, but not yet. Terri undulated hips against his face, clutching, moaning and calling his name, until finally, they bucked wildly as she came.

Luther pushed to stand, wiped his mouth, and stepped back, taking in the beautiful sight of her writhing on the bed from what he'd just done to her. He had to keep his distance. Luther paced back and forth, and eventually sat down in the chair across from the bed to ease the pressure building inside him, a desperate need so maddening that he was afraid he'd hurt her if he didn't calm the fuck down.

Damn! She looked delicious! Glistening dark skin, soft thighs, full, round breasts. Terri's hand slipped between her thighs, disappearing into the folds of where his tongue had been, and met and held Luther's gaze, daring him to stay in that damn chair.

He stripped naked, walked over to the bed, braced himself on one knee, wrapped one arm around her waist, picked her up and pushed her closer to the headboard. Luther kissed her again, and drove inside her, balls deep, and stopped. Terri tried moving her hips, but he pressed down on her, stopping her from pulling too much too soon from him.

"Look at me," she whispered, cradling his face between her hands.

Terri's dark eyes locked onto his.

"I see you, sweetheart," he murmured.

Luther saw a woman he wanted, desperately needed, but couldn't have. Terri's pussy pulsed, and Luther lowered his face to the pillow, and methodically, slowly, eased in and out of her until time, space, reason—disappeared.

"Ohhhh—shit!" he exclaimed.

"Luther," she called out, digging nails into his back, bringing him back to this moment.

He pushed up and looked into her eyes, concerned. "I'm hurting you?"

She nodded and pulled his face closer to hers. "Don't stop."

There was more than chemistry between them. More than similar backgrounds. Luther and Terri had a special connection, the kind he never even had with Ava. The kind that entwined two people deep enough to cum at the same time.

❧

LUTHER STAYED THE NIGHT. Terri slept in his arms and he was so content with having her next to him that he didn't move.

The savory scent of bacon woke him up the next morning. Luther slipped into his jeans and followed the aroma to the kitchen, that was surprisingly a whole lot cleaner than it had been the day before.

"Good morning," she said, staring back at him with wide, pretty eyes. "If you plan on staying long enough for breakfast, tell me how you like your eggs."

Luther pulled up a bar stool and leaned on the counter. "Scrambled is fine."

She returned a timid smile. "Good. Cause that's the only way I know how to make them."

He laughed.

"There's coffee," she motioned her head to the pot next to the sink.

He had to pass her to get to it and on the way, tugged on her elbow, leaned down and kissed her good morning, like this was part of their daily routine. He wished with everything in him, that it was. But the truth revealed itself in a flash. She wasn't his and she never would be. After breakfast, Terri told him of her plans. "I texted Nona this morning, told her that I was coming and that'd I'd be there next month."

Luther's heart sank at the thought of her leaving.

"She asked a bunch of questions and I told her I'd explain when I got there."

"You selling this place?"

"Going to try to." She shrugged. "Know anybody who might interested?"

"I'll ask around," he said, hoping she hadn't missed his reluctance.

Terri was putting on a brave front, but he could tell she wasn't okay.

"I'm just disappointed that I'm going to miss theater season," she laughed. "And I'm going to miss Mavis and Lucy."

"They'll miss you too."

She became quiet and introspective for a moment. "It did feel like home here, for a while. More than just about any other place I've ever lived."

"I wish things had turned out differently, Terri. I wish I'd been the one to scoop you up and take you to the hospital the night you twisted your ankle," he admitted, forcing a smile. "Does Nick know you're leaving?"

Leave it to him to kill a mood, even one as short-lived as this one, but he had to know.

"I told him," she said, tears glistening in her eyes. "And I did make it crystal clear that it was over between us."

Relief set in, along with the certainty that Nick would come through this just fine. Of course, he wouldn't have had to come through it fine if Luther hadn't fucked up and ended up with Terri.

"It was never like this with him," she tried to explain. "I liked him. I wanted it to work because he's this great guy. Nice, funny, smart."

Luther shifted, an uneasy feeling washing over him, talking about his son at a time like this.

Terri seemed to notice and quickly changed the subject. "Do you think you can send me a copy of the soundtrack you're writing for the festival?"

"Absolutely," he smiled.

"Good. I know it'll be great."

He leaned over and kissed her. "When the dust settles, Terri, you're going to remember that *you're* great. You don't need some punk-ass producer to tell you that."

She bobbed her head slightly. "I suppose. I just don't know what I'm going to do with the rest of my life, Luther. I've only ever counted on one thing and it was acting." Terri shrugged.

They finished breakfast, made slow love on the sofa, and an hour later, Luther stood at the door, hands driven deep into his pockets, dreading that this would be the last time he saw her.

"You messed me up, shorty," he admitted, leaning against the door.

Terri smiled. "Yeah, well, I'm pretty messed up, too."

"You're going to be okay," he assured her, then leaned down for a lingering kiss. "You're gonna figure it out, and come out on the other side shining like a silver dollar."

Terri pursed her lips together and nodded. "Maybe someday," she sighed. "I will miss you, though."

He raised her hand to his lips and kissed it.

"Call me—sometimes?" she asked.

No. He never would.

Terri walked him out onto the porch and Luther turned one last time and kissed her. She wrapped her arms around him and held on—but not long enough.

"Bye, Luther," she pushed away and stepped back.

Luther made his way to his car, but before he opened the door, all hell broke loose.

Nick's BMW skidded to a stop in front of Terri's house. "What the fuck!" He exclaimed, climbing out of the car and marching into the yard, glaring first at Terri, then at Luther.

"Nick," Luther heard her say.

"This mothafucka is why you stopped seeing me?" He motioned his hand at Luther. "You're fuckin' him?"

Luther felt like he weighed a thousand pounds. He couldn't move. Couldn't breathe.

"Mothafucka!" Nick marched toward him and lunged at Luther, landing a hard right to his father's jaw and then a left to the side of his head.

"Nick! No!"

"Is this the kind of shit you do? Fuck for the sake of fucking no matter who it is or who you hurt?"

Bracing himself, Luther wrapped Nick up in a bear hug just as he was about to take another swing. "Hold up! Calm the fuck down!"

"Calm down?" Nick shouted, wrestling with Luther, shoving him back against the car. "You fuck my girl and— Let me go!"

"Stop!" Terri's voice might as well have been coming from another planet, it sounded so far away. "Nick!" she appeared next to the two of them.

"Get off me," Nick demanded, trying to jerk free of Luther's grasp. "Get the fuck off me!"

Reluctantly, Luther let him go and pushed him back, preparing for another attack.

"Nick." Terri's voice shook. She placed a hand on his arm, but he jerked away from her too. "I'm—I'm so—sorry."

"So, this is who you are?" He loomed over her. "You fuck with me then you fuck with him? Is this that Hollywood shit?"

"I'm sorry," she repeated, tears filling her eyes.

"Son, don't," Luther interjected, moving Terri out of the way.

Nick glared back at Luther. "Don't? Don't what? Lay up with the same woman as you? Is that what you mean, Pop?"

Luther lowered his head. His heart pounded. "This wasn't— Goddamnit, son. I'm so sorry."

"Yeah. You're fuckin' sorry. You're a joke, Luther." He stared at Terri like she was infected. "You both are."

"We didn't plan for this to happen," Terri tried explaining.

Luther stood, numb, watching his son storm off, back to his car and peel away from the curb.

"Are you all right?" Terri asked, reaching for his face.

Luther swatted her hand away and climbed inside his car.

"Luther," she said, blocking him from closing the door.

"Move, Terri."

"I—"

"Move!"

He had to fix this. Luther had to fix this with Nick. Nothing else mattered. Nothing.

❧

"FUCK," he exclaimed, enraged, slamming his hand against the steering wheel.

She hadn't spoken to him in weeks, not since giving him that sorry ass speech about walking away from their relationship because her career meant so damn much to her. How the fuck could Nick have missed it? Every time he had ever mentioned the woman's name to Luther, that mothafucka got all sheepish looking, pretending not to give a damn about her when the two of them had been fuckin' the whole time.

"Fuck!" he grunted over and over again, making his way out of town.

Nick's phone was blowing up, but he didn't give a damn. Luther was dead to him, and Terri—

Goddamn! How in the hell did he ever let himself fall for her trifling ass? She'd played him from the beginning and Nick had been dumb enough to catch feelings. A car raced up behind him and honked. It was Luther. Nick sped up and so did he.

"Fuck it," he growled, skidding off to the side of the road leading to the highway.

Nick was out of his car before he'd even come to a full stop.

"Son," Luther said, getting out from behind the wheel. "I never meant to hurt you, Nick."

The two marched toward each other, Nick with his fists curled. "Nah, you didn't hurt me, man," he shouted. "You fuckin' embarrassed yourself. You humiliated yourself, Luther, and you look like a goddamn fool. But that's what you've always been to me," Nick drove his finger into Luther's face. "A fool!"

Luther dropped his head and had the nerve to look wounded. "You're right. I made a fool of myself and I never meant for you—"

"To find out?" Nick interrupted. "You knew, I cared about her! You and me were mending some fences, and that mattered, Luther."

"It still matters."

"Fuck you, man. You never gave a shit about anybody but yourself and still don't."

"That's not true."

"Bullshit. You standing there smelling like her and telling me that? Really?"

"Nick—"

Nick backed away, lowered and shook his head. "Selfish sonofabitch," he muttered, then looked back at Luther. "I was actually starting to think I was too hard on your ass."

"I deserve this," Luther had the nerve to say.

His words fell on deaf ears. "No, you don't. You don't deserve my time or my anger, man. Never did. All those times, growing up, when I'd put your ass on a pedestal, only to end up scratching my head wondering why? What the fuck made you so goddamned special? So, you played a fuckin' guitar while my mother was hooked to a dialysis machine three days a week. That shit didn't make you special. A real man would've been there, Luther. He'd have said, fuck the road—the music and he'd have kept his ass at home."

Luther looked away.

"She needed you. We both did. But you only showed up when it was convenient for you. When she was feeling good your ass came through like some lame ass knight in shining armor buying up big ass televisions, video games and diamonds like that shit was supposed to be enough to fill in the gaps you left because you were too damn busy doing what you wanted to do."

Nick and his mother had both been dealt a shitty hand. They didn't deserve Luther and he sure as hell didn't deserve either one of them.

"You're right," he admitted.

"I don't need you to tell me that. I said all this to remind myself of who you really are, because sometimes, I forget."

"Nick, I didn't—"

"Keep my damn name out of your mouth, Luther and go back and finishing fucking that ho. I don't give a damn about you or her." Nick walked back to his car. "Stay the fuck away from me," he shouted, driving off, and glancing back at Luther through his rearview mirror for the last time.

THE WATER'S EDGE

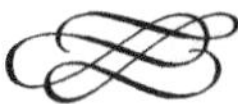

Two days ago, World War III erupted outside her front door. The confrontation between Nick and Luther, with Terri stuck in the middle like a zit in an ass crack, sickened her. Nick was so furious that it scared her. Of course, he had every right to be but not because Terri was his woman. She never had been. But she'd been intimate with him and with Luther. When the dust settled, she had all the faith in the world that he'd come to see that Terri wasn't the prize that he'd lost. His relationship with Luther was that prize, but because of her, it was gone forever.

Her phone had been turned off since it happened. Terri had spent the last two days drinking, sleeping, waking up to pee, drinking some more and going back to bed. Her whole fuckin' life had unraveled more than she'd ever thought it could—even more than it had after getting fired in Atlanta. Nothing, she thought at the time, could've been worse than that. She was wrong.

❧

SHE WAS GOING to miss this tree. Terri managed to drag herself out of bed and take refuge underneath it for the last few hours, soothed by the gentle rustling of the leaves and the caress of its hundred-year-old shade. Louisiana Fall was starting to creep in, and Terri sat outside wearing an oversized sweater, some shorts, and house slippers that should've been tossed a long time ago. She'd given up on trying to latch on to any thought remotely optimistic. There was no light at the end of the tunnel. There was nothing to look forward too except leaving.

"David Randall called me," Roxy told her this morning.

Terri groaned and rolled her eyes. "I don't give a damn about David Randall and his silly show, Rox."

"You're going to be mad at me," Roxy responded.

Terri was too numb to be mad.

Roxy continued. "He asked how you were doing," she reluctantly stated. "And I sort of opened up to him on your behalf."

She sighed. "Meaning?"

"He called you boring, Terri," Roxy shot back. "I couldn't help but to prove him wrong."

All of a sudden, Terri felt like she wanted to puke. "What did you do, Roxy?"

"I told him about you living in Devastation, Louisiana," she began.

Terri instinctively knew that, that wasn't all she'd told him.

"And I mentioned a little bit about a love triangle," she added.

"Roxy," Terri groaned.

"His eyes lit up, Terri. Girl, I know, I know probably overstepped my bounds—"

"Probably? Are you serious? You had no right—"

"I know, but he damn near shit his self, he was so excited. And when I mentioned the movie role and audition and all the shit—"

"You— Why? Why would you humiliate me to that moron? What makes you think I want to impress him?"

"Because now he wants to offer you your own show, T," Roxy hastily admitted. "Your show. Just you, and I think it'd be a great way to build fire for your brand, Terri. I think that roles will come pouring in if you'd just—"

Terri hung before Roxy finished.

The absurdity of it all wasn't lost on her.

Nick and Luther. Nick and Luther. Nick *and* Luther? Reality television. Roles offered then snatched away— How the hell did she end up like this? It was as if someone else had lassoed her brain, her common sense, and rode off with it, leaving the rest of her dumbass behind scratching her empty head, bewildered, battered, bruised, and humiliated.

Nick's face flashed in her mind every time she closed her eyes. That look of utter revulsion left her feeling like something slithering out from underneath a rock. Terri felt dirty and stupid, like she had had no control over her mind or her body. Every time Luther was within a foot of her, all she wanted to do was wrap her legs around the man, even when she had convinced herself that wasn't the case. But it was. It had always been the case. No matter how hard she tried to make it make sense in her mind, or tried justifying it, nothing she told herself felt true. She'd wanted Luther more than she'd ever wanted Nick. Period.

"There you are."

Terri gagged a little at the sight of Lanette appearing in her back yard.

"I knocked," she said, coming over and sitting, uninvited, by Terri. "But you didn't answer. You never do. Since your car was here, I knew you were home. You've been hiding inside like a hermit for the last month. What compelled you to come outside and breathe the free air?"

She hadn't seen or heard from Lanette since the day she'd picked her up from the hospital, and she hadn't wanted to.

"What do you want?" Terri asked with the kind of acidity that could burn through metal.

Gone was any empathy she had for the woman. Terri was a husk of her former self, so things like concern for her fellow neighbors had dried up and blown away in the wind.

Long, silky strands of sandy, blond hair, framed her narrow face. She looked like she'd disguised herself to keep Terri from recognizing her. Terri had been avoiding her from the moment she closed on this house.

Lanette wore a jean jacket over a maxi dress, with a pair of really cute cowboy booties that Terri coveted, even in her current state.

"You know everybody's talking," Lanette stated.

No. Terri was not putting up with this woman's nonsense today. "Go home, Lanette."

Lanette cast a side eye glance at Terri. "Ronetta Drake saw Luther and Nick pull away from your house a day ago. 'Nick looked pissed,' she said. Luther followed him. Ronetta followed them both, but I don't think they saw her, because they were too busy fighting."

"Go home," Terri repeated, gritting her teeth.

"People talk about me all the time," Lanette continued.

Was Terri invisible? Was this lunatic really that daft? "Lanette—"

"It's a small town, so other people's drama has a way of being seen like looking under a magnifying glass. Of course, whatever went on here, and I can only speculate," she grinned, "must've been some juicy shit for those two to go at it the way Ronetta said they did. Which one did you fuck?"

"Are you insane?" Terri blurted out, glaring at Lanette who seemed like she was in another world.

"What?" Lanette asked, looking Terri square in the eyes.

"You heard me. Are—you—crazy?"

Lanette looked away, her lips quivered and tears filled her eyes. "I believe so, Terri," she sadly admitted. "I believe I must be. You think I am?"

Terri returned an introspective nod. "Perhaps, but I want you to leave me alone. And I mean it, Lanette. I really mean it."

"I know," she said, her tone filled with earnest. "But I can't, Terri."

"Why the hell not?"

Lanette shrugged and sighed, gazing out across the yard. "You saved me." She smiled. "You don't even know it, but you did. Now, I'm just returning the favor."

Terri laughed, "I don't need you to save me, Lanette."

"Somebody has to," she looked at Terri, scanning her from head to toe. "You look a mess."

"Will you get the fuck out of my yard?" Terri yelled.

Lanette huffed and rolled her eyes. "You try to act like you've got your shit together, but you don't. No actress, not a good one, would move to a place like this on purpose."

Tears escaped down Terri's cheeks. "I'm trying real hard not to punch you in the jaw," she admitted, rage seething in her veins.

"You ever feel like you're in the world but not part of it?" Lanette continued, her gaze drifting skyward. "Like you're the moon or some distant planet orbiting around everybody else and you try to get close, but you can't because gravity won't let you."

"What?" Terri asked thoroughly, and utterly confused.

"I know. Right?"

"What are you talking about?"

"I'm talking about me, Terri. I'm talking about you. I see you," she said, pointing in Terri's face.

Lanette's statement, the way she stared into Terri's eyes, left Terri speechless and begged the question, how do you argue with insanity?

"I see your fear, Terri," she said, smirking. But there was no malice in her expression. Surprisingly, and for the first time since Terri had known the woman, there was a softness in her eyes. "I see your vulnerability and your brokenness."

"No, you don't," Terri muttered in disbelief.

"Oh, people like me see everything because nobody thinks we're paying attention... because nobody pays attention to us." Lanette smiled and placed a warm hand on Terri's. "You're really good at hiding your pain, especially from yourself. But broken people recognize broken people. You see it in me, too. Have from the beginning. Haven't you?"

A wave of emotion flooded her chest. Maybe it was the alcohol, or maybe Terri was just tired, but a strange, unsettling kind of kinship suddenly tethered her to this woman.

"For me," Lanette said, pulling off her wig, exposing sandy-brown cornrows of her natural hair. "It's the hair."

Terri marveled at her. It looked so real.

"I choose to hide my pain in hairstyles that change almost every time the wind blows," she laughed, nervously twirling strands from the wig in her lap, around her fingers. "Most times it works. A new wig, some braids, a pretty fro can make me feel right as rain."

That dark madness Terri was so used to seeing in Lanette's eyes abruptly returned.

"Other times, ain't enough hairstyles in the world to lighten my mood, and so I—" She shrugged. "You, on the other hand, hide in the characters you play, especially the one you play every day, believing that she is you."

The weight of Lanette's words resonated and weighed heavily on Terri. Crazy or not, Lanette nailed it.

"You ain't *that* famous," Lanette continued. "Oh, you're more famous than anyone here, but you're no Halle Berry."

Terri looked away.

"Don't be sad."

Terri sobbed.

"I imagine that it's always hard seeing your true self for the first time," Lanette continued. "But then, as soon as you do see her, you kill her off like the rookie cop you played in that television show. I suspect that you have never really lived. Have you? Never truly loved."

Terri sat speechless, locking gazes with a crazy woman who had her all figured out.

"People like you go to the grave, a fraud if you're not careful." Lanette draped an arm over Terri's shoulder. "The only reason you're broken now is because you've lied to yourself too damn long. And that's okay. Most cowards do. But the shit's hit the fan now, Terri. Pain does that. It forces you to open your eyes and take a good, long, hard look at the real you and not the fake bitch you've been pretending to be. The real Terri is tired of hiding and being fake, and you can't bury her anymore."

Fake?

"If this is what it means to be *real*, then you can keep it," Terri murmured.

"You say that now, but you've needed this," Lanette gave her a good squeeze. "You needed to wake the hell up and to be you, messy and silly—you, Terri." Lanette slipped back on her wing. "So, what did happen between you and Luther that got Nick so mad? Details, girl. I'm here for them."

Terri never said a word. Lanette was right. Terri had been playing at being Terri for as long as she could remember. The real her had only ever revealed itself in moments, especially since she'd moved here, away from the noise of her disappointments and expectations.

The real Terri liked being an honorary board member of the Devastation Community Theater Committee and working with Mavis and Lucy and their incredibly great and awful play. Terri liked fixing up this old house, and five-star hotels. She liked Nona and even Roxy, even though she was mad at her. She even, maybe sort of liked crazy Lanette.

"I loved a man once," Lanette finally said, adjusting her hair.

Terri groaned. "I'm not in love, Lanette."

"It's a funny thing about love," she said with introspection.

"I'm not in love with anybody."

"I didn't realize it until it was too late." She looked at Terri. "And he was long gone."

Lanette left without saying goodbye, leaving Terri alone with too much to contemplate. Was she in love? With Luther? If she was, then it wasn't the fairy tale kind of love. That was for damn sure.

BAD MOON

"Hey, Nona," Terri said to her best friend, on video chat.

Hours after Lanette left, Terri had gone back to packing only to end up staring at empty boxes and getting absolutely nowhere.

"Hey, girl." Nona sipped her tea, looking absolutely flawless, as usual.

Not a hair was ever out of place with that woman. She always managed to look cover model ready.

"You're still coming," Nona probed. "Right?"

"Yeah. Of course."

Nona gave Terri the side eye. "But..."

"But nothing. I'm coming. I need to."

Sympathy filled Nona's eyes. Terri had given her the rundown on losing that part to another actress, but she hadn't mentioned getting caught by Nick with Luther. It's the reason she'd called, but now, Terri couldn't bring herself to even mention it.

"You just need time, sweetie," Nona reminded her. "A good, long self-care retreat will do you good, and you don't even have to cook if you don't want to... or clean. You'll have free use of the pool, the gym... the kids."

Terri laughed, "Gee, thanks."

"And you'll have all the time in the world to find yourself, whatever that means for you. Terri the actress or Terri the something even better that she never knew she could be because she's had tunnel vision her whole life. And you'll get to your happy, T. I promise you."

Terri teared up. "My happy."

"And maybe when the dust settles, you'll meet someone nice, dangerously sexy and aloof with everybody except you, who'll worship the ground you walk on and know martial arts and have muscles like Dwayne "The Rock" Johnson. Powerful enough to slay dragons and beat back silly ass producers who don't know a good thing when she's standing right in front of their silly asses."

This time, Terri laughed, "Wow. Dwayne 'The Rock' Johnson, huh?"

"He's going to be the shit," Nona finished. "I can't wait for the wedding."

"Slow your roll, Nona," she responded, softly. "I need to get my act together, first."

Terri never equated happiness with having a man in her life. The very thought was archaic to her, but a connection had been made with Luther, even if fleeting and forbidden. Enough of one to show her that —yeah—she could get with the idea of being part of a team. Terri shook off the thought.

"You still there?" Nona asked.

"I'm here."

"Is something else going on that you're not telling me?"

Terri smiled. "You doing that best friend mind-probe thing again?"

"Been doing it since the seventh grade. What aren't you telling me?"

Terri had spilled all the beans about her life to Roxy lately, but it dawned on her how she'd managed to keep her oldest and dearest friend in the dark about what had been happening in her life. Why? Because it was okay for Roxy to know how fucked up she was and not Nona, the most perfect person she knew?

"I met someone," Terri offered.

"O-kaaaay," Nona replied. "Like a romantic someone?"

Terri sniffed. "Yeah."

"Well, that's good. Right? Or no? No."

"It's not—"

Good Lord! Why'd she even mention it? It wasn't as if Terri wanted to drudge up the dreadful details of the sordid threesome. Nona had always thought so highly of Terri and if she admitted what happened with her, Nick, and Luther… Besides, Nick was never what he should've been, or could've been in Terri's life. She'd tried. Hadn't she?

"It didn't work out," she stated, simply but not with Nick in mind. With Luther.

Nona sighed, "If it was meant to be, Terri, it would be. You finish packing and get your ass down here. I've got a masseuse, champagne and chocolate waiting here for you to remind you of how beautiful and worthy you are, sis. You deserve all the good things in life, Terri. I wish you knew that."

They ended the call with those words ringing in Terri's ears, convicting her even more than she'd already convicted herself. Nick had been so angry. No, the two of them weren't seeing each other, but now he knew why. Him knowing was the part she had to find a way to make peace with.

And what about Luther? Being with him was like slipping on a warm, worn robe and slippers, the perfect fit and comfortable. But the look in his eyes the last time she'd seen him bore through her like hot iron. He'd destroyed the person he loved most in the world, his son, and in doing so, he'd destroyed more of himself.

A part of her knew better than to reach out to Luther to see if— What? What would seeing him accomplish? Not a goddamned thing. But, Terri got up and got dressed, anyway.

❧

EVERY CONVERSATION in the room came to an abrupt halt when Terri walked into Luther's, and every eye in the place fixed on her. Terri scanned the room for Luther, but when she didn't see him, made her way over to the bar.

"Hey, Yolanda," she said, smiling.

Yolanda turned to Terri, propped her hand on her hip and cocked a brow. Gone was that warm, welcoming, star-struck girl she'd come to know and love.

"Is Luther around?"

Yolanda took her time answering, "He's upstairs."

"Thank you," she muttered, before sheepishly wading her way through the room and heading up the wrought iron winding staircase to his apartment.

Terri took a deep breath before knocking lightly on the door. Luther, unshaven and unkempt answered, looking like he had just crawled out of a cave. He paused, met her gaze, then turned and left her standing in the doorway.

Wearing a wife-beater and jeans, Luther made his way to the kitchen, pulled two beers out of the fridge and handed one to her. Terri took it, but she had no intentions of drinking it. He twisted off the cap on his bottle, sat down and finished half of it before coming up for air.

She sat on the sofa, placed her bottle on the table and leaned back wondering why in the hell she'd come here at all.

"I thought about calling him," Terri admitted. "But I don't think he'd want to hear from me."

Luther shrugged. "That makes two of us, Terri."

This time next month, Terri would be in Houston, getting a massage and drinking champagne with nothing but sour memories of what had happened here. She stared at Luther, looking old and weathered, beaten, wondering if what had snapped inside him could ever be repaired.

"What are you going to do, Luther?" she asked, more to herself than to him.

Luther cut his eyes at her, then looked away. "What I'm doing."

Her question had been unnecessary. The wound shared between the two of them was so raw, she knew it'd never close. That magic connection she'd once felt with this man, was severed. Luther was just a man. Someone she used to know.

"I'm sorry for my part, Luther," she eventually said.

Luther believed he should be the one to shoulder all the guilt, but she knew better.

He finished his beer and stared at the empty bottle in his hand. "I'd never wanted to fix something more in my life than my relationship with my son," he said, his voice cracking. "I couldn't go back in time to fix the past, but the future," he paused. "I could do something about that."

For some dumb reason, Terri said something even more asinine. "Maybe you still can."

Luther leaned forward, resting his elbows on his thighs. "How much did I want to, Terri?" he asked, looking at her, the light that once filled his eyes, gone. "If that's truly what I believed, how in the hell could I risk the most important person in my life to mess with you?"

He was hurt. Luther was angry and defeated, and maybe he didn't mean for his words to cut so deep, but they did.

"*Mess* with me?" she repeated, furrowing her brow. "Is that how you see it?"

Luther groaned and lowered his head.

"The part with Nick in it, yeah. That's a mess." Terri swallowed, holding back sentiment he didn't deserve after a remark like that. "But you and me, Luther… When I'm with you, I don't feel like a mess."

"Terri, stop," he protested, obviously frustrated or drunk or both.

"My life is a mess. My career is a fuckin' mess," she continued. "I never believed I needed what I felt with you until I had it, and so, no, Luther, I will not let you refer to some of the best moments in my whole, pathetic life, as a *mess*. I won't let you diminish what I felt being with you; whole, at peace," she counted on her fingers, "safe, sane, good enough."

"Why is everything about you?" he blurted out, glaring at her. "You. Your career. The leading force in your life is what you do for a living, Terri, isn't who you are. It's what you do, and I get it. I get that you've been better to *it* than it's been to you, but when it's all said and done, you get to get out of here, move past this nonsense, get over me and Nick and focus all your time and attention where it's always been—on you, honey."

Terri couldn't believe she thought this man was ever capable of rescuing her from herself. "You mother fucker," she muttered, staring at him like he'd just crawled out of a dirty pond.

Luther shrugged. "Nailed it."

Seeing him now, stripped down to the lowest common denominator of himself, Terri stopped being impressed. "I may be guilty of feeling sorry for myself from time to time, Luther, but I'll be damned if I spend the rest of my life rolling around in self-pity like a pig in slop."

He grinned. "Oh, so now I'm a pig? I'm a pig because I feel like shit for letting my family down, for not being there for my wife and son when they needed me most?" Luther's bloodshot eyes locked onto hers.

"Did Nick really mean that much to you, Luther?" she asked, knowing good and damn well she was hitting below the belt. "When you made love to me, did he matter?"

Luther released another deep groan and lowered his chin. "What happened between us sours in my stomach every time I think about it. It cost me everything—the only thing in the world that still mattered to me—my son, Terri. Me being selfish. Me being greedy—for you—cost me Nick."

"I don't even know why I came here today."

"Makes two of us."

The last time the two of them were together, it was as if two galaxies had come together to form one. As wrong as it was, nothing had ever felt more purposeful, more right than sharing bodies and space with this man. But look at them, now. The two of them so destroyed over this trespass they'd spend a lifetime paying for it.

Terri would tuck her tail between her legs and slither out of Devastation with her shame and her regret, no longer wondering "what if". She'd dodged a bullet with Luther. But he was a survivor.

Eventually, he'd shuck off the humiliation of this fiasco and shave and polish himself up to look brand new again. People in town would always gossip about what happened but not to his face. Nick would slip in and out of town to see everyone but his father, and Luther's heart would break every time he did. But he'd go on, more convicted than ever to the fate he'd sealed for himself, until he was old and gray.

Terri hung her head, awestruck by how she'd gotten everything so wrong. Why had she come to see him? What did she expect? Luther reveled in guilt and regret, but hadn't she been doing the same thing? If nothing else, seeing him now confirmed one thing. She did not want to end up spending the rest of her life living this way. She would not let the past dictate her path forward.

As Terri started to leave, Luther went back to the kitchen, pulled out another beer, planted himself in that leather chair again and uttered. "Have a safe trip."

A hush fell across the restaurant again as Terri descended the stairs. Yolanda glanced over her shoulder at Terri, glaring at her, like everyone else, as she left for the last time.

POISON MIND

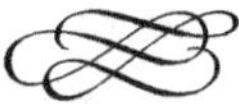

Unlike Luther, a man driven by passion and right brain thinking, Nick was more like his mother, where logic and rationality ruled. Those two things are what made his profession a perfect fit for him. Weeks had passed since he saw Terri kissing Luther on her front porch.

Nick was filled with a kind of rage he didn't know was possible. The kind that drove him to come close to beating the shit out of Luther. The only thing that stopped him, was realizing in that moment that, Terri wasn't worth taking another man's life.

It was Nick's nature to know the reason for a thing. For the last few weeks, the question of "why" had consumed him. Terri owed him an explanation. That's the only thing he wanted from her. He'd called her dozens of times since that morning. This call would be his last. Nick was about to cut his losses and give up ever getting the answers he needed, until she surprised him.

"Nick," she said, simply.

"Surprised you answered," he admitted, after a long pause.

Terri didn't say anything, but she didn't hang up, either. He'd had time to come down from his rage, and hopefully she'd be straight with him and at least give him some closure.

"I'm not going to beat around the bush, Terri," he said. "I need to know why? And why him? Why my father?" Terri was so quiet, Nick thought that maybe she'd hung up on him, after all. "You there?"

"I'm here," she responded, barely above a whisper.

Nick thought he'd had her pegged. He thought he knew her and what he thought he knew, made him want a future with her. Sure, she was beautiful, but to him, she was more than that. Terri had a worldliness about her that he was drawn to. Everything from her wry sense of humor to the torment she'd expressed over her career drew him to her—in the beginning. Time away from her had given him a clearer perspective of his motivation for wanting a relationship with her. Terri needed fixing. And Nick had grown up trying to "fix" things—his mother, his own broken heart from losing her and being let down by Luther. Terri was just another damaged thing.

"Was it me?" he asked, considering the possibility that maybe what happened had something to do with his schedule, the distance—sex.

"No," she quickly responded. "No, Nick. It wasn't you. Don't ever think that."

Nick regretted putting himself at fault for what happened, but he had to know. "You could've— Damn, Terri! You could've fucked with anybody. Anybody else. Why Luther?"

"It's not like you're making it sound."

"It sounds like what it is. You had sex with my father. Nothing about that is remotely vague."

"It wasn't just about sex, Nick," she stated, her voice cracking.

So many thoughts had been coming back to Nick since finding the two of them together. The coolness between Terri and Luther, the reluctance to even make eye contact. He didn't think much of those things back then, but hindsight brought clarity to details. Back then, he just assumed their interaction had something to do with Luther's aloofness and Terri's movie star persona. But now he knew that both of them were working overtime trying to hide something.

"It wasn't the first time?" he asked. "Was it?"

Terri took her time answering, "No."

He suspected that it wasn't but hearing it was still a kick in the gut.

"So, if it wasn't about sex," he began, wondering if he really wanted to know the truth. "Then what was it about?"

"I hated myself for what happened. Neither of us meant for it to, but—"

"You didn't answer my question. I was the man in your life, Terri. What could you possibly get from Luther that you weren't or couldn't get from me?"

"We were dating, Nick. Neither one of us ever said that you were my man."

He wasn't going to let her turn the tables. "We were seeing each other. You fucked me too. Remember?"

Another long silence between them. The comment was rude. True, but he was over trying to be kind.

"If it wasn't about sex, then what was it?"

"I don't—"

"Don't," he stopped her. "Don't pull that shit. You know. So, tell me. You owe me this."

"The first time— I don't know what—why… We were talking and one thing led to another and it happened."

"You read that from a script? That shit is cliché, Terri. The truth. Please."

"What do you want here, Nick?" Terri paused. "That I felt a strong connection to Luther? That I was more attracted to him?"

"Is it the truth?"

Yeah, she made him feel like shit, but he knew when he made this call that it wouldn't end with him feeling better. Nick needed answers.

"He made me feel—"

"Feel—what?"

"That's just it," she continued. "Luther tapped into a part of me that I didn't even know was there. More than just playing a part on film or in real life."

"Is that what you were doing with me? Playing a part?"

"I didn't know I was, until Luther and I— You were—are everything *right*, Nick. Handsome, successful, funny, smart."

"And that was a problem?"

"Chemistry was the problem. You felt it. I didn't, but, I kept hoping I would. I kept waiting for that moment when something sparked in me, something that made me long to be with you when you were away, that never wanted you to leave."

Nick raked his hand across his head, got up, walked over to the window, and stared out at his uncle Don lighting up a cigar in the back yard. He'd felt those things for her. Hearing that she didn't was a blow he wasn't prepared for. So, what was she really saying?

"Do you love him?"

"Would it matter if I did?"

Her response hurt. "Answer the question."

"I don't want to answer the question, Nick," she retorted.

"You owe me."

"I owe you an apology," Terri responded. "I owe you my regret and shame. But, honestly, what I feel or don't feel for Luther is none of your business."

With those words, she solidified everything he'd concluded about her since finding Luther at her place. Terri was one of those women, out of touch with her own worth, wearing confidence like Saran Wrap. Pretty on the outside, a messy entanglement of insecurity inside, preferring to chase thugs and players, thinking they could change assholes into decent men with that golden good-good between their thighs.

"I don't expect you to understand," she continued.

"Honestly, Terri," he sighed. "It's not worth understanding. If you thought you were special to him, then I'm sorry for you. All he's ever truly cared about is himself and that's all he will ever care about."

Nick didn't wait for her to end the call. He did, realizing Terri deserved his pity more than his disdain.

❧

"I SMELL IT," he said, walking up to his Uncle Don, ten minutes after ending the call with Terri.

The old man looked at him. "It was the only one I had all day."

"The only reason I'm here is because Aunt May knows you're sneaking cigars, too, and she wants me to remind you that it's not good for your heart because she thinks you'll stop if I tell you. But we both know that's not the truth. Right?"

The old man shook his head. "Shit, boy. I been smoking since I was eight years old. How you expect me to stop now?"

"I just told her I'd tell you," Nick said, turning to leave. "See you in a few weeks to tell you again."

"You seen ya daddy?"

"Not yet," Nick said. "On my way."

"I ain't so old that I can't tell when you lying, son."

❧

NICK STOPPED by Irma's for lunch before getting on the road back to New Orleans.

"Hey, stranger," Yolanda said, taking the seat across from him as soon as he sat down.

"Miss Yolanda," he said, wiping his mouth. "How you doing?"

Yolanda's pretty eyes fixed on his. "Good. Really good. Haven't seen you around lately."

"Don't act like you don't know why. This is Devastation, Yo. Everybody knows everything. And as *astute* as you are, I'm sure you know what I mean."

"You know she left," Yolanda told him.

He was surprised to hear it. Nick just assumed she was still in town.

"No. I didn't know. Probably for the best," he said, dismissively.

Their story would become legendary in Devastation, gossip passed down from generation to generation until it became skewed into something unrecognizable. Fortunately, Nick had two advantages. He lived in New Orleans, and eventually, if he was lucky, he'd die of old age and it would become more nonsensical than it already was.

"You think you'll ever come by the bar again?" she asked.

"Don't hold your breath."

"You think you can forgive him?"

Nick smiled and left it at that.

"He can't forgive himself, either," she shared.

"Yo, I get that you're his little sidekick, but I really don't want to talk about this."

"It's just that, you can't help who you love," she said, leaning over the table.

"I don't give a damn about who loves who. Can I please eat in peace?"

"So, for instance, if I were to tell you that I loved you—"

Nick suddenly stopped eating and looked at her, waiting for the punch line.

"That would make my point. Right?" she reasoned.

He laughed, "Your hypothetical love for me would not make a point that I care to entertain."

"It's not hypothetical. It's true."

He chuckled and shook his head. "I've known you since forever, Yo."

"That's about how long I've loved you." She smiled.

"You mean like a crush."

Yolanda rolled her eyes. "I'm thirty-four, Nick. I know the difference between love and crushes."

Nick put down his fork, leaned back, and studied her, finding it impossible to tell if she was serious or joking. "Where is this going?"

"I told you. I'm trying to make a point."

"What point?"

"That you can't help who you love." She leaned back. "I've tried not loving you, especially whenever you would show up with a new woman in your life. All through school, I was your friend, your buddy, but you never looked at me like I could be anything else."

"I never saw you as anything else, and I didn't think you saw me as anything else."

"Because you weren't paying attention."

Was she really trying to make a point or really telling him that she was in love with him? And if she was—in love with him—then what did she expect him to do about it?

"Somehow, you telling me this is—what? Supposed to make me forgive Luther?"

"Not forgive. What they did was fuckin' shitty, but maybe it can help you to understand."

"I don't want to understand him, and I honestly don't believe that what happened between him and Terri had anything to do with love. At least, not on his part."

"You made up your mind about him a long time ago, and he's been balancing on the edge of your opinion of him and the truth of who he is ever since he moved back here."

She knew the story of Luther's absence in Nick's life. He saw no reason to rehash it.

"All I am saying is that love speaks its own language, its own frequency. If you're not tuned in to it, you won't hear it. Luther and Terri were on the same frequency and they couldn't help but be drawn to each other."

Nick put down his fork and pushed his plate away. "Frequencies and love language— That's no excuse to do what they did."

"Not an excuse," she said, standing to leave. "Maybe, just an explanation."

Yolanda took a step toward the door, then turned, walked back over to him, leaned down, and planted a soft kiss on his lips. "I have wanted to do that since kindergarten."

She walked out, smiling over her shoulder at him.

WRECKAGE

When all the magic of the world disappeared, music remained, a salve to spread over festering wounds and offer relief, even temporarily. Luther leaned back in a cedar Adirondack chair on the deck of Angie's Padre Island beach house, lightly plucking at the strings of his guitar, humming a random melody.

Two months had passed since he last spoke to her. Terri's house was empty, and Nick hadn't returned any of the 2,000 messages Luther had left for him, so he finally gave up.

"You still have that house in Padre?" he asked, calling his friend, Angie.

"I do."

"Can I borrow it?"

"Sure. When?"

"Now."

Luther headed north to Shreveport, swung by Angie's place, picked up the keys and had been in the house for a few days. The collaboration between his guitar, the ocean, the breeze, and seagulls created the kind of symphony that only God could make. Luther closed his eyes, bobbed his head and let nature take the lead as he played.

If he could title this song anything, he'd call it "Peace Be Still" because, for the time being, it managed to still peace inside him. A lifetime of regret could never be stilled for long, though. Once again, he'd committed a crime against someone he loved, and the price it cost him was his son.

Nick would never forgive him… and he shouldn't. Luther didn't deserve a pass, so he wouldn't bother asking for one. Not from Nick. Not from God.

He wanted more than anything to apologize to Terri. To know that she was going to be alright. Nick, he'd be fine. A young, good-looking kid, a doctor, no less, would move on from this and come out better than ever on the other side. Fate and the odds were on his side. He'd hate Luther, but deep down, hadn't he always?

Nick was used to his father not being in his life. As much as the thought pained him, Luther knew that his son would get used to it all over again. But was Terri alright?

"You wanna tell me what's up?"

Angie's voice sliced through the waves of sound flooding Luther's head, snatching him back to the moment. He looked up at her, standing just inside the doorway and he smiled.

"Where's Lou?" he asked, continuing to play.

She'd told him that the two of them would be coming up to check on him because he *sounded* funny.

"Putting the bags upstairs in the bedroom," she said. "You could've used the main one. We'd be fine in the guest room."

He shook his head. "Nah, I'm good."

She came out and sat on the steps. A few minutes later, Lou emerged, looking like Ruby Dee.

"Hey, Big Luther," she said, kissing the top of his head. "Got woman problems?"

He chuckled. "Who told you?"

She sat down across from her wife. "Angie said you sounded funny," she answered.

"Did you really think I didn't know?" Angie asked.

Luther stopped strumming and looked at her.

"I was your Spades partner on tour for how many years?" Angie asked. "And you think I can't read you?"

"Let me guess. You caught feelings and she broke your heart?" Lou finally asked, peering at him. "First time for everything, I suppose."

Luther cocked a brow.

Did Terri break his heart? Or did he break his own?

"Well, am I right?" Lou concluded.

"Closer to right than wrong, Louise," he responded, continuing to play.

"Is it true?" Angie asked.

Luther stopped strumming. They didn't live in Devastation, but they didn't live far enough away to not get wind of gossip, either.

"I knew something was going on between you and that woman," Angie continued. "Knew it that night when I stopped by the bar."

"She really was Nick's girlfriend?" Lou probed.

Luther really wasn't in the mood to talk about it, but he knew that these two wouldn't let it go.

"They were seeing each other," he reluctantly admitted.

"Did you love her?" Angie asked.

"I don't know, Angie," he sighed.

Shit! How many times had he been asking himself that question? He needed her. He wanted her. She was a wish, a dream, a hope. Was that love? Luther used to believe he knew what the word meant. Now, he wasn't so sure.

"You fuck around with your son's woman, risking everything you have with that boy, and you don't know if you love her or not?"

"It was never supposed to be a risk," he told her.

"Why?" she challenged.

"Lou," Angie chimed in, trying to come to his defense, but there was no defense against Lou once she set her sights on you, and right now she had her sights on Luther.

"Because you weren't supposed to get caught," Lou concluded with a wicked smirk.

"Because it wasn't supposed to happen at all," he argued.

"How many times did it happen, Luther?"

He didn't answer.

"Because if it happened one time, and you say that it was never supposed to happen again, I might say, okay. You messed up. Got caught. Damn the bad luck. It was still wrong, but damn the bad luck."

Luther set aside his guitar.

"More than once," Lou surmised. "You tested fate and lost, Luther."

"Shut up, Lou," he told her.

"Of course, I'm not shutting up," she said, coolly. "Did you think it was all right to mess with that woman as long as you didn't get caught? Did you think it was fine to betray your son like that?"

"You know I didn't."

"To which one?"

"Both. And why did the two of you come here?"

"It's my house," Lou answered.

"Our house," Angie corrected her.

Lou didn't seem to hear her, choosing instead to keep her laser gaze fixed on him, convicting him even more.

"Did you really risk your relationship with your son for some pussy, Luther? Just pussy that you can get any damn where?"

"Why didn't you stay your ass at home?" he snapped.

"Because *she* wanted to come see about you." She motioned her head toward Angie.

"Then you should've let her come by herself."

"Why?" she grimaced. "Your own son can't trust you with his woman. I sure as hell ain't gonna trust you with mine."

"Lou," Angie shouted. "Get inside."

Lou took her damn time going inside the house, glaring at Luther until she disappeared behind the door.

"You could've stayed home, Angie," Luther eventually said.

"I know, but I was worried about you."

"I'm fine."

"Nick?"

He sighed, "He'll be fine."

"You think the two of you will get past this?"

"Doubt it."

"And you're okay with that?"

"Hell no, I'm not okay with it, but it's not up to me. Do I blame myself? Yes. Do I take full responsibility for my actions? Again, yes. Does my son have a right to hate my fuckin' guts? Absolutely." He raised his hands. "End of story."

"And what about her?"

He shrugged. "She's gone. Moved to Texas."

"Remember that time we were on the road with Babyface and the bus broke down outside Seattle, I think," she reminded him.

"Yeah. I remember. Playing Spades against Troy and Big Mike," he reminded her. "We came real close to reneging in that last round."

"I gave up my Ace to Big Mike's joker," she recalled, smiling. "Because I knew you had that high joker."

"How'd you know?"

She shrugged. "I knew you. I could read you. You looked at me. I don't know. It just— I knew. Connection, Luther. When it's right, you don't need words. In that moment, you understood just like I understood, that we might not win that game if one of us didn't do something. You had the high joker. We only needed one book."

"But this wasn't about cards, Angie. It was about so much more."

"I know. As hard as the two of you were trying to hide it that night, I sensed it... a connection between you and Terri, which was why I assumed y'all were together."

He chuckled, "I think you're full of shit and saw drama because you wanted to see it."

"You're full of shit if you think it wasn't obvious. If nobody else noticed, it's because they never played Spades with you before."

He shook his head, slightly.

"There's no greater feeling than sharing space with someone else who you feel belongs in that space, Luther. Yeah, what you did was hella wrong, and you don't deserve your son's forgiveness. You also don't deserve to live the rest of your life alone."

"Angie—"

"You don't, Luther. I know how much you've beaten yourself up over Ava. You're not a bad man. You've done some fucked up shit, but you're one of those led by his heart and not his head. Know what that makes you?"

He looked at her. "A fool?"

Angie laughed, "Exactly, but shit, Luther," Angie turned her gaze to the ocean. "Even fools deserve to be happy."

He wasn't convinced.

"I'm going to ask you again," she continued. "Do you love this woman?"

Luther gathered his courage, enough to admit the truth. "That connection you just went on and on about?" he looked at Angie.

"Yeah?"

"I felt it with her," he confessed. Luther tried swallowing the lump swelling in his throat. "That was something I never even felt with Ava. So, yes, Angie." Luther strummed a chord. "I'm in love."

He'd said it. Luther had finally admitted what he'd rather choke on than ever admit to another living soul. God! He loved Ava more than he thought it was possible to love another living soul, but there was something between them, a barrier, a gap, space, where the two never quite united despite how hard they both tried.

"It was never hard for her to tell me to follow my dreams—to play." Hot tears stung his eyes. "Ava saw me at my worst when I wasn't playing. I was miserable, angry, and resentful. Thought I could learn to live without the music, performing, and maybe in time, I could've. But rather than have to deal with my ass every day, feeling like she was responsible for stealing my dream, she'd tell me she was fine and that I needed to make money to keep the bills paid."

"She gave you her permission," Angie concluded. "Right or wrong, you took it."

He nodded. "I did and I hate myself for it."

"You can't go back and change it, Luther. You can't fix your broken relationship with Nick. So, what's left?"

Luther picked up his guitar again and broke out chords of James Bay's, *Hold Back the River*, looked at Angie and started singing.

Lou burst through the door, glaring at Luther, taking a seat next to

Angie, and with a look, warned him not to even think about trying to steal her woman's heart.

Luther and Angie laughed.

❧

DAYS LATER, Angie and Lou had decided to take a walk on the beach, leaving Luther in the house alone. He stared at the cell phone in his hands like it was going to sprout wings and fly away. Terri's number was the last number he'd called. He'd lost count of how many messages he'd left. Luther reached out to her anyway, knowing he was the last person she wanted to hear from. He couldn't blame her. Luther had been toxic the day she'd come to his place, toxic and unapologetic about it.

Without thinking, he lightly tapped her name with his thumb, dialing her number.

"This is Terri Dawson. Leave a message."

Luther released a heavy sigh and closed his eyes. "Let's see," he paused. "Where'd I leave off?"

He started to hum and tap a beat on his thigh. Luther closed his eyes and started singing.

"Redemption and me don't see eye to eye.
Forgiveness don't know my name.
I'd like to try—just the same.
Talk to me, baby girl.
Pick up the phone and—
Let me apologize."

He chuckled. "It doesn't exactly rhyme, but…" He hung up.

Damn! He missed her.

PUSHERMAN

Terri still could not believe the man was actually here, casually sauntering alongside Nona's pool, daring to try to break the ice with super awkward small talk.

"Growing up, my sister and I used to spend summers in Houston with our grandparents, getting fat and happy on Dr. Pepper and red licorice whips."

David wore a white button down, the sleeves casually folded back midway up his forearm, with jeans and casual slip-on leather shoes.

"I'd have never guessed you had anything to do with Texas," Terri said, not bothering to hide the sarcasm. "The summer heat must've been brutal on you."

He tucked his hands in his pockets and gave her the side eye. "You're telling me. A California boy in Southern Texas during the hottest part of the year?" He glanced at Terri, stretched out on a chaise, wearing a pair of cutoffs and an oversized tee shirt. "Tor and ture."

He was so fuckin' Hollywood. Nine months ago, he'd fired Terri under the guise of being "boring". Now he was here, in Houston, poolside—beating around the bush in a conversation leading up to offering her a new gig.

"A fish out of water," Roxy, looking as perfect and as polished as ever in a red form fitting, knee length sheath, chimed in. Red was a power color and that dress was powerful enough to cover both Roxy and Terri.

Terri quietly marveled at the revelation that she'd never seen Roxy in flats and jeans or a sundress. The woman always looked as if she was head of the board of directors of some corporation.

"You plan on calling Houston home, Terri?" David probed. Of course, he was fishing. Roxy had filled Terri in on the reason for this little gathering. He wanted her back and he was willing to bring his ass all the way to Texas to get her.

"Maybe," Terri replied, curtly.

David looked as if he expected her to elaborate. She wasn't going to.

"So, I guess you've heard about the petition floating around to get you back on the show," he asked, finally sitting at the foot of Terri's chaise.

"Last I heard it was up to a million signatures," Roxy added.

"One-point-five," he clarified.

"You want me back on the show," Terri asked, tired of this man beating around the damn bush.

"No," he quickly responded. "I'm here to offer you your *own* show."

Terri raised a brow. "My own show? But, you said I was boring."

"To me," he shrugged. "You were. But to more than a million people, you bought balance, class, and grace to the continuous train wreck that is *Vivacious Vixens of Atlanta*."

Terri considered what he'd said. "Then how the hell do you think I can carry the weight of a whole reality television show on my own if I'm balanced, classy and graceful?" she challenged. "Those things only work if everybody else is a disaster."

"You could bring your own disaster," he offered with a gleam in those beautiful, green eyes of his.

Terri glanced at Roxy, returning a sly grin.

"You out here telling my business?" Terri asked.

"I gave an overview," Roxy explained. "Very general."

"But I got the gist of it," David said. "You're a beautiful woman, Terri. What made you boring, was that you thought being an actress was the only thing that made you interesting. You leveraged off that, when what makes you interesting is you, living your life, whatever that means."

"Living my life?"

"Date. Fall in love. Fall out of love. Make mistakes. And this thing with Desmond, that role that went to someone else? Everyone knows disappointment, Terri. People are drawn to shit like that, to getting our hopes up only to have everything come crashing down around you. Hell, we could even include me firing you in this storyline. Viewers would eat it up."

"And did I mention that Desmond's got a new script and is really excited about it, T," Roxy added, looking at Terri.

David looked at Roxy. "You didn't tell me that."

She smirked. "I know. I was saving it."

He turned to Terri. "I mean, we could start filming in a few weeks, Terri. Get Desmond to agree to do a cameo on the show—maybe?"

"I haven't said that I'm even interested in Desmond's film," Terri offered.

Roxy rolled her eyes and sighed. "Of course, you are."

"Great," David exclaimed. "The fact that you're on the fence about this major film role, that you were hand-selected for, is even better. It's drama. It's intense. And remember, Lyle from The ZZ Bar in Atlanta?"

Terri drew a blank.

"Tall, dark, guns the size of my thighs," he continued. "He owns the place and flirted with you during Dee Dee's birthday party?"

Terri vaguely recalled him. "Yeah. I think so, his breath smelled like dirty socks."

"I can add teeth brushing to his contract," David said without missing a blink. "The point is, he did well with fans too. We could arrange an introduction—see what happens between the two of you?"

"This kind of exposure could mean everything for future roles, Terri," Roxy added. "You'd be calling the shots for the first time in your career, instead of standing on the sidelines, waiting for someone else to *let* you play. But not only that," she sat down next to Terri. "Imagine what else you could leverage from this? A make-up line, natural hair products, whatever side hustle you can imagine could become huge."

❧

TERRI SAT at the edge of the pool, dangling her feet in the water. David had left half an hour ago, leaving plenty of food for thought, a cheesy grin and parting words, "I'll be in touch.".

She'd been at Nona's for nearly three months now, chillin', releasing, meditating, and adjusting to life as a brand new pescatarian.

"Not letting go of the cheese, sis," she'd protested when Nona suggested that Terri go all-in vegan. *"And I'm still on the fence about giving up the seafood, too."*

"That man practically got on his hands and knees begging you to agree to do your own show, Terri," Roxy said, sitting behind her. "Which is unheard of for the emperor of reality television," Roxy laughed. "And Desmond's been blowing up my phone, chomping at the bit to get you to agree to do his new film."

Terri introspectively stared over the crystal, blue water of Nona's Olympic sized pool. Leave it to that woman to have a pool the size of the gulf.

"Looks like I'm finally that chick," Terri muttered, more to herself than to Roxy.

"You've always been that chick, T," Roxy responded. "Other people are finally waking their asses up to see it."

So, why wasn't she doing black flips into the pool? Why wasn't she giddy times a thousand, reveling in the fact that she was on her way to having everything she'd ever dreamed of?

"What happened last time wasn't Desmond's call, Terri," Roxy reminded her. "The studio flexed and gave the role to Joy. He's still sick over it. But he assures me that this role is even better and that there's no way he's going to let what happened before happen again."

The old Terri's ego would've ballooned to the size of the moon over something like this. But the old Terri was more resilient and hungrier than this new Terri. She was closing in on forty-five and had happened upon the realization that if she was ever going to make a shift and break from this holding pattern, she'd been in most of her life, she needed to do it now.

"My booty's still sore from being dropped on my ass the last time," Terri joked.

Roxy laughed, "I know. I know, but this time we can count on a different ending."

Terri thought long and hard before answering, "I'll think about it."

"Okay," Roxy answered, her tone rather shaky. "I'll send the script when it's done, and you can decide from there."

"Thanks, Rox."

❧

"So, LET ME GET THIS STRAIGHT," Nona said, sitting at the massive breakfast bar of her massive kitchen, in her massive home, eating massive sized grapes.

Terri chopped mushrooms for the vegan wild rice, mushroom soup she'd become addicted to.

"Two big time producers are circling you like hungry vultures and you told Roxy that you'd *think* about it?"

Former model, Nona, headed up her own organic-uber natural skin care line and was raking in millions. Her equally beautiful hubby owned several local luxury car dealerships and everything about these two looked and smelled like money. Terri had asked to be adopted by the beautiful pair, but they'd refused citing they were more interested in adopting infants.

"You're really serious about walking away from your career," Nona said, sounding all kinds of surprised. "I thought you were just bullshitting, again."

"You never listen to me, Nona."

"I do listen," she said, plucking another grape from the bowl. "I just don't believe you when you say you don't want to act anymore. It's all you've ever talked about."

"I'm tired of riding this rollercoaster," she said. "Nine months ago, I was a boring nobody fired from a shitty reality show, and now all of a sudden, I'm a hot ticket? Just when I make peace with creating a new life for myself, somebody comes in and ruins it."

"By offering you everything you ever wanted?" Nona said, sarcastically.

"Exactly. I used to live for this kind of drama, but now I'm just worn out."

"I get it. And having all those boyfriends in Louisiana probably wore your ass out, too."

Terri laughed, "Shut up."

It was funny that she could laugh about it, now. Humiliation still sullied her reputation around the fringes, but Terri was gradually coming to terms with the fact that, for a time, she'd crossed unimaginable boundaries she never thought she was capable of crossing.

"You are welcome to stay here for as long as you need, T," Nona reassured her. "But don't give up on your passion just because it's kicked your ass from time to time. I've seen what you're working with, girl." Nona smiled. "You have a gift, and it sure would be a shame if you decided not to share it with the rest of us."

"Dreams change, Nona," Terri reminded her. "Or at least, people do. I have."

"You keep saying that, but you're wounded, which is the only reason you think you've changed. You're scared."

"Fed up, is more like it." Terri set her chopped mushrooms aside. "It's never been like this for you."

She smiled at her best friend, marveling at the fact that Nona seemed to have the Midas touch in every area of her life.

"You wanted to be a model. You were one of the best. You wanted the perfect husband. You got him. You decided to start your own business and it took off."

"I mean—yeah, but—I'm me."

Terri snarled, held the knife up and pretended to bring it down on Nona's head.

"You're brilliant, Terri. You've got too much talent and too few opportunities to show it, but ask yourself, what will you do if you're not acting?"

"For more than twenty years I have been scratching and clawing through this industry. Every now and then, landing a small victory always felt like it was the beginning of everything I'd ever wanted... only to end up feeling like I was back at the beginning all over again."

"Life doesn't unfold the same way for everybody, Terri." Nona said. "You can't waste your time comparing your life to anyone else's. What looks good on the outside, comes at a price. I promise you."

Ryan, Nona's tall, beautiful, black-haired, blue-eyed love of her life, descended the stairs, looking like a member of some European monarchy.

"Time to go, love," he said, kissing his wife lightly on the temple. "Are you sure you don't want to come, Terri? We'll wait for you to get dressed."

"Nah, I'm good," Terri assured him. "I'm going to make a pot of soup and eat it. Unless you want me to save you some."

He chuckled, "You enjoy every last drop."

That British accent was spine tingling.

"We'll see you later, T," Nona smiled, as they left.

"Bye."

"And stay out of my things," Nona called back.

"Okay," Terri lied.

Nona had the best stuff. The woman was a foot and a half taller than Terri, but they wore the same size in jewelry and handbags, and Terri admired herself in those things every chance she got.

Terri ate her soup on the lanai surrounded by palm trees. Self-examination was necessary and required solitude. She learned that from a meditation app she'd subscribed to recently.

For the first time in her life, she realized how lonely she was and how lonely she'd always been. Terri had tricked herself into not noticing that she had isolated herself from the rest of the world, even

Nona and her own parents. Her career had become everything, homie, lover, friend, which was why she'd clung so desperately to it. Being clingy was hard work and she wasn't so sure she had the strength or the interest to be that woman anymore.

She finished her soup and started thinking about the inevitable. Terri had just closed on the house and needed to go back to Devastation to pack up what was left of her things. Naturally, she was going to try and sneak in and out like a ninja. Those nosey ass town folk would work themselves into a gossip mongering frenzy when they got wind of her being back in town. She just wanted to fade away like a bad rash and leave people with the memory of that movie star who used to live in the house on Dupelo.

I'LL BLEED

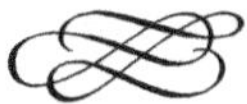

"Don and them damn cigars," Nick's aunt grumbled, climbing out of the back of one of the limos, taking them from the gravesite to Luther's.

The family had all made the decision to meet at his bar and grill after the funeral. It was the first time Nick had seen his father in over three months. He'd shut the place down for the day for the family to pay their respects and, of course, eat. Thankfully, Luther was busy playing host and Nick wasn't staying long so the two didn't have to interact.

Yolanda was there too, helping out.

"You doing all right?" She asked, setting a slice of pecan pie in front of him.

The woman had told him she loved him, and Nick was still waiting for her to say, "sike."

"I'm alright," he said, feeling a bit awkward. "You doing alright?"

"You still tripping over that conversation we had, Nick?" She smiled, and he'd seen it a million times, but this time Yo's pretty smile hit different. "Don't get weird," she warned him. "I'm still me. You're still you. Let's keep it moving."

And just like that, Yolanda flitted away like the lovely butterfly she was.

Half an hour later, Nick went around the room saying his good-byes. "Grandma," he took hold of her hands. "I'm about to head out." Nick kissed her cheek.

"Tomorrow ain't promised, Nicholas," she told him. "Say your peace before it's too late. He still your daddy."

He smiled. "I can't help that, Grandma."

"Talk to him before you go. For me?" she pleaded with her eyes. "Please?"

If the woman asked him to snatch the moon out of the sky, he'd do it. The word 'no' was not in his vocabulary when it came to this woman.

She squeezed his hands. "Please, Nick."

His grandmother knew that he could deny her nothing. She was Luther's mother, but she'd been there for Ava in the darkest times, even more than Ava's own mother.

"Only because you asked," he reluctantly agreed.

"How much older was he then you?" Nick heard one of his cousins ask Luther about his brother, Don, sitting in a booth across from him.

"Nineteen years." Luther smiled. "My whole life, he acted like he was my daddy."

"Don acted like everybody's daddy," the cousin added, laughing.

"Got a minute?" Nick interrupted.

A hush fell over the room.

"Of course," Luther said looking up at Nick.

"In private?"

Luther excused himself and led the way up the stairs to his place.

"Can I get you a drink?" Luther offered.

"Nah. I'm on my way out," Nick sighed. "I just told grandma that I'd say something to you, and this is me saying something to you."

Luther filled a glass with some kind of alcohol and sat on the sofa.

"Understood," Luther responded.

He studied his father, feeling absolutely nothing for the man. Did he still have questions? Did he still care about Luther and Terri? No. Nick didn't give a shit about either one of them. Terri's actions had been unexpected, but Luther's—not so much. Not that he ever believed his father would stoop so low as to sleep with Nick's woman. But Luther never gave a damn about anybody but himself. That much had always been true.

"This will likely be the last conversation we'll ever have," Nick surmised.

Luther lowered his gaze to the glass in his hand. "Then I won't waste it apologizing or making excuses."

"Good, because we both know any apology from you is worthless. Mom knew it. Every time you said it, she—"

"Leave her out of this," Luther said, staring hard at Nick.

"Like you left her out of your life, fucking around out there on the road?"

"I didn't fuck around," he said with so much conviction that, for a nano-second, Nick almost believed him.

"Right," he chuckled. "You lying to the wrong man, dude. I've seen first-hand what you're capable of."

"I loved Ava, Nick."

"Take that lie with you to the grave, Luther. I don't believe it. I never did."

"I don't give a fuck what you believe," Luther declared. "You're a grown-ass man, Nick, not a kid. Believe what you want. She knew and I knew. Nothing else matters."

Nick had always assumed he knew why Luther didn't give up life on the road for his wife. "She wanted to believe in you because she loved you."

"She *knew* me," he insisted. "You"— Luther shook his head— "Never did."

"I knew home, Luther. I knew what she went through," Nick responded with a shrug. "You don't have a clue. While you were out there fuckin' around, strutting around on stage, I saw what she went through. I watched her suffer."

"And I felt it." His chest heaved. Luther's eyes bore into Nick's. "I felt the pain you couldn't see. I felt it and I ignored it, Nick. But ignoring it—her— it didn't have shit to do with another woman."

"Then why didn't you bring your ass home?"

"Because I chose, Nick," he bellowed, his voice cracking. Luther collapsed onto the sofa, looking fuckin' defeated. "She kept telling me that it was okay. She was fine, and I didn't need to come home."

"She was lying."

"Ava knew what music meant to me." Luther became lost in introspection, talking more to himself than to Nick. "I loved her. I'd loved her for as long as I can remember. But when it came down to it—when I had to choose between her and music" — he looked up at Nick.— "I chose."

Nick sat down and raked his hand down his face. "That's some selfish shit, Luther. It was just music. It was a job."

Luther's eyes widened. "Is medicine just medicine, Nick?"

"If it came down to medicine or someone I love—then yeah."

"Then you're a better man than me," Luther admitted, pausing for several moments to gather his thoughts. "I heard what I wanted to hear," he confessed. "And then lied, telling myself that she was my heart and soul, all while resenting her for being sick, and making me feel guilty that I'd rather be playing music than sitting at home with her."

"Do you hear yourself?" Nick retorted, disbelief over Luther's confession engulfing him.

"She wanted me to choose," Luther continued. "Every time she told me that I didn't have to come home, that we needed the money—that she was fine—she wanted me to choose—her," he looked at Nick. Tears filled his eyes. "I knew it and told myself that she was my everything." Luther paused again, looked down at his clasped hands, and sighed. "By the time I came to my fuckin' senses it was too late. By the time I crawled out of my ego—"

A cold silence settled between them. Nick's version of why his father stayed away made more sense than this confession. If Luther was selfish enough to choose music over his wife, then...

Nick swallowed the lump swelling in his throat. "Did you ever give a shit about me?" He shrugged. "I mean, if you didn't care enough for her to come home, did I matter?"

Luther reluctantly raised his gaze to meet Nick's. "I didn't know you, son. You were hers. Your whole life I'd been on the road, Nick. We've always been strangers."

"I was a kid. I was *your* kid, not just hers, Dad." Nick's eyes clouded with tears. "I needed you, too."

Luther pursed his lips. "I know."

Nick leaned back, staring at the man like he was seeing him for the very first time. This was the most honest conversation they'd ever had, and Nick had no idea what to do with it.

"I sacrificed her for music," Luther continued. "I abandoned you both because my dream meant more to me than my own life. When I came home the last time," he choked back tears, "I saw my beautiful wife, withered like some dying flower, and looked into the empty, hollow eyes of my son, who hated me." Luther leaned back, too. "There was no fixing it, Nick. I'd lost my chance. I blew it. I let you both down and had no right to call myself husband or father. That's my penance, son. I'd sold my soul to music, and the price I paid was her and you."

"You're saying you're cool with all that?"

"I'm saying, I never deserved either one of you."

Nick paused. "I agree."

Again, the two men sat silently until Nick realized there was nothing more to be said and stood to leave. He stopped.

"We were on our way to—something," Nick said, shoving his hands in his pockets. "It wouldn't have ever been perfect, but better."

Luther hung his head. "I know."

"So, why risk it, Luther? Even a mediocre relationship with your son should've meant something. We were on shaky ground, man," Nick reminded him. "So, why would you risk our relationship for a woman?"

Luther didn't answer right away, and Nick didn't push. But he needed to know, not because he cared for her. Terri never owed him anything, but, Luther did.

"She reminded me of the things I promised myself I couldn't have," he said.

"Not good enough," Nick argued.

"Of course, it isn't, Nick, but you asked, and I'm telling you." Luther stood and walked over to Nick. "Terri resuscitated that part of me that died with Ava."

"You didn't die with Ava. You felt guilty over her, but like you said, that's your penance."

"Nothing with Terri was planned, but when I was close to her, whenever we spoke, my heart beat, Nick. I mean, I've been the walking dead since your mother died. I thought that no other woman could impact me the way Ava did, but—and I know you don't want to hear this—"

"Terri did?"

"It was wrong," he blurted out. "And I—I tried to push past it. I tried to ignore it and move on, but— She ignited a light in me that had been put out for years. Like the night I played with Cleo in New Orleans," he said, raising his brows. "I hadn't felt that good in so long, son, that I'd even forgotten to feel guilty about it."

Nick remembered that night. He had never seen his father in that light, and it was something he would never forget.

"I don't expect you to understand," he finally said. "I don't expect you to ever forgive me. But I will love you for the rest of my life, and I am sorry that I was not the father you needed, son."

Every son looks up to his father expecting to see perfection. Nick stood there, looking at his, and saw a husk of man he'd never known. A man so immersed in living his dream that he'd lost sight of the people who'd loved him despite himself. Nick stared at a tortured man who, too late, appreciated what he'd had and lost.

"You never had to choose, Luther," Nick found himself saying. "It was never either us or music. It's your passion. I get it. But you were ours."

Luther and Nick locked gazes.

"When you know better, you do better," his mother used to tell Nick that every time he failed a test or said or did something stupid.

Meaning, if you got another chance, take the lesson from the first time, and put it to good use.

Nick turned again to leave. "I need to get back."

Luther nodded. "Be safe."

"You too, Luther."

Nick started down the stairs and stopped. Permission wasn't something Luther would ever get from Nick. Forgiveness, for anything the man had done, might not ever come. Nick would never know why he felt the need to tell Luther this, but it seemed important.

"I hear she's in town."

Luther cleared his throat. "I heard that too."

"Me and you have a lot of issues," Nick explained. "For me, she's not one of them. I'm just saying."

"Understood," Luther responded.

Maybe Nick was the wrong piece of the puzzle for Terri.

"What's meant for you will find you," his mother also used to say.

If Terri and Luther ever managed to find their way to each other again, that was on them and had nothing to do with him.

WORDS I NEVER SAID

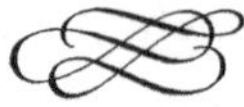

"Hey Terri," Lanette said, coming into the house without being invited, wrapping both arms around her in a powerful bear hug. "I'm so glad you're back."

Lanette wore a short, sharp, jet black bob with precision cut bangs.

"Thanks, Lanette," Terri said, pushing away from the woman who always managed to track Terri down like a bloodhound.

"Girl, I have missed the hell outta you," Lanette exclaimed with all the warmth and sincerity of a stink bug.

"Really?"

Lanette's eyes widened as she pushed passed Terri and started peeking inside unsealed boxes. "Got anything you want to get rid of?"

"No, Lanette."

"What about this?" she asked, pulling out a lamp shade Terri bought from Wayfair.

Terri took it from her. "I said no."

"Is this what you do? Move away when bad things happen?"

Terri was learning that the most grating thing about Lanette was not necessarily *what* she said, but *how* she said it. Her delivery sucked.

"We all have our coping mechanisms," Terri responded.

"People ain't even talking about you that much anymore. You might as well stay."

"I've sold the house, Lanette. I'm sure you know that."

"I do," she said, pulling a throw pillow from another box. "This is cute."

"Oh, Terri," she said, taking a figurine from one of the boxes admiring it. "This is beautiful. Can I have it?"

"Lanette, put it back," Terri insisted.

"But I love it. Where'd you get it?"

"Paris."

"Texas?"

"France! Now put it back."

"You know, I'm super busy. It was good seeing you again." Terri took hold of Lanette's elbow and guided her toward the door. "Might as well say our goodbyes now in case I never see you again."

"Why wouldn't you see me again?"

"Well, I—"

Luther!

"Hey," Lanette bellowed at the sight of him climbing out of his car. "Man, I didn't think you were coming. You know how long I've been stalling?"

"Stalling?" Terri muttered, watching Lanette hurry over to him and greet him with a high-five before leaving.

"I owe you one," he said.

"You owe me big," Lanette said over her shoulder.

Did the thought occur to her that Luther might show up at her door while she was here? Yes. He'd called a hundred times since she'd left, and Terri wasn't surprised that he'd come to her house once he found out she was back. That didn't mean she wanted to see the man. He'd finally stopped leaving singing messages on her phone. Terri had enough songs from Luther to make a whole album.

Terri abruptly slammed her door shut. Moments later, he knocked.

"I just want to talk, Terri. Just for a few minutes."

Terri braced her back against the door and folded her arms. "So, talk."

"Face to face."

"I don't need to see your face, Luther."

It wasn't just him she wanted to get away from. It was everything that'd happened between them—among them, Nick included. Terri hadn't heard from Nick, which was as it should've been. Luther needed to follow Nick's lead and let go.

"I need to see yours."

Terri didn't respond.

"Please," he said.

"Take your medicine, T," she murmured to herself, rolling her eyes. "Be a big girl."

This confrontation with Luther was like a bitter pill she needed to swallow. Terri needed to woman-up and get this over with. Reluctantly, she opened the door and stepped away, giving him plenty of room to enter without getting too close. Bad and sexy things happened whenever he got too close.

Luther was still Luther, meaning... still fine as hell, but so what? He was *still* a regret.

Luther drove his hands into his pockets and teetered back on his heels a bit, like a big kid.

"It's so fuckin' good to see you," he said, his eyes lighting up like she was Christmas morning.

Whatever feelings she'd had for him before, which Terri had never quite named, were gone. They'd dissipated into the air like steam. Relief had settled in that felt an awful lot like peace.

"What could we possibly have to talk about, Luther?"

She felt sorry for him and embarrassed for him, for all those silly messages he'd been leaving her these last three, nearly four months since she'd left town. Luther was a shell of a man who'd lost everything and everyone who'd ever loved him and never recovered from those losses. Terri had let herself fall into the trap of his magical façade and left town a humiliated mess. So, yes. She was done.

THERE WAS no way Luther was letting her leave town without seeing her. She'd been dodging his calls for months, but she was here now and the two of them needed to close the loop on this—relationship.

"When are you leaving?" he asked with a shrug.

"Day after tomorrow."

She looked like she'd dropped a few pounds. Not that she needed to, but he just noticed. Terri's curly natural hair had been straightened, loose curls framed her beautiful face.

"How've you been?" Luther finally asked.

"Good. You?" she asked, coolly, folding her arms, defensively across her chest.

"Okay."

It was still there, that pocket in space that Luther felt drawn to every time she was close enough.

"You made it to Texas?"

She smiled. "I did."

"Houston. Right?"

"Yep. Big, old, gigantic Houston. Feels like, I don't know, Jupiter, compared to this place. I got used to small town living faster than I anticipated. I'm going to miss it."

"Then don't leave," Luther blurted out without meaning to.

Terri gave a slight shake of her head. "I think we've covered the small talk, Luther," Terri said. "Let's wrap this up. Please?"

Ouch!

"How are you and Nick?" she asked, sounding almost as if she actually cared. Curious was probably a more accurate assessment.

Luther took a deep, contemplative breath and released it slowly. "We are—" Hell, Luther didn't know what they were. The last conversation they'd had a day ago was nothing more than clarification.

"We are. The issues he has with me go beyond anything that happened between you and I."

"The situation between us didn't help."

"It didn't. I love him."

"Of course, you do."

"And that's it."

"I'm sorry to hear that, Luther."

"Don't be. I take full responsibility for my relationship with my son. I hurt him a long time ago, but I can't ever be that father he needed as a kid. So when and if he's ever ready, we'll have to learn to try and build a different type of relationship. He's a grown man. One I respect." He paused. "So, what's next for you?" Luther asked, still feeling awkward and lost, and still very much enamored with this woman.

"I don't know," she sighed. "Still trying to figure it out. I don't see myself making Houston home, though."

"Then where?"

"Hard to say. I've lived in half a dozen cities in my lifetime, and I really am ready to settle down."

"You found a home here," he suggested.

"I just closed on my house," she said. "And, well, *you* live here."

She was cute when she was being insulting.

"Well, I mean—"

"Redemption and me don't see eye to eye?" Terri interjected, surprising him with his own, corny song lyrics. "Forgiveness don't know my name?"

He smiled. "Wow. You actually listened to my messages?"

"It's true, Luther. There's no redemption for you or me. We blew it. We blew it with Nick and each other. You and I were a huge mistake and there's no changing that."

There was nowhere to sit in this place. All the furniture was gone, and boxes littered the floor. The scene was set for him to say his peace and leave.

"What do you want to say to me?" she asked, taking a step closer, as Luther hung his head. "What could you and I possibly say to each other, now?"

Luther met and held her gaze. "I wanted to say that I was sorry."

Terri shrugged. "Me too. I'm sorry, too. For everything that happened between us and for what we did to Nick. There. That's it, Luther. There is nothing else."

"I'm sorry for things I said to you, things I didn't mean," he continued. "I'm sorry for hurting my kid and my wife."

She nodded and offered a slight smile.

He huffed. "I'm sorry for doing shit that I always have to be sorry for."

Goddamnit! Luther was sorry for his whole fuckin' life. This shit was getting old, saying it—hearing it, feeling it.

"I get it," she said, her demeaning softening.

"But I'm not sorry for any moment I spent with you," Luther admitted. "I'm not sorry for what I feel for you."

Terri leaned her head to one side. "How do you think you feel for me? We talked. We fucked. Was anything either of us thought we felt for each other even real?"

"I can't speak for you," he told her, inhaling the familiar scent of Terri Dawson. "But I'm old enough to know real."

"Real what, Luther? Love?"

Love. What he felt wasn't simple enough to be summed up in one word.

"Can you love anyone as much as you love your music?" she asked. "Ava. Nick. Me?"

"What's music got to do with this conversation?" He suddenly felt defensive, the way he always did when that part of his life came into question.

"I've seen you play, and it is magical."

Luther tried to recall Ava ever telling him that. She never did. His music was never a part of their lives together. When he was home, his guitar stayed in the closet most of the time, except for family gatherings when someone would ask him to play. Ava stopped asking, probably that moment she realized he loved that guitar more than he loved her. At least, that's what she believed because Luther failed to show her different.

"I don't understand what music has to do with this," he repeated.

"You and music. Me and acting. Can I love you or anyone as much as I have loved my career? See, that's what I think we had in common. A love so compelling that it blinds us to everything and everyone around us. Obsessions. You and me connected on that one real fact about ourselves and that's all."

"That's not all," he argued, determined not to let her diminish what he felt. "Not for me."

Terri took a step back. "Do either of us really know how to love another person?"

"We know how to love each other, Terri," he surprised her and said. "Better than anyone else ever could."

Terri shook her head and turned her back to him. "I don't love you."

"Fine," he added. "But you understand me. Like I understand you. You see who I truly am and not who you think I should be."

Terri turned to him. Maybe Terri didn't love him, but that didn't mean she couldn't. She was hurt, despite trying to hide behind this don't give a shit façade. He knew her, too. And Terri wasn't fooling him.

"I see you, Terri. I mean, I really see you and I know you, better than any other man ever could. Is that love? For people like you and me, what the fuck does that even mean? Acceptance. Appreciation. Applause. Admiration. Consideration. Creation."

Terri's eyes widened because Luther spoke her language. His life had been a rollercoaster of passion and regret, joy and guilt. Since Ava's death, it had just been him, standing still, trying not to ripple the water. And then Terri came along, and all he wanted to do was make waves. Luther never wanted to hurt Nick, but Nick was never meant to be in the middle of this.

"I don't want you to go," he finally admitted, taking hold of her hand.

Terri wiped the rogue tear streaming down her cheek. "I don't know how to stay, Luther."

"You just do."

"And what about Nick?"

"Nick is—not a part of this anymore, Terri."

Did he feel like shit for still wanting this woman who'd been with his son? Hell yeah! Enough to let her go? Not anymore.

"But he was. And that's hard for me, Luther. Not because I loved him, but because you do."

"More than he'll ever understand, Terri. More than I can ever say, but the damage is done between me and Nick. He made that clear."

"So, you just let him go? No," she shook her head and pulled back her hand. "I won't be a part of that. I won't be responsible for the two of you not working this out and coming back to each other."

She didn't understand. Frustration ballooned in his chest because Terri believed that a reconciliation between him and Nick had anything to do with her anymore.

"You sacrificed him once for your music, Luther," she continued. "Don't do it again for me."

She was right. Luther hadn't learned a damn thing. He was doing it all over again, choosing his own selfish happiness over someone he said he loved. If he really wanted to be a better man, he'd let her go.

Neither of them spoke for several moments before Terri finally broke through the fragile silence.

"I have to go back to Houston. I can't stay here."

Luther took hold of her hand again, raised it to his lips and kissed it. "Then you go," he said, his voice cracking.

A moment of truth rose to the surface in Luther. Staring into her eyes, he knew that when she left, she'd take a big part of him with her.

Luther raised her hand and pressed her palm to his chest, over his heart. "You are here, Terri. And somehow, someway—someday," he grinned. "We'll find a way to meet up in the middle of some goddamn where."

With tears streaming down her cheeks, she surprised him and managed a nervous laugh.

"Deal?" He asked, hoping and praying she'd say yes. He could never promise her perfection, but Luther could guarantee his attention… his devotion. She could leave town, but, Luther couldn't let her leave *him*.

Terri shrugged. "Can I think about it?"

It wasn't the answer he wanted to hear, but it was the one she needed to give him. He released her hand and took a step back.

"Yeah."

❧

TERRI HADN'T PACKED a thing since he'd left, hours ago. Luther and Terri were pieces of the same puzzle. She wasn't the woman for Nick. Never had been. Luther, obviously wasn't the father for him either. Dr. Hunt had been collateral damage in a collision he never should've been a part of. Luther and Terri recognized themselves in each other and were drawn to their reflections. If either of them could ever stop feeling like shit about it, maybe, just maybe they could make this work.

"Hi," she said, sitting on the floor of her empty bedroom, hovering over her phone.

"Hey," Luther responded.

Was this phone call a mistake? It wouldn't be the first one she'd made and damn sure wouldn't be the last.

"Maybe you could come visit me in Houston?"

After a long pause, Luther finally answered, "I can absolutely come visit you in Houston."